LEARNING TO BREATHE AGAIN

FINDING LOVE IN WAKETON
BOOK TWO

KELLI HENEGHAN

Published by
Kelli Heneghan

Edited by Nathan Squiers for Literary Dark Editing
Cover art by EmCat Designs

For the one who gave me the courage to BREATHE...I love you.

ACKNOWLEDGMENTS

Again, I have to say a huge Thank You to my family for all the encouragement and support.

To my friends who made sure I kept both feet on the ground. Laura, I promise, one of these days, you'll be on the cover!
To Nate and Meg: you two are the greatest! Thanks for sticking with me and helping me get this thing done!

And to all of my readers, THANK YOU! You've made my dream come true!

She only wanted a
place to stay and
some time to *heal*;
He was only trying to
help out a *friend*

CHAPTER 1

*B*ayleigh morrow stared at her phone in disbelief. How in the hell did it only have two percent battery life left? She had forced herself to keep the damn thing turned off during her overnight layover in New York just so she'd have a full battery today. Damn smart phones always needing a signal. The fact that this one was way over-due for an upgrade wasn't helping the matter.

Gritting her teeth, she turned her phone off and slid it into her backpack. Like everyone else in the free world, she didn't keep phone numbers written anywhere. She and her brother didn't talk to each other often, a fact she wanted to change with this visit.

Her flight from England to New York had gotten in too late last night to make any connecting flights to Texas. She'd stayed at JFK all night and slept upright in a chair with her feet propped on her luggage, her brief attempts to doze interrupted by departure calls and announcements. She'd thought luck was on her side when they were able to get her on a flight to Austin that left New York at six that morning.

But no, her plane had been late arriving in Austin and the line for car rentals had been unbelievable. The coffee stand she'd tried to get breakfast at burned the bacon for her breakfast sandwich and there hadn't been time to wait for another one. And to top it off, the traffic in Austin had been hellacious. After an eleven- hour flight across the Atlantic, having to sleep in the airport, and then the delays here, she had thought that would be the end of her troubles. But, no. The damn phone had to go and die on her.

Now she was two hours outside of Austin, filling up her gas tank with a credit card she hadn't used in at least three years. She gave a mental fist bump when the card worked. Next up on her list, finding her stupid car charger for the cell phone.

She leaned into the back seat and started rummaging through her bags. *I know I packed the damn thing. I took it to Europe and never needed it there. Figures I need it the minute I step foot on the ground here.*

"Where the hell did I put it?" She muttered, digging through the suitcase for the third time. She stood up and huffed out a frustrated breath, blowing her hair out of her eyes. She remembered throwing the charger into the suit-case. Hadn't she? She closed her eyes, picturing the apartment back in London. She'd kept it in a drawer because she never drove anywhere in Europe. She was positive she'd pulled it out of that drawer. Her phone only needed to be charged once a day or so because she kept it turned off most of the time. There weren't many people in Europe who needed to call her cell phone.

Short of dumping everything out of the suitcases and her bags, she wasn't going to find it. She shivered as she stared at the diner attached to the gas station. Despite the sun shining, it was still February and the wind was cold. She decided she might as well get a snack and something to drink for the road since she'd had to stop for gas. Maybe someone inside could tell her if there was an electronics store nearby.

Moving her car so she wasn't blocking the pump, she pocketed the keys and walked up to the double doors, eyeing the almost empty tables and the two waitresses drinking coffee at the counter. She felt like she'd just stepped back in time into a diner from the 1950's. There were ten booths, and even from the door she could see the cracked vinyl seats. Most of the booths were along the windows, with one large one in the back corner. A few smaller tables scattered around the middle of the diner, and plenty of seating up at the counter for people who were alone, such as herself.

With every intention of just ordering a cup of coffee and asking for directions, she slid onto a stool at the counter. The aroma of hamburgers and French fries and fresh baked pies had her mouth watering and her stomach grumbling, reminding her she hadn't eaten a real meal since leaving London yesterday.

"Hey, there. Do you know what you'd like to order?" The younger waitress set a glass of ice water down in front of her.

"I'll take a cheeseburger and fries, and a Coke. But could you put the Coke in a to-go cup?" Bayleigh smiled at the waitress.

"Of course, doll. Be happy to. It'll just take a few minutes to get that going for you." The waitress gave her a wink and stepped up to the window between the kitchen and the dining area and called out the order to the cook in the back. Bayleigh watched the banter between the cook and the two waitresses while she waited for her food.

She glanced at the clock on the wall. Time was of the essence here and she really needed to get back on the road. The cook and the waitresses seemed to think she had all day, though. They weren't moving very fast behind the counter. Maybe she shouldn't have ordered anything. But man, oh man, did the smell of those burgers and fries get her appetite to wake up.

"Here ya go, hon. You just let me know if you need anything else. My name is Tory."

"Well, Tory, I do have a question for you, if you've got a few minutes?" Tory turned back to her and glanced around the diner with a wide-eyed dramatic stare.

"Gee, hon. Not sure my customers can be put off," she teased as she leaned a hip against the counter across from Bayleigh. "Whatcha need?"

"Directions to an electronics store. My cell phone is almost dead and I need to get to Waketon before it dies," she bit into her burger, almost moaning in appreciation. European burgers just weren't the same. Now *this* was a burger.

"Hmm," Tory tapped a long fingernail against her lip. "Only stores I know are in Austin. You said you're headed to Waketon?" she waited for Bayleigh to nod her head. "Yeah, you don't want to have to go all the way back there." She turned and motioned the older waitress over.

"Betty, this gal needs an electronics store. Do you know of one near here?"

Betty came over and stood near them, hands on her hips. "Honey, if Wal-Mart ain't got it, I don't need it!" she cackled. "Wal-Mart is just on down the road a couple of miles," she informed her, pointing in the general direction Bayleigh was going to be headed in to get to Waketon.

Bayleigh thanked them and finished up her meal as fast as she could without choking herself. She didn't have the time to go back to Austin, nor did she want to make that drive again today. She'd just find this Wal-Mart and keep going. Wal-Mart was sure to have the charger she needed.

She found the Wal-Mart Betty liked so much, but because she had an older smartphone, and not the most recent upgrade, they didn't have the charger she needed in stock. The poor guy at Wal-Mart took pity on her and let her use the computer at the customer service desk to print off a map from the Internet. What a mistake *that* was turning out to be.

Now, here she was, two hours later, sitting on the side of the road, frustrated and cursing enough to make a sailor blush.

She tossed the offending piece of paper on the seat beside her and released a heavy sigh, leaning her head back and trying to think past the jet lag and exhaustion. It was a little past four in the afternoon, but she was in the Hill Country of Texas, lost, still no way to get in touch with her brother, and ready to call it quits. At least for today. If she knew where the closest decent hotel was, she'd park herself there for the night and try this again tomorrow.

Biting her lip in an effort to control her emotions,

Bayleigh sat back up and gave herself a mental slap across the face. *"Be tough, be resourceful. You're not stupid. You can figure this out! Think outside of the box!"*

A car sped by her, startling her. She double checked the door locks, hitting the button over and over as her heart raced. Her hands shook and she gripped the steering wheel until her knuckles were white.

Damn it, I am not going to fall apart now!

Until that fateful night, she'd never suffered panic attacks, and now there wasn't a single day that went by that something didn't trigger one. The landscape outside her windows did nothing to soothe the frantic urge to run. In a few weeks, the fields around her would be overflowing with the Texas bluebonnets and Indian paintbrush. Right now, though, with the gray clouds covering up the afternoon sun, it struck her as bleak. Her frantic gaze moved over the horizon, seeking something to use to center herself. Her eyes settled on the red barn in the distance.

There, focus on the red barn. Breathe in, hold...breathe out...focus. Find that safe place. Go to that damn safe place! The thready wheeze coming from her chest increased her anxiety level by at least tenfold.

Red barn isn't working...what else, damn it, what else is there? She continued to scan the horizon.

A hawk, wings spread, glided through the air. Floating. It caught a draft and circled around, dipping his left wing down, then his right.

Beautiful.

Hypnotized, she followed the hawk's progress, and the anxiety loosened its hold and her breathing became even again.

Score one for imagery in motion!

After a few more cleansing breaths, she jammed the gear stick into drive and pulled out onto the road. There had been an office building a few miles back down the road, and at least one vehicle parked in the front; maybe whoever was inside could give her better directions. Or at least let her use the telephone to call her brother to come and get her.

Her brother. Jason. God, how many times had she thought about calling him in the last couple of months? She should have, she knew that. Once she'd decided to return to Texas, the phone should have been in her hand. And she should have told him long before that even though her life had gone from sugar to shit. But she never made that call.

After Will blamed the whole thing on her, she had started second guessing herself. What if her brother sided with him? She could live without Will, their relationship had been a disaster from almost day one. But her brother? She needed her brother on her side.

I can do this. It's going to be okay. What else could possibly go wrong when I'm this close?

CHAPTER 2

*P*arking her car in the small lot next to the pickup truck, Bayleigh studied the small building. A solitary pick-up truck sat in the parking lot and the place was well kept. Knowing she wasn't going to get any answers just sitting out here, staring at the building, she forced herself to turn off the ignition and pocketed the keys.

With a deep breath and a short prayer for courage, Bayleigh slid out from behind the wheel of her small car, taking the time to stretch and try to ease the cramped muscles in her back and shoulders. Her knee and thigh protested every movement she made as she gripped the handrail on the stairs and pulled herself up them. She gritted her teeth and pushed herself forward.

She paused for a moment at the top before taking those last few steps forward to the wood paneled door. The plaque beside the door caught her attention: "Williams and Winters, Attorneys At Law." There was something about those names teasing her memory, but she was too tired.

Struggling to pull open the solid oak door, she was able to wedge it open enough with her hip and step through into the reception area.

A bell chimed down the hallway, announcing her arrival. She glanced around, unsure of what to do when no one came to see who had entered. Muffled curses echoed from one of the offices.

"Hello?" she called out, craning her neck to see into the back hallway.

An impatient male voice called back, "Yeah, what do you want?"

Bayleigh rolled her eyes. *Great, someone else having a shitty day.*

"I'm sorry to bother you, but I'm lost. My cell phone died and I can't find my car charger and I was hoping you might be able to help me." The quietness of the office was unsettling her. Maybe this wasn't a good idea. She debated turning around and leaving. With her recent panic attacks, especially the one she just had in the car, she wasn't sure she could handle a strange man right now.

She could hear the unseen man as he cursed again and then muttered something about 'just put her out of her misery' and 'making things easier' and something about 'setting him up."

Good Lord, what kind of attorney's office did I choose to stop at for help? She turned towards the exit and reached for the doorknob.

"I thought you needed help?"

Without warning, the voice sounded from behind her. She jumped, her heart now in her throat.

"Sorry. I didn't mean to startle you," the voice was softer, but still male.

She spun around and stepped backwards, cursing herself for not putting her pepper spray in her pocket.

WHOA, face of an angel. The phrase ran through his mind. *A very startled and scared angel, but still, an angel. Blonde hair and everything. And familiar-looking.*

"Both my partner and my receptionist are out of the office and the computer decided this was the perfect time to act up. She hates me," he glared over his shoulder before turning back to her, a slight grin on his face. "If my partner wouldn't kill me for it, I'd shoot her. Now, what's this about being lost?"

"OH GOD," was Bayleigh's first thought, followed by *"well, damn"* as she took in every detail of the man standing across from her. Jet black hair, chocolate brown eyes, well-worn jeans. Polo shirt stretched tight across broad shoulders. *Smoking hot* seemed to be the only description her brain could come up with at the moment.

Giving herself a mental shake as she caught the frown on his face, his words registered and she went still. "Wait....who hates you and who are you going to shoot?"

She felt behind her for the doorknob, keeping her eyes locked on him. He was big. He had to be over 6 feet tall. And muscles. Lots of muscles. Her heart started to pound. The room seemed to be closing in on her and her mind was trying to take her back to the last room she'd been cornered in, with *that man. That man* had been tall, too, and muscular. More muscular than this guy. She felt her chest getting tight again and the hated yet familiar hitch in her breathing started.

Crap! Focus. Stay in the moment! She couldn't afford to lose sight of where he was, what he was doing. She struggled to get her breathing under control.

"My computer hates me, and I'm going to shoot her one of these days." His arms were relaxed at his side, his hands visible to her. He took a few steps backwards, putting a few extra feet between them.

"You refer to your computer as a she?" She tracked each of his movements and tried to focus on his words. But now she was getting confused. Who referred to their computer as a person, and why would they want to shoot it?

He raised an eyebrow, "Yes. I tend to call her Miss B, short for Miss Bitch. She's temperamental and you have to have the right touch in order to get her to give up what you want. Right now she's locked up tighter than Fort Knox and is not letting me access my files."

Bayleigh studied the man across from her. He was keeping his distance and his comment about the computer was kind of funny. Her heart was still racing but her breathing had evened back out. As long as he stayed on the other side of the room, maybe she could get through this.

Clearing his throat to get her attention, he repeated his question. "You said something about being lost. Where are trying to get to?"

Bayleigh shook her head, not sure what episode of *The*

Twilight Zone she stepped into, but shuffled forward just enough to hold the map out to him. "I'm sorry. It's been a long day and I'm a little out of it. I'm looking for my brother's place but I can't seem to find the road the map says I need to take. I'd call him, but as I said, my cell phone is dead." As soon as he took the map from her, she stepped back, out of reach. "Do you think you could help me?"

The man glanced down at the paper as he took it from her. "Hmm. Who's your brother?"

"Jason Morrow, he's a doctor." His head snapped back up and she frowned. "Do you know him?"

"Yeah. I was in the wedding a few months ago when he and Nicole got married. I thought I recognized you. He flashes pictures of you and that band around all the time." He held the map back out to her. "They've got you going down Old County Road 29, which doesn't connect to Jason's and Nicole's property. You need FM 29, not that that information will do you any good. Jason's not there."

"Oh, is he at the hospital, or do you know where I could find Nicole, then? I'd like to meet her."

"He and Nicole headed up to Dallas for a long weekend. His wife would be my partner who isn't here to save her blessed computer from certain doom." He leaned back against the receptionist's desk and stretched his long legs out in front of himself, and she noticed he could recognize her tension as he moved by the way he stilled.

"I think half the town is convinced Jason is lying about having a half-sister. I'm Jack Williams, by the way." The man offered his hand in greeting, leaning forward to shorten the distance between them, causing Bayleigh's muscles to grow even tighter.

"Jack Williams?" She bit down on the inside of her lip before she forced herself to reach out and accepted his handshake. His hand was calloused, as if he were used to doing hard labor. All the lawyers she'd ever met had smooth hands and soft skin that had never seen a hard day of manual labor. But this man had rough skin, and a deep, natural tan, even in winter, that spoke of hours spent outdoors.

The significance of his name hit her. "You're one of Jason's best friends! I knew there was something familiar about the names on the door but I was too tired to place it." And then what he was saying sunk in. "Jason and Nicole aren't here?"

"No, they left yesterday evening. Hey, are you ok?" Jack straightened as her eyes filled with tears.

Bayleigh sniffed, looking around and grabbing a tissue from the box on the receptionist's desk. "I'm fine, honest. Like I said, it's just been a long day. Sorry," she dabbed at her eyes.

What was wrong with her? She hadn't cried, not once, since this whole ordeal started. The stress of the last few days must be getting to her. Or she was just more tired than she realized.

"NOT A PROBLEM." Jack's intent gaze never left her face. He should have recognized her from a couple of pictures Jason had but who expected long lost sisters to show up out of nowhere? Plus, in his own defense, Jason's pictures did not do this woman justice. This woman was hot.

Whoa, that kind of thinking needs to stop. Remember this is Jason's sister. He and Nicole will kill me for sure.

Jack cleared his throat, forcing his focus back to the lady standing in front of him. "So, when did you get back to the States? I'm sure Jason and Nicole would have delayed their trip if they'd known you were planning on coming here."

"I landed in New York late last night and caught a flight to Austin this morning and drove straight here. It was kind of a spur of the moment thing." She shifted, trying to take some of the stress off of her knee. She was pushing the limits again.

"What's wrong with the leg?"

"WHO SAYS ANYTHING IS?" Bayleigh stopped looking at the door and focused her attention on the man a mere few feet away. Had he stepped closer? Her hand closed around the doorknob, ready to make a run for it if needed, damage to her leg be damned.

"You're favoring your left leg." He glanced between her hand on the doorknob and her leg before meeting her eyes. He crossed his arms over his chest, daring her to deny it.

"I am not. I'm fine." She forced herself to put more weight on her leg. Her leg started to buckle and the room spun. Christ, now she was fainting on top of crying? Awesome first impression.

No, wait, the room had spun because he had swung her up in his arms. She stiffened at the realization that he was carrying her. She could feel his arms like bands of steel supporting her upper back and under her thighs.

"Please, put me down. I'm ok. Please, just let me go!" Bayleigh struggled in his arms, trying to get away. She could feel her chest tightening again as his arms tightened against her struggles. *Fight!*

"IT'S OK. I'm not going to hurt you. I just didn't want you to fall." He soothed as he carried her to the couch in his office, his arms tightening even more. "And if you don't stop that, I'm going to drop you!" he warned. He didn't know what this lady's story was but something was off and his protective streak was coming out. He laid her down on the couch and slid his arms out from under her, ignoring the sensations brought to life that that simple movement stirred up.

"Now, want to rethink that story a bit?" he raised an eyebrow and cocked his head to the side, waiting.

"I'M FINE, promise, just let me go!" she moved to push herself up but he held her in place with a firm hand on her shoulder. *Away! Must get away! Now!*

"Really? I don't know too many people who almost collapse just from trying to prove that they can put weight on a leg," he told her with a frown. With a heavy sigh, she stopped trying to get up off the couch. He dropped his hand from her shoulder and stepped back as soon as she stopped pushing against his hold. "So?"

She squared her shoulders and sat up as much as her position on the couch would allow. "I injured my leg and I've been traveling for thirty-six hours straight to get here. I

15

had a five hour layover in New York, which I spent in the airport because I didn't want to chance missing my flight to Austin this morning. I couldn't take my pain killers or my muscle relaxers because I knew I'd be driving when I got to Austin, and I didn't want to take a day to rest in between flights and driving. I just pushed myself too far."

Bayleigh refused to break eye contact with the man standing over her. "So, if you would be so kind as to allow me the use of your telephone, I will contact my brother and see what he suggests I do."

"Of course." He nodded and turned to grab his cell phone off the corner of his desk, pushing a couple of buttons before handing it to her. "I'd like to talk to Jason, when you're done. Just call out when you're finished talking to him."

Bemused, she glanced down at the phone in her hand, seeing he'd brought up her brother's contact information. With a deep breath, she hit the dial button on the phone. It was answered on the second ring.

"This better be important, Jackass. We're trying to have some alone time here." Her brother's disgruntled voice sounded in her ear.

"Hi, Jase. It's me."

There was a brief pause. "Bayleigh?"

"Yeah. I'm, uh, I'm in Waketon." Bayleigh didn't even try to blink back the tears this time. Christ, she needed sleep.

"What the hell? I mean, when did you get in? Why didn't you call me?" Jason fired the questions at her, not giving her a chance to answer. And then his voice softened. "I would have met you anywhere, you know."

The wave of emotion that rolled over her almost had her sobbing. She should have called him long before now, but she hadn't wanted him to know how screwed up she'd let things get in her life.

"Slow down big brother! I landed in the states yesterday." Bayleigh took a deep breath and forced herself to block out the emotions. She needed to focus on the 'here and now', not the past. Soon, she would tell him everything. But right now, she needed the time to pull herself together and heal.

"So, I kind of showed up at your friend Jack's office because I was lost and my cell phone had died. He told me you're out of town for the weekend." Realizing Jack would tell Jason that she was hurt, she decided to at least tell him that part of her story. "I also hurt my leg a couple of months ago. I almost fainted on him because I overdid things today."

"What'd you do to your leg?"

Should have known the orthopedic doctor would want details, she thought with a grimace. "I injured my knee, tore some ligaments and did some damage to the muscles in the thigh, nothing that can't be fixed with time." She massaged her thigh as she told her brother the story. With any luck, that big brother radar he had wouldn't work over the phone.

"How the hell did you do that?" Jason asked.

Bayleigh bit her lip. "I fell while running but it's fine now." Not knowing how he'd react stopped her from sharing the whole story. She'd lost the right to dump her problems in his lap a long time ago.

"And why wasn't I called when it happened?"

"It wasn't anything serious. I spent a few weeks in a hospital and then stayed with a friend until the doctors agreed I could travel." She hoped he didn't catch the slight hesitation in her voice when she answered. Her brother was going to lose it when he found out the truth concerning what had happened to her. But she'd long ago learned to overcome and adapt to whatever life threw at her.

"Will you stay with Jack until we get back on Monday?"

"Ahh, I was just going to go to a hotel."

"That would be okay, if the hotel in town wasn't closed right now for remodeling. And Waketon only has the one decent hotel."

"Well, shit," Bayleigh muttered, closing her eyes. "What the hell am I supposed to do?"

"Stay with Jack. His place is big enough," Jason suggested.

"I can't do that!"

"Sure you can. He's a former Army officer, injured in the line of duty and everything. He's also one of my best friends. Hell, he and Nicole treat each other like siblings, so he's like family. On top of all that, he got Nicole to give me a second chance, so I owe him my life."

"Well, he hasn't offered yet. Why can't I stay at your place?"

"Because we had a busted water pipe the other day, which is why we took a long weekend. The contractors are supposed to be fixing it while we're gone. And trust me, he'll offer to let you stay with him. Plus he has a hot tub. You can relax and let it work its magic on your leg. It'll help relieve the muscle soreness."

"Jason, don't you dare make him offer..."

"I won't have to. Trust me, Bayleigh."

"Fine. He wanted to speak to you anyway. But I'm warning you, Jason. Don't you dare tell him to let me stay with him! He may be your best friend, but he is still a stranger to me!"

"Great. And Bayleigh..."

"Yes, Jason?"

"I'm sorry we weren't home but we'll see you on Monday. I'm glad you came back, sis." Those words alone told her in an instant she had made the right decision to come to Texas.

"Thanks, Jason." She swallowed past the sudden lump in her throat. "Let me get Jack for you." Covering the phone with her hand, she called out to Jack and waited for him to walk back into the room.

"Where's the bathroom?" she asked as she handed the phone over and pushed herself up off the sofa.

"Down the hall, first door on the right," he told her, the phone already up to his ear. "Do you need help walking down the hall?"

"I'm good," she waved him off and headed down the hall. She needed to come up with a good excuse as to why she couldn't stay with him, and fast!

JACK TOOK THE PHONE, keeping his eye on the hallway. By standing there, he'd be able to see the door for the bathroom open when she left it to return to his office. If he was going to talk about Bayleigh to her brother, he sure as hell wasn't going to get caught doing it.

"So, how's the trip going?"

"Just great," Jason admitted. "So my sister showed up."

"What's her story?" Jack lowered his voice a notch.

"What do you mean?"

"Well, I've never met your sister before, but something doesn't quite look right. She damn near fainted on me when I asked her what was wrong with her leg and she tried to put her full weight on it. A strong wind would blow her over," Jack glanced down the hallway, lowering his voice. "And she's skittish."

"Skittish? What the hell do you mean by skittish?"

"Just that. Like a newborn colt. She was ready to either bolt, or scratch my eyes out the second she knew I was behind her." Jack's eyes narrowed as he thought back to the scene in the outer office. "I don't know what it is, Jason. She said she's been traveling for at least thirty-six hours, but by the dark circles under her eyes, I'd say she's gone more than that without any decent sleep. My gut is screaming at me that there's more than just a lack of sleep," Jack scrubbed a hand over his own face. "Any ideas why my gut is telling me that?"

Jason hesitated. "She never told me the details, but something happened last summer. I saw an article online about her being stalked. She wouldn't talk to me about it at the time, and then everything happened with Nicole and her accident. Bayleigh said she was fine and that idiot boyfriend of hers said she was fine."

"She has a boyfriend who let her travel that distance, in her condition?"

"I think they broke up last fall. Again. Maybe this time

it was for good. I try to stay out of her love life as much as possible."

"Did you break it to her that she can't stay at your place and the hotel is closed right now?"

"I did."

"You okay with her staying with me out at my place?"

"You know I trust you, man, and believe me, she takes the term 'stubborn' to a whole new level," Jason sighed. "Look, please, just keep your eye on her for me. If she needs anything, get her up to the hospital and have one of my partners look at her for me. Tell them I'll square it with them on Monday."

"Will do. I'll let you know if she decides against staying with me. Otherwise, we'll be leaving here and heading to the ranch in a few minutes." He disconnected the call and shoved the phone in his pocket and moved over to his desk to turn off his computer monitor.

Stupid piece of junk. I should just throw the damn thing against the wall. I can afford a new one.

His glance went back to the doorway and he wondered what was taking Bayleigh so long. There had been a spark of awareness in his body when he'd touched her. He wasn't one for all that touchy-feely crap, at least he hadn't been in over ten years. Not since the last woman who he'd allowed into his heart had pulled it still beating from his chest and stomped on it.

But the emotions stirring in his chest, just from catching Bayleigh when she almost fainted, had him wanting more. He wanted to fight her demons, to hold her in the night, and catch her every time she stumbled and fell. There was a look in her eyes he wanted to erase and replace. He'd never felt this kind of pull towards another woman. It would be a lie to say he wasn't spooked by it.

Maybe it was the look of innocence or the steel under the fatigue he'd seen peeking through when he thought she was going to attack him in the outer office. But something in her called to him. The question was, could he or would he bother to answer it?

He smiled at her as she stepped back into the room. For now, he could at least help erase some of the exhaustion from her eyes.

"So..." He picked up his keys and grabbed his Stetson off the hook on the wall. "Jason said he'd told you the bad news about the hotel and his place. I have a couple of extra rooms. You are more than welcome to stay with me until they get back on Monday."

"Did he put you up to offering?"

"No. He and I both know that Nicole will skin me alive if I don't offer you a place to stay. Southern hospitality and all that," he told her with a wink. "I know I'm a stranger and all, but in all honesty, the closest decent hotel is at least an hour away."

"An hour?"

"At least. And I am not going to believe you if you try to tell me you can make it that far."

Bayleigh took a deep breath and tilted her head back to stare up at the ceiling. *Why me?* "Fine. I'm not left with much choice, am I?" she lowered her head and met his amused gaze.

"You always have a choice. This is just your best option right now." Jack intoned with a grin in her direction. "Let's go, then." He indicated for her to following him out to the main room. While he made sure all of the lights were out and doors were locked, she waited by the door.

Leading the way outside, he set the alarm and locked the door. He turned to where she was leaning against the wall, the dark circles under her eyes seeming even darker in the fading sun.

"Why don't you leave your car here tonight? It's at least twenty minutes out to my place, and with it starting to get dark, I don't want you getting lost again. I promise I'll bring you back out in the morning to get your car." He reached towards her to take her arm. It didn't escape his notice her sudden tension as his hand came up.

"I'm not going to hurt you, Bayleigh." He whispered, lowering his hand back to his side without even touching her. He looked down at her hands, clenched into fists at her sides, and then his gaze traveled back up, taking in her heaving chest, as if she'd just finished a five-mile run, to her face. Her very pale, deer-caught-in-the-head-lights-looking face.

He kept his eyes locked on her face as he took two steps back. "Better?" He asked her, making sure he didn't make any sudden moves towards her, or try to touch her again. He'd seen that look on a couple of clients before. Domestic abuse cases. He hoped to God that wasn't the case here.

"I promise you're safe with me. The door to your bedroom has a lock. I'll even give you a weapon if that's what you need."

She swallowed hard at that, and breaking eye contact, she looked over at her car. *Jason said I could trust him. I have to trust someone.* "Do I need a weapon?"

"Not against me. You have all the power you need, just by saying the word 'no'. Got it?"

"I..." She moved a few steps away from him, cleared her throat and brought her eyes back to his. "I'll get my bags out of my car. I would appreciate the ride. I guess I'm more tired than I thought."

"Bayleigh, tell me which bags you need and get in my truck. I'll get the bags." He stepped in front of her, keeping enough distance between them to try to avoid freaking her out, but needing to stop her.

"Again, the whole Southern hospitality, Nicole will kill me thing. Okay?" He teased when she hesitated. Holding his hand out for the keys, she stared at him for at least another ten seconds before dropping her keys into his hand.

"The two suitcases, the canvas carry-on and the backpack, which doubles as my purse. And the guitar," she told him.

"Here. You can start it, if you want, get the heater going," he handed his own keys to her and started towards her car. After grabbing the bags she'd indicated, he locked her car and carried everything over to his truck. After getting her bags situated in the cab of the truck, he slid behind the wheel of his pickup, setting her keys on the seat between them.

"Do you need me to stop anywhere before I head out to my ranch?" He offered, as he put the truck in gear and started to pull out of the parking lot.

"No, I've got everything I need."

"Well, try to relax, then. It'll take me about twenty minutes or so to get out to my place." Jack's eyes raked over her from head to toe. With the way she was holding herself so still and tight right now, he was surprised her bones weren't breaking under the pressure.

He was going to find out what the hell had happened to this chick to put that distrust in her. And while he was at it, he'd work on figuring out why it was so important to him to erase that look in her eyes. She was Jason's sister, for Christ's sake. His *much younger* sister. What the hell was he thinking?

CHAPTER 3

*N*ot one word was spoken between them the entire ride out to the ranch. What kinds of questions were now floating through Jack's mind? She could think up a dozen in no time *she'd* be asking if their situations were reversed.

But this guy seemed content to sit in the driver's seat and just drive. She'd caught him glancing over at her a couple of times, concern lining his eyes. He'd adjusted the heat once, and the volume on the radio a couple of times, but other than that, he'd ignored her.

She wondered what her brother and Jack had talked about earlier, when she'd left the room. For the last nine months or so, she'd tried to limit phone calls with her brother. Emails allowed her that cloak of invisibility, and less worry for him. At least, that's how she justified it in her mind.

But now, she didn't know what to do, and things were so screwed up, she didn't know if they could ever be fixed.

They crested a hill and her breath caught at the view

below her. She wasn't sure what she'd been expecting, a small, non-descript farmhouse, maybe, or even a double-wide trailer, with a few rusted out pickup trucks up on blocks next to it. They were in the middle of Nowhere-ville, Texas, for Christ's sake.

But this? This was something worthy of a write up in *Architects' Monthly*. This house had the same type of bay windows the house she remembered from her childhood having. She'd loved curling up in those bay windows and watching summer thunderstorms, her mother working on something at the kitchen table nearby.

She closed her eyes against the sudden pain the memory brought with it. That time and place was gone. Long gone and never to return. She realized they had stopped and she opened her eyes again, turning to the man beside her. "Wow. Nice place you have here."

"Thanks. I think I drove a couple of the architects and builders to drink," he paused in the act of opening his door. "I'll help you down from the cab."

Wanting to be out of the truck before he got to her side, she rushed to open her own door and jumped to the ground. "Damn it." She hissed out between clenched teeth as her knee buckled again. She collapsed back against the truck and squeezed her eyes closed on the wave of pain that shot through her. Why couldn't her body cooperate for a little longer?

She cried out when the heavy weight of a man's hand settled on her shoulder.

"Bayleigh? Are you with me?" Jack's deep voice carried a note of concern and broke through her thoughts. She opened her eyes and focused on his face. She nodded once and attempted to push away from the truck, screwing her face up in pain when she attempted to put weight on her knee.

"Oh, no you don't," he told her with a firm shake of his head, making her sit back down inside the truck. "Do me a favor and stay here for a few seconds. I'll go get the door and then carry you in. Your knee has had enough punishment for one day."

He spun on a booted heel, striding across the driveway to the covered porch, taking the steps two at a time. He thrust the key in the lock and shoved open the door, not even stopping to remove the key before turning to head back to her.

"Ok, here we go. Put your arms around my shoulders and just relax." His lips were against her temple. As soon as his hands slid across her shoulders and under her legs, ready to lift her, her whole body tensed and her breath hitched in her chest, her pulse jumping. And just like that, the downward spiral started.

Bayleigh tried to concentrate on his eyes and his words, but he was *touching* her. The panic was rising up inside and overtaking her. It didn't matter that he was only trying to help. She was cornered, trapped. She couldn't run away this time. Her breaths were short and choppy and her chest was tight. She could feel the blood pounding in her head.

"Can't...breathe..." she wheezed out, her hands pushing on his chest, as her vision blurred from either the lack of oxygen or the tears running down her cheeks, she wasn't sure which.

Please don't let me pass out. I can't protect myself if I pass out.

"Shit." Jack's own eyes went wide and then he shifted her higher in his arms and quickened his pace. He hurried to get her into the house, heading for kitchen and settled her onto of the chairs before turning to the cabinets, muttering under his breath.

Bayleigh leaned forward, hands on her thighs.

"Here." Jack shoved a brown paper bag in her face. "You're hyperventilating. Breathe into the bag." He shook the bag to get her attention.

Keeping her eyes on him as he retreated back to the other side of the kitchen, she opened the bag. It took a few minutes but the rock that had taken residence in her chest eased off of her and she was able to take a more comfortable breath. Her skin was cold and clammy and her hands were still shaking. The tremors would linger for a while, she knew, but the claws of anxiety were loosening their hold on her.

"So how often do you get panic attacks?" Jack leaned against the counter, keeping his distance.

Bayleigh pulled the bag away from her face long enough to answer. "It's just the exhaustion." *Deny and sidestep.*

Jack shot her a dubious look but didn't refute her. "Well, I can help you solve that problem, then. Your bedroom is just down the hall. I'll help you to it," he straightened up from the counter.

"I can make it..." She lowered the bag, raised her chin and stood. Her thigh muscles tightened into a knot as soon as she attempted to put her weight on her leg and her knee gave out.

Shit. Shit. Shit. She collapsed back into the chair, shoulders slumped. *Breathe. Just breathe.*

"As I was saying, I can help you...and while you are resting, I can fix us something to eat." He gave a hard look, crossing his arms over his chest, daring her to contradict him again.

Bayleigh swallowed hard and studied Jack from across the room. She couldn't make it down the hall on her own, not unless she crawled. Worse, he knew it, too. He was just waiting for her to try it.

"Instead of carrying me, could you just, maybe, let me lean on you or something?" The rough whisper of his denim jeans and the 'click' of his boot heels on the tiles alerted her that he was on the move, but she wasn't expecting him to be right in front of her when she raised her head. She gasped, drawing back. *Too close. He's too close!*

His eyebrows drew together and he took a step away from her. "Sorry." He held his hand out, palm up.

She looked between his outstretched hand and his face. He had such beautiful eyes, full of concern for her. Jason had said she could trust him, and she trusted her brother.

"It's ok, Bayleigh. Believe it or not, I get it," his hand didn't waiver.

With her heart pounding so hard and fast in her chest she was sure he could hear it, Bayleigh wiped her hand on her thigh. A slight tremble was still evident in her fingers and she pressed her lips together as she placed her hand in his, allowing him to ease her out of her chair. She wobbled a bit as she stood and his hands dropped to her waist, causing her body to tense.

"Sweetheart, you are hell on my ego," a wry smile crossed his face as he stood there.

She breathed in deep, her senses overwhelmed with the subtle scent of his spicy cologne, the warmth of his hands on her waist holding her. She couldn't deny if they'd met *before*, she'd have been all for the flirting. But now, she just couldn't let go of that all-consuming fear. The injustice of that made her want to scream. Instead, she clenched her jaw and looked up. Her determined gaze meeting his concerned one.

"You sure you can walk?" He raised an eyebrow as he removed his hands from her waist.

"I'm fine. It's just sore. I think...I...I shouldn't have jumped out of the cab like I did. Stupid mistake." She grasped the hand he offered with a tight grip, accepting his support. She could do this. She had to do this.

"I could have told you that *before* you jumped out of the truck," he lifted his eyebrows when she glared at him.

By forcing herself to ignore the pain radiating from her knee, she took the first step, congratulating herself on having to use his arm as a crutch only a little. She couldn't let him carry her again, she didn't think she could take another panic attack. That was one of the things she'd neglected to fill Jason in on. She knew Jack wouldn't buy into the exhaustion theory if she did have another one and she just wasn't ready to tell him or Jason the whole sordid story. Not yet.

There was also the whole issue of what to do if they didn't believe her, or understand what she was going through and turned their backs on her. Like Will had.

Her ex hadn't understood, she knew that much for

certain. He'd blamed her for the whole thing, never once admitting to his own failures that led to this mess. He'd made the other band members choose between them, causing her to quit the band and head home to Texas.

"Earth to Bayleigh." Jack squeezed her hands, bringing her attention back to him.

"Sorry. I was..." she looked around and realized she'd managed to make it all the way to the bedroom and they were standing in front of the bed. Her eyes darting between him, the bed and the door, she tugged her hand free from his and took a step back away from him.

Frowning as he let go of her hand, he motioned to a door. "You have your own bathroom," he scrutinized the room. "I think you have everything you need. There's extra blankets in the closet, if you need any."

"Thank you." She wrapped her arms around her waist.

He turned, facing her once again. She stiffened as he took a step towards her, causing him to stop and take two steps backwards. Compassion shone in his eyes, along with understanding as he again looked in her eyes. "I don't know who hurt you, pretty lady but you are safe with me. I promise you." His voice was soft and the words went straight to her heart, warming the darkest recess of her soul.

He looked down at her fists briefly. "You are safe here," he repeated forcefully, as his eyes came back up to meet hers. There was something else in his eyes; was it a flash of desire? She took a ragged breath, and with a jerky nod blinked to clear the tears.

He turned away and paused at the door, one hand on the doorknob. "You need to rest. I'll get your bags later." He hit the light switch as he stepped into the hallway, pulling the door closed behind him, leaving her alone in the room, the only light coming from the setting sun through the window.

As soon as his footsteps faded down the hallway, she threw herself backwards on the bed and covered her face with her hands. How many times in a day was she going to embarrass herself in front of him? She'd gone *weeks* without a flashback or panic attack. She had both within minutes, in front of him.

And the look in his eyes. Was he interested in her? It had been so long since anyone had looked at her with anything but pity, she was afraid to read too much into it. But what if he was interested? What was she supposed to do? Could she push the panic down far enough to explore the attraction?

And for some strange reason, she *trusted* this guy. And not just because her brother had given his stamp of approval, either. But what if he was like her ex, and found her at fault for anything and everything? God, she should have never come here. She should have taken Maddie up on the offer to hide in the mountains, where she'd have been alone.

Other than her ex, Maddie was the one person who Bayleigh had trusted enough to tell about the panic attacks and nightmares. And he didn't care. He blamed her for the whole mess. Maddie had tried to get her to talk to someone in the hospital, but Bayleigh just wanted to get her knee taken care of and escape. She had hoped getting away from there would allow her to just bury it and forget. But even halfway around the world, the fears chased her.

As a tear slid down her cheek, she turned on her side

and curled into a fetal position and tucked her hand under her cheek. She'd call Maddie later. Maybe she could still join her in Kentucky, with her family. Once her knee recovered from this little set-back and she'd seen her brother, she could leave and keep running.

CHAPTER 4

*A*s soon as jack left bayleigh's room, he went to his home office and started searching the Internet for information about her. Her reactions whenever he got too close to her and the way she was hyper-aware of every single movement he made, he would bet his monthly disability check he got from the Army on her having been a victim of some kind of abuse. The question he wanted answered right now was by whom and for how long. His fingers tapped against the keyboard as he typed in her name and waited for the information to appear.

He was amazed at the amount of information that popped up on his screen, just from her name alone. It seemed as if the majority of the band's success wasn't given to the band itself, but the strength of the music they played. And she wrote the majority of their music, according to most of the articles he read. She was quite the talented songbird, it seemed.

He finally stumbled across the information he was looking for. He could feel the anger simmering under the surface as he skimmed the article, before going back and reading it in more detail. He wondered if Jason knew. And then remembering the slight hesitation in Jason's answer when he'd asked about why she was skittish. He figured Jason had done his own Google searches.

She'd been stalked by some crazy bastard. He'd broken into her apartment. She'd managed to get out of the apartment with a few bruises from being 'slapped around,' according to the article. Her neighbors had heard her and called the police. And to top it all off, it had been the owner of the bar where they'd been performing since going to England.

No wonder Bayleigh looked like she hadn't slept in a month. He was guessing she hadn't slept in a year. It also explained the trust issues.

He exited the page he'd found the article on and went back to Google, typing in *stalking victims* this time. Domestic abuse and stalking weren't his forte when it came to the law. Hell, those types of cases didn't come up too often in Waketon. And if they did, people tended to use the 'good-ole-boy' system to take care of it. But it did happen every once in a blue moon, and he always referred the cases to attorneys out of Austin or San Antonio. Bigger cities would have better resources to help those victims. Plus he didn't want to screw up in court and cause more damage.

Shit. Now what the hell do I do? I can't just tell her I looked her up on the Internet and invaded her privacy. He pushed back from the desk and with a heavy sigh, shutting down the computer. His stomach growled, reminding him he hadn't had anything for dinner yet.

Glancing at the clock, he saw that his houseguest had

been asleep for over an hour. Deciding now was a good time to bring her bags inside, he headed outside to grab her luggage and took it back to her bedroom. He opened her bedroom door just enough to set everything just inside of it; she didn't even flinch as he set everything down. After that, he headed back out to the kitchen, trying to remember what he even had on hand worth eating that wouldn't require a lot of prep time. Or thawing. It would help if he knew what she liked to eat but, hell, beggars couldn't be choosers.

Pizza. He could always make a pizza, he thought, as he looked in his pantry. He wasn't cordon bleu but he could make a mean pizza. Grabbing all the ingredients he needed, he had a pizza thrown together and in the oven in a matter of minutes. He hoped one would be enough for both of them.

He glanced at his cell phone on the counter and debated with himself whether or not to call Jason. But he'd already invaded her privacy by doing that search on the Internet. He couldn't bring himself to betray her trust by telling her brother on top of it. Besides, it was up to Bayleigh to decide who was told and when. It was Jack's job to keep her safe until Jason got back to town.

His job. He did not like thinking of her in those terms. She was not a 'job', damn it. She was a woman who had been put through the ringer and needed a chance to heal.

And he wanted to be the one to help her heal.

What the hell am I thinking? I couldn't even 'be there' and give Diana the attention she needed when I was with her. Bayleigh already had a dumbass for a boyfriend, if Jason is right. I am so not the guy for her.

Hearing her door open and close down the hall, he

turned and braced himself against the countertop, arms relaxed at his side, legs crossed at the ankles. His ears caught the sound of her uneven footsteps as she made her way down the hallway. He shook his head. *Damn stubborn woman. Wouldn't kill her to call out and ask for a hand, would it?*

He wanted to go to her, scoop her up in his arms, shield her from whatever demons were out there. Again, what the hell was he thinking?

Jason's sister. Nicole's sister-in-law. She has a boyfriend. Somewhere. She is off limits! The lecture he was giving himself was not helping, he decided as he waited for her to join him.

BAYLEIGH MADE her way to the kitchen, feeling a little more refreshed after her nap. The hot shower had helped, too. Her knee was the size of a large grapefruit though. She knew if the swelling wasn't better by tomorrow morning, she'd need to have Jack take her to the ER and let them take a look at it. Her breath hitched and she forced her thoughts away from the possibility of the ER as she stepped into the kitchen. She'd worry about that if and when the time came.

Her gaze slid around the room, settling on Jack as he leaned against the counter. "Um, hi," she greeted, pushing her hair back behind her ear.

"Hey, there. How's your knee doing?"

"A little better. It's swollen, but it's holding my weight," her eyes drifted to the coffee pot. "Is the coffee fresh?"

"Yes, but I'll warn you, I make it strong. Nicole says it can be used to strip paint."

"I like it strong," she started to step towards the coffee pot but stopped as Jack waved her away.

"Sit down and I'll bring you a cup. You should stay off that leg as much as possible," he turned to the cabinet and reached in for a mug. "How do you take it?"

"Just black," Bayleigh moved over to the table and sat down, wrapping her hands around the mug when he set it down in front of her. "Thank you." She forced herself to relax as she breathed in the aroma. "And thank you for bringing in my stuff, too."

"You're welcome." Jack refilled his mug and sat down across from her at the table. "I made pizza for dinner. I hope that's ok?"

"You made it?" she glanced over at him, her eyes meeting his for a second before flitting away.

"Yes. I mean, I buy the crust already made and keep a few in the freezer. I tend to have pizza at least once a week. It's great for those nights I don't have any plans in town."

"Oh, God, I didn't even think about that...did I interrupt anything by showing up?"

Jack gave a short laugh at her stricken expression. "Not like what you are obviously thinking," he winked at her. "I had thought about stopping and seeing my aunt and uncle tonight on my way home, mooch off of them like I tend to do about five nights a week." He shrugged his broad shoulders and smiled across the table at her. "My aunt and uncle raised me so they're more like parents to me than anything else. Nicole feels the same way. She tends to eat there whenever Jason is on call."

Bayleigh nodded and stared at her coffee. "I'm looking forward to meeting her."

"Yeah, Nicole is great. I think you'll like her. I know she's looking forward to meeting you, too." Jack studied her across the table, taking in the tension in her shoulders. "Tell me about your band."

"It's Will's band. He started it years ago. I just sing back-up when I'm needed." Her finger was tracing patterns in the wood on the tabletop. "And I write some of the songs."

"Will's the front man, right? The lead singer?"

"How'd you know that?"

"Your brother does talk about you every now and then." Jack stood up as the timer started buzzing. "Pizza's ready. What would you like to drink? I have beer, soda, water. I can find some wine if you'd rather have that, and I always have whiskey," he offered as he pulled the pizza from the oven, setting it on a towel on the counter.

"Water is fine. Can I do anything to help?"

"Nope, I had everything set out, ready to go," Jack grabbed a couple of plates and napkins from the counter and carried them over to the table. He grabbed a bottle of water out of the fridge for her and a beer for himself, setting those on the table as well, before turning back to the stove and grabbing the pizzas, carrying them over to the table as well.

"I didn't know what kind of pizza you'd like, so I hope you like everything on yours," he told her as he set it down on the table, grabbing the pizza cutter.

"It looks good," she told him, helping herself to a piece of each one. She picked a piece of the pepperoni off and nibbled on it.

"Help yourself to whatever you like, and don't be shy,"

Jack instructed as he served himself a couple of the bigger slices. He noticed her frown as he popped the top off his beer, making a note to himself to work that into the conversation later.

"So, the band..." he tilted his bottle towards her. "You guys must be pretty good to be touring Europe."

"They're not really touring, they are just one of the opening acts in a couple of pubs. They've got themselves a faithful following, but they're a long ways from being a success."

"I looked them up on-line. Article I read said you write most of the music for them."

Her eyes flew up to his and her fingers stopped pulling the pepperoni off the pizza. "Which article?"

"I don't know. Something on the Internet." Jack's eyes watched her as she swallowed hard. "You ok?"

"I'm fine. Just surprised anybody mentioned me, is all."

Jack nodded and started eating his pizza, watching to make sure she ate more than just the pepperoni off of hers. "From the way the journalist wrote it, he was surprised more people weren't talking about you."

"Yeah, well, I'm just the backup singer. So, what's your story?" she changed the subject as she picked up her slice of pizza and took a bite.

"My story?" he raised an eyebrow at her.

"Yeah, you know, where'd you grow up, where'd you go to college? That kind of stuff."

"I was your typical small town, all-American kid. I was born and raised right here in Waketon. I even played on the high school football and basketball teams. I managed to graduate with honors and headed to Texas A&M for my undergrad, then moved on to the University of Texas for law school," he gave her a wink. "Now, I'm just a small town lawyer."

"Who owns a large chunk of land," Bayleigh's eyes strayed to the window, where the sun was sinking below the horizon, causing the hills to cast long shadows over the land.

"Not that large of a chunk, just what was left to me when my grandfather died. My uncle and cousin got the majority of it."

"How much land is there?" She leaned forward, peering out the window next to the table, trying to see out.

"Between my uncle and cousin, me, and Nicole we own a total of 600 acres. Nicole owns about forty acres, I think, and I own closer to fifty. She and I both let our uncle use it for grazing and what not. Neither of us have the inclination to actually ranch."

"So why own so much land?"

"It's the heritage, for both of us. Nicole's land was left to her when her dad died. She threatened to sell it off many times over the years, but my uncle managed to always talk her out of it. She'd lease out pastures for grazing, or she let my uncle just use it most of the time, if no one signed a lease on it. And for me, well, it gave me a place to come home to when I needed it."

"I could use a place like that," Bayleigh commented as she crumpled up her napkin and tossed it onto her plate.

"You're more than welcome to stay here for however long you want. And I'm sure Jason and Nicole will offer you a place to stay when they get back."

"But these are your places. It'd be nice to have my own," her eyes strayed back to the window.

"My place wasn't always here. I had to build it. It took time and energy. And a hell of a lot of patience," he grimaced. He pushed back from the table and stood up, holding his hand out to take her plate. "Don't get up. It'll just take a few minutes to clean this up," he instructed as he tossed the paper plates into the trash can and made quick work of putting away the leftover pizza. He rejoined her at the table when he was done.

"What's Nicole like?" she asked, her voice quiet.

"She's amazing. She's smart, beautiful, and sassy. She can out argue almost any lawyer around. She's the best partner anyone could ask for, that's for damn sure. Your brother was the luckiest son of a...gun around when she decided to give him a second chance."

"How long have you known her?" her lips quirked up when he stopped himself from swearing.

"We grew up together. My uncle is married to her aunt. They raised me when my mother took off, and took Nicole in when her parents died. Their own son Mitch is only a few months older than I am, so the age span between the three of us is about eighteen months." He paused to take a sip of his beer. "Mitch is now married to Nicole's best friend Carly and they're expecting their first baby."

"Were they mad I didn't come to the wedding?" She was back to tracing designs on the tabletop with her finger.

He took in the bent head and rounded shoulders. The clink of his bottle against the wood table as he set it down caused her to jump. "Bayleigh, look at me," he waited for her eyes to meet his across the table. He eased his hand

43

across the table and laid it over one of hers. He felt her tense, but she didn't pull away. He rubbed his thumb across her knuckles. Her hand started to relax under his. Her eyes were wide but she wasn't panicked.

"To answer your question, no, they weren't mad. Disappointed might be a better word for it, maybe. Not that they talked to me about it, but believe me, if Nicole is unhappy with someone, doesn't matter who it is, everyone around her will know."

She bit her lip, looking back down at the table. "I wanted to be there. No one would have paid any attention to me being gone except Will." Stopping and clearing her throat, her voice was more of a whisper as she stated "I should have come home." She tugged her hand free of his.

"So, Miss Backup Singer. What do you do for fun?" he changed the subject as he finished off the beer, sensing she was about done with conversation.

She glanced between him and the empty beer bottle and the hallway to her room. "What do you mean?" A guarded look came down over her features as one of her hands went to her lap.

Jack would bet money that she had pepper spray in her pocket. Her other hand that was still resting on the table was flexed, as if she were ready to sink claws into skin to defend herself if needed.

"It's not a trick question," he pushed his chair back and stood up, tossing his beer bottle into his recycling bin before resuming what had become his 'normal' stance around her: across the room, arms at his sides, feet crossed at his ankles and leaning back against the counter. As non-threatening as he could make himself. "I have a few suggestions."

"I just bet you do," her voice had an edge to it.

He raised an eyebrow before continuing. "I have a hot tub, which after the last few days that I've had, and after the day you've had, would feel pretty damn good, I think. But I also can see where that might not appeal to you. I'm just giving you your options," he rotated his neck on his shoulders, emphasizing his own need for the stress relief.

"I also have a pretty extensive DVD collection, if you want to watch a movie, and there's even microwave popcorn we can make. Or, there's always the simple quiet of your own room, with the lock on the door." He crossed his arms over his chest. "It's all up to you."

"And if I choose my own company, alone in my bedroom with the door locked?" her eyes narrowed as she studied him from across the kitchen.

He wasn't sure why she was testing him but he knew she was. He tilted his head to the side a bit and shrugged his broad shoulders. "I'll go ahead and use the hot tub, read over a few briefs, catch the news and then head to bed, just like I always do. If you want to join me in the hot tub, it's through that sliding glass door. Or if you'd rather wait until I'm done, feel free to use it later." He pushed away from the counter, moving towards the hallway.

"Nicole always leaves an extra bathing suit in the dresser in your room. She won't mind if you borrow it," he called back over his shoulder. He was hoping she'd join him but knowing now what she'd just been through, he wasn't going to hold his breath.

. . .

BAYLEIGH MADE her way back to her bedroom and closed the door but stopped short of locking it. She eased down onto the edge of the bed, across from the mirror on the dresser, and stared at her reflection.

Now why did I act like that? He's just trying to be nice. Jason said I could trust him. She glanced down at her hands, which were gripping the edge of the mattress so tight, her knuckles were white. *Not all men are assholes. I have to learn to trust again.* She took a deep breath, trying to force herself to relax. She closed her eyes and thought about the man just down the hall.

She knew that he had figured out what had happened to her. It wasn't like her reactions fell into the 'normal' category. She was well aware of the articles on the Internet. There wasn't much about the attack, but a few of the tabloids had jumped on the story: American singer attacked and beaten in her rented apartment, and the guilty party was the owner of a popular nightclub; it was the stuff that sold newspapers. But he wasn't acting any different towards her.

He was still courteous, even protective of her. And she was being rude, staying in her room like this. He was letting her crash here, without prying into any of her personal story. And all she'd done was pull back from him, and just now out in the kitchen, she'd pretty much accused him of having ulterior motives when all he'd been trying to do was ask her what *she* wanted to do for the night.

With a heavy sigh, she stood and pushed herself off the bed, walking over to the dresser. He'd said Nicole kept a bathing suit here, maybe it'd fit her. She found it tucked into the top drawer, and she pulled it out, holding it up.

A simple one piece with a modest style and in her size. But could she do it? Could she prance around in front of a man, wearing next to nothing? She stepped into the bathroom with the swimwear clenched in her fist. The towels he had stocked in the bathroom drew her attention. They were large, over-sized bath towels, made for tall people. Wrapped around her, it would cover her from just above her breasts all the way to her knees.

She could do this. She'd make herself do this. Besides, she wanted to get to know Jack. She wouldn't deny she was attracted to him, as much as that scared the crap out of her right now. But she hadn't felt this kind of spark with a guy for a long time, long before she and Will had called it quits. And after his treatment of her once she'd decided it was time to end it for good, she hadn't wanted to get involved with anyone else.

One way to find out if the attraction was mutual, she decided, tossing the bathing suit onto the bathroom counter. Before she could talk herself out of it, she was changed, a towel wrapped around herself and she was making her way out to the hot tub.

JACK WAS STRETCHED out in his hot tub, head back against the side, when he heard the patio door slide open and close. Struggling to hide his grin and keep his eyes closed, he listened to her feet shuffle across the deck and stop near the spa. When he'd walked past her door on his way to the hot tub, he heard her in her room, opening and closing dresser drawers. He had hoped it had meant she was looking for that bathing suit he'd mentioned but he also knew she could have been putting away her own clothes.

When he didn't hear any other sounds coming from the pool area, he cracked one eye open, turning his head towards where he'd last heard her. "You getting in?"

When she didn't answer, he opened both eyes to look at her. She'd found Nicole's bathing suit and had wrapped herself in a towel so that only the straps of the suit showed as they crossed over her shoulders. He made a mental note to himself to buy smaller towels in the future.

Jesus, are you trying to get yourself killed by your best friends? Stop with that line of thinking!

"Not sure yet," she muttered, looking down at the water.

"You should drop the towel, if you are," he told her with a smirk.

"Still not sure," she repeated, biting her bottom lip, looking between him and the water. He laughed and stood up, offering her his hand.

"Come on, Bayleigh. You won't regret it. I promise," he watched the emotions chase each other across her features: the indecision, fear, shyness, courage and determination. He cocked an eyebrow and grinned at her. "Trust me."

TRUST HIM. She could hear Jason's voice echoing in her head, telling her he trusted this man with his life. Knowing she should and letting go of her fears and doing it were two very different things. She swallowed hard and met his gaze, allowing the towel to drop to her feet. She took those last few steps to the edge of the hot tub, her eyes dropping to the water once she was at the edge.

Now, it was Jack's turn to swallow hard. Somehow, he managed to keep his eyes on her face. The modest swimsuit was sexy as hell on her. He offered her his hand, helping her step into the tub. She let out a hiss as the heat enveloped her.

"You'll get used to it," he assured her, as she eased onto one of the bench seats. He sat down across from her and then reached over and activated the jets. His head dropped back against the edge and he closed his eyes. "Just relax, Bayleigh."

BAYLEIGH TURNED so she could lay her leg across the bench and direct one of the jets at it as she massaged her knee and thigh. Her eyes strayed over to him every few seconds, as she took in the scars on his chest and abdomen. She hadn't allowed herself to stare as she got into the hot tub, but she was pretty sure she'd seen some scars on his leg, too. Her fingers traced over the small scars on her own leg as she again looked towards him, seeing his eyes now open and looking right at her.

"Go ahead and ask, I don't mind," he invited.

"I'm sorry...I didn't mean to be rude."

"I'd keep my shirt on if I didn't want them to ever be seen," his hand went to the marks that crisscrossed his ribs and upper abs on his left side. Her eyes followed the motion. He watched as she opened and closed her mouth a couple of times, as if to ask him, but she didn't voice her thoughts out loud.

He grew frustrated with the silence and decided to just tell her, save her the trouble of figuring out how to ask. "I was in the Army, in Afghanistan. My transport hit an IED." He dropped his head back, staring up at the glass ceiling. "My leg is worse. One of the doctors told me I was lucky I got to keep it. At the time, I just wanted to die. Most of these were just from shrapnel. They required stitches but they weren't serious."

He closed his eyes against the wave of emotion that churned in his stomach. It had been years since he'd talked about this to anyone outside of his family. But if he was going to ask her to spill her secrets, he had to be willing to share his. He cleared his throat as he realized he was the one being silent now.

"The pain was pretty fu—uh, fricking intense," he gave her a lopsided smile to apologize for his near slip. "My injuries wound up getting me an honorable discharge from the Army. I found a rehab center in California I liked. It was pretty close to where Nicole lived at the time. She stuck by me for most of my rehab, even when I was cussing her out and telling her to go away. Which is more than I can say for the lady who was supposed to be the love of my life." For a brief moment, he allowed the old bitterness to take hold and rear its ugly head. He knew he should have grabbed a drink tonight before getting into the hot tub.

"Rehab took about 9 months and then it was time to move back to Texas. I got into law school in Austin, graduated and opened my practice." He watched the blinking lights of a plane as it flew across the sky. "That's my story."

"Some story." Her eyes traveled across his chest. "How long were in Afghanistan?"

"Sixteen months. I was injured eight weeks before we were due to be rotated out." He rolled his shoulders before sliding down into the water, getting the jets to hit him further up his back.

"And the others?" She asked, her voice so quiet he almost didn't hear it above the jets.

He closed his eyes, his gut really churning now. God, the others. He could still hear the screams in his head sometimes. "Three of us survived the IED's blast. I'm the only one who made it home." He took a chance and allowed himself to look at her. He was expecting to see her face filled with disgust, or revulsion, or something. Instead, all he saw was compassion.

"We did some USO stuff when we were in England. The injured, they're happy to have anybody visit them," she told him. "It makes you appreciate life, when you hear the stories of what our troops have to do, and go through, every single day. You don't need to feel guilty that you survived, Jack. Just remember to live for your buddies."

He swallowed hard and nodded, not trusting himself to speak. How could this woman know what made it so hard to reveal those dark days to others? Survivor's guilt, that's what the therapist had called it. He was the only one on that transport to survive. Not wanting to dwell on those thoughts right now, he shoved them away. His view strayed up to the ceiling again and this time, hers followed. He heard her gasp.

"Oh, wow. I didn't realize...The whole ceiling is glass!"

"Yup." He latched onto the opening to change the topic. "I wanted to be able to use the pool year round, but I like to see the sky. "This was one of those things that drove the builder nuts." They both had their heads tilted back, staring up at the magnificence of the night sky.

"It's beautiful."

Jack nodded his agreement and lifted his hand from the water, pointing towards the stars. "That bright spot over there is the International Space Station."

"It never amazes me how many stars there are..." She tilted her head and pointed at something. "What's that?"

He had to shift closer to her to see what she was referring to, surprised she didn't tense up. "One of the planets, I think. I'd have to look online to see which one. I know the constellations, at least the big ones, but that's about it," he admitted. "This is what I missed when I had to live in the city. You can't see the stars for all of those city lights." He leaned forward and turned off the jets before settling back into his spot again. "It's even better when you enjoy it in the quiet. Nights like this, when there aren't any clouds in the sky and it's just the stars and the moon for light...it's perfect."

He allowed his gaze to slide over to Bayleigh. She still had her head back, looking up at the stars. He wondered what her story was, who had abused her, and why she wasn't telling her brother the truth. He knew she was going to need counseling and a gentle hand, and a man who could stand by her, to help her get through it.

He found himself wishing he could be that man. Could he do it? Could he allow a woman access to his heart again, while being there for her? Diana, his ex, sure hadn't thought he could do it. It had taken her one bad night, seeing him struggle with nightmares and flashbacks, for her to turn and run. He knew it took a hell of a woman to put up with men like him, scarred not just physically but emotionally. But now that the reverse situation was staring him in the face, someone needed him to be there for them while they put their life back together...could he do it? For this moment in time, he wanted to try.

She turned towards him just then and smiled. "Thank you."

He raised his eyebrows, but made no other movements. Had he said any of that out loud? Or was she reading his mind now?

"I fell into your life today, giving no thoughts to what I might be disrupting, but you've opened your home to me and haven't pushed for anything," she explained. "And I know you keep saying that crap about southern hospitality...but you don't know me from Adam. So, thank you," she repeated. Her eyes drifted back up to the ceiling and then lowered to meet his. She sat up and turned, pulling her knees up against her chest. "I'm sure you'd like to know what happened to me."

"It's your story to tell, Bayleigh. I'll listen if you want to tell me but it's not a condition on you staying here or us being friends." Jack's gaze never wavered.

"If I was up to telling anybody, I think it would be you," she looked away. "I should have come back before now."

"Why didn't you?"

"I didn't want to admit it was over," she shrugged her

thin shoulders. "Besides, I needed to get away from them. I was hoping the distance would help with some of it."

"Take it from me, lady. The distance won't help as much as you need it to. But if you need anything—a shoulder to cry on or strong arms to help hold you up, I'm here for you." He flexed his bicep for her, trying to get her to laugh, pleased with himself when she did.

"I owe you my thanks, again," she whispered as her gaze drifted to his lips. Hesitating for a second, she leaned forward and pressed her lips to his cheek in a soft kiss.

Jack was too shocked to do anything but nod at her when she drew back, a slight flush on her cheeks. "I think I'm going to go back to my room now." She stood up and stepped out of the hot tub and grabbed her towel. She had it wrapped around herself and was heading for the sliding glass door before he could do anything more than wish her good night.

Really should have been drinking tonight. Jack shook his head as he watched her hurry back into the house. He wasn't sure if he wanted Monday to get here sooner...or never.

What the hell was he thinking? He needed for Monday to get here so he could hand her over to Jason. He didn't need the complication of a woman in his life. 'Love 'em and leave 'em that was his motto. Had been ever since that bitch of an ex had left him lying in the hospital bed.

He wasn't a believer in 'happy ever after'. Not for guys like him. Life had hardened him. He found female companionship when he needed it, women who weren't looking for long-term commitments. And so far, that plan had worked well for him.

So why was he sitting here thinking about not wanting Monday to get here? Monday meant Jason would be back in town and his sister could go home with him, where she belonged. Right? Except there was something about her that called to something deep inside of him. And it wasn't just the raging hard on he had at the moment, either.

Christ, like a fucking hormonal teenager, the second she'd shown up in that bathing suit, his cock had taken notice. It wasn't that the bathing suit was too small, or hadn't fit right. At least, not that he could tell. But all he could think when she dropped that towel earlier was how he wanted her to drop the suit along with it. And then just now, when she'd given him that chaste kiss on the cheek, he was surprised he hadn't gone up in flames.

He waited until he was sure the coast was clear before he stood up. Hell, he was in trouble. T-R-O-U-B-L-E. He groaned at the thought as he stalked down the hallway to his bedroom, refusing to give into the temptation to pause outside of her bedroom to listen at the door. He was not a love-struck teenager, damn it. Of course, it would help if certain body parts would listen to that argument, he thought as he entered his bathroom and turned the shower on but left the temperature on 'cold'.

Stripping off his wet swimming trunks, he stepped into the shower, muffling a curse as he ducked his head and stood under the freezing cold spray. "Damn it, go down! She is off limits!" he muttered as he titled his head back and clenched his teeth together. Reaching up, he tried adjusting the shower head until the spray was aimed at his groin.

"Start behaving or we'll be having nothing but freezing showers until Monday," he warned himself, bracing his hands against the walls of the shower and forcing himself to stay under the stinging needles of the spray. "Let this be a warning to you, too. Listen to the brain upstairs and quit taking it upon yourself to show interest. Got it?"

He stayed in the shower, torturing himself, until he could no longer feel *any* of his appendages. Exhausted, he climbed into bed, and closed his eyes, sending up a silent prayer that sleep would come fast and easy for at least one night.

CHAPTER 5

*J*ack woke up earlier than usual the next morning, groaning when he saw the time on his clock. Once his body had warmed back up and his mind had started thinking about the houseguest down the hall, all the blood had rushed back into his cock. At that point, he'd resorted to taking matters into his own hand, so to speak. All that had done was taken the edge off.

Knowing it was pointless to try and go back to sleep again, Jack climbed out of bed and pulled on his work-out clothes, and headed for his in-home gym, or in this case, in-*barn* gym. He paused after he opened the first door, and stared out over the horizon. The sun was just coming up over the horizon and he breathed in the early morning freshness. He loved this time of day. The peace and quiet, the newness of it all. The chance to just be alone with his thoughts.

The sharp call of a crow startled him out of his musings and he turned to enter the barn, flipping the switch to turn on the lights. He moved over to the stereo he had in the corner and cued up his music, but didn't hit play yet. He jumped on the treadmill, and started off at a brisk jog. Within minutes, he was at a full out run, at a brutal pace. One he knew he wouldn't be able to sustain for long. But he liked to push himself. He liked to prove that he could still do it, despite the injuries from the IED.

A couple of trucks passed by the barn on the private road behind it, which made him think his uncle and cousin must have some of the stock up on his land. He'd have to remember to text the foreman later and make sure. Otherwise, he had trespassers. Wouldn't be the first time. He heard a third truck approach but this one slowed and turned to come up to the barn. *Damn. Well, saves me the text.* He slowed his run but didn't get off the treadmill.

"You in here?" a voice called out before stepping through the door.

"Treadmill!" he called back, recognizing his uncle Steve's voice and he slowed his pace a little more.

"Saw the doors open, thought you might be. You didn't stop by or call last night." Steve leaned against one of the posts in the center of the barn. "Everything ok?"

Shutting down the treadmill, Jack stepped off and grabbed a towel from the stack he kept near the weights. He'd only completed three miles, so he wasn't out of breath, but the sweat was pouring off of him. "I'm fine, Pop." Steve was the only father figure Jack had ever known. He'd never been able to call him dad, "Uncle Steve" always seemed too formal, too distant for what he was to him. So they'd agreed on the term "Pop".

"Jason's sister showed up at the office yesterday, a little worse for wear. I offered to let her stay here," he chose to ignore the lifted eyebrow. "Jason and Nicole will be home Monday."

"She could come and stay with us. Mitch is gone for a few days, and Helen and I are heading to San Antonio for a few days. Carly would appreciate the company."

"We're fine here."

"Uh-huh." Steve chuckled, pushing away from the post. "Boys are moving the herd to the North pasture today and repairing some fencing. Helen and I will be leaving this afternoon for our weekend in San Antonio. We'll talk to you next week." He slapped his nephew on the back as he passed by him. Jack listened to his uncle drive away and then hit play on his stereo, moving over to the weights. He settled himself on the bench and began lifting, losing himself in the repetition of movement, not stopping until every muscle in his arms and chest burned from the exertion.

He groaned, dropping the hand weights he was holding, wincing at the *clank* that seemed to echo through the barn. He grabbed a clean towel and wiped the sweat off his face, glancing at the clock. He'd managed to get in his full work-out already. Wondering what his houseguest was up to, he pushed to his feet and secured the barn, heading back up to the house and a shower.

HAVING GOTTEN up earlier than usual and putting his body through his normal workout, by the time he finished his shower, he was in desperate need of that first jolt of caffeine. The house was still silent, the hum of the refriger-ator almost deafening in the morning stillness. He put on a pot of coffee. Not wanting to wait for the whole pot to brew, he deftly switched out the pot for his mug, watched for it to fill, and then switched it back, without spilling so much as a drop. He inhaled the rich aroma, and then carried his first cup into the living room to watch the morning news. Which is where Bayleigh found him a little while later.

"Good morning." She greeted him as she eased into the room. He smiled over at her, waving at the seat beside him, noting she'd helped herself to coffee.

"Sleep ok?" He asked as she walked over to the couch. He watched her with a critical eye, trying to see if she was still favoring her knee.

"I slept. I took one of my muscle relaxers after I got out of the hot tub, so I think I was asleep before my head even hit the pillow. How about you?" She brought her coffee cup to her lips and blew across the top of it. He'd never thought of how a woman cooled off her coffee as 'sexy' before, but with her, it was a definite turn on.

"Uh...fine. I was up early though." He turned back to the TV and nodded towards it. "We've got a cold front moving in late tonight. Thunderstorms tonight and then the temps will drop, so they're saying we'll have freezing rain by tomorrow morning. If you need anything from any stores, we should go get it today." His eyes strayed back to her.

"I can't think of anything. I'd just like to get my car, at some point, if you're going to your office at all." She took a sip of coffee. God, didn't she know her lips were a lethal weapon?

"Not a problem. We can leave here in about forty-five

minutes or so. I was just going to make omelets for break-fast, if that's ok with you?" He stood up, heading back towards the kitchen. He had to distance himself. Now. He'd had enough thoughts about that mouth last night, he wasn't sure how much more he could take.

"Omelets are fine. Can I help?"

"No, I've got it covered," he assured her, mentally groaning as she followed him. He reached into the refriger-ator and started pulling out ingredients. After watching him for a moment, she muttered something about going to get dressed. He sighed in relief when he heard her bedroom door close. Christ, he needed to get a grip. And fast.

He set the frying pan down on the stove and turned the burner on with a flick of his wrist, before cracking the eggs into a bowl and beating them with the whisk. The omelets were ready and on the table, along with glasses of orange juice, when she returned.

"Wow. A man who can cook. I'm impressed," she teased, taking her seat.

"Well, small town living tends to do that to you." He shrugged as he sat down across from her. "And I hate eating alone, so I don't go out very often."

"Oh, come on. A good looking guy like you? Are the women in this town blind or something?" Her eyes went wide and her shoulders shook and even from where he sat across from her, the wheezing was audible. "I'm sorry...I mean...I'm not..."

Jack said her name as loud as he dared, trying to break her focus on whatever was in her past. He needed her here, in the moment. "It's ok. Most of the women here are blind. Just ask Nicole. She's still trying to figure out how Jason lasted until she came back to town without someone snagging him." He told her when her gaze settled on him. He didn't draw attention to her clenched fists, or the way she'd reacted to her own comment but by the way her breathing was evening out and her fingers were no longer gripping her fork, he knew she was calming herself down.

"So while I'm finishing up a few things in the office, what are you going to do? You're welcome to come back here and hang out."

"I might do that." She took a deep breath. He didn't hear any catches to it. "Would I be able to use your computer? I, uh, quit the band so I'll be needing to find a new job. Soon."

"Yeah. Help yourself to the desktop in my office here. I don't have a password on that one, since I do all my legal work on my laptop now." He groaned. "Crap. My laptop. I forgot I locked the system up yesterday and I didn't think to tell Nicole about it. And Stacy's out of the office today, too."

"I could take a look at it," she offered.

"How much do you know about computers?"

"Does it matter if you've already locked it up?" She raised her eyebrows. When he gave her a mock glare, she laughed. "I have a degree in computer science. I was a double major and I just never took a job in the field. I'm sure I can figure it out."

"I see." He studied her across the table. "Well, as you pointed out, I don't have much to lose. Can you be ready to leave in about ten minutes, then?" He waited for her to agree before he stood up. They cleared the table and then went to their rooms to grab last minute items, before meeting back in the kitchen.

He handed her a travel mug, filled with fresh coffee. She looked at him, surprise in her eyes. He smiled and stroked her cheek with one finger in a gentle caress. "I drink a lot of coffee. I just thought, since it was the first thing you grabbed yesterday when you woke up from your nap, and again this morning, you might like another cup."

"Thanks." She told him, a slight blush coloring her cheeks.

It didn't escape his notice that she hadn't pulled away, flinched, or in any way had a negative reaction to his reaching out and touching her cheek. He led the way out to his truck and they drove back to his office. They listened to the radio. The winter storm that was supposed to hit the Hill Country the next morning was the big news of the day and had everyone in a tizzy.

He parked in the lot at his building and led the way inside. She sat down and booted up his system and started muttering about "idiots who don't know a damn thing about computers" and he chuckled. At least she'd given him apologetic smile when she realized he was still standing there. Not sure what to do with himself, he headed out to the reception area and opened up his email on Stacy's desktop, sending a few replies. Twenty minutes after leaving her alone, she called out his name. When he went found her, she was buffing her nails on her shirt.

"You do realize this system is pretty easy to use, right? I'm surprised you managed to lock the whole thing up." She smirked.

"Yeah, Nicole tells me that every time, too." He leaned

over her to tap on the keyboard, checking a couple of files. "You, my dear, are amazing." Straightening, he spun the chair around to face him, and pulled her to her feet. He waited a brief second to see if there were any negative reactions, but she just stared at him. "So, do you like red meat?" Her hands were still held in his and he ran his thumb over her knuckles.

"Uh, yeah, why?" her eyebrows drew together.

"Because, without you, my business would be in danger of financial ruin. The least I could do is take you out for a steak dinner."

"Financial ruin, huh? What will I need to wear?" She scrutinized her jeans and sweater.

"Something tight and slinky." He winked, laughing when she pulled a hand free and punched his shoulder. He allowed himself to look her over from head to toe. "What you're wearing would be fine."

"I have this sudden urge to go shopping."

"I told you, what you have on works. Why do you need to go shopping?"

"Because" her cheeks grew warm and she refused to meet his gaze.

"Bayleigh?" Women and clothes, two things that men were never meant to understand.

"I want to dress up for you." With her chin tucked into her chest, the words were pitched so low he almost didn't hear them.

"Oh." Anything more intelligent escaped him. When was the last time a woman wanted to dress up for him? Not because she wanted him to take her somewhere fancy, but *for him*? A weird feeling hit him in his stomach as he studied her bent head. "Well, let me give you some directions to downtown. There are a lot of shops around the town square, and Nicole and Stacy are always going on about them." The scratch of the pen over the paper seemed loud in the silence of the room.

"I wrote my cell number on there, too. In case you need saving again." He handed the paper over to her when he finished and she tucked it into her pocket. She moved towards the front office and the door. "Think you can find your way back to my place?" He followed her.

"I think so, I--oh!" she stopped and turned without warning and he plowed into her. His arms came up and wrapped around her, steadying her. Her hands were trapped between them, her palms flat on his chest. "I'm sorry, I didn't realize you were behind me" she tilted her head, the apology falling away.

Without thinking, he reacted. With her hands on his chest and the tenderness in her expression as she peered at him through her eyelashes, he couldn't help himself. Lowering his head, he kissed her. She gasped but didn't try to move or push him away. His lips covered hers. He wanted to be gentle. But this was more than the chaste peck she'd given him last night. Tongues were involved this time.

He stroked her back with his left hand, his right hand resting beneath her rib cage. He wanted her closer, wanted to feel her against him. Her hands clenched against his chest. *Damn, she's reached her limit.* Prepared to stop, she surprised him by pulling him in closer, her hands now fisted in his shirt. He stroked her tongue with his, retreating, pushing in...a dance as old as time. And she responded to each movement. Against the hand on her ribs, he could feel her heart as it raced and his own pulse sped up. She moaned, or was that him? Hell if he knew, or even cared at this point.

He needed to put the brakes on now, before he did something stupid, like sweep everything off the desk and lay her down. That image should not be in his mind. He broke off the kiss, resting his forehead on hers. Her breathing was ragged, but it didn't have that wheeze it would get with her panic attacks. His hands rubbed over her back in soothing strokes, enjoying the moment of holding her in his arms. The occasional car drove by outside, and the ornate clock on the wall ticked, the sound loud and obnoxious in the near silence of the outer office. It was just the two of them for now. He simply held her and waited. Her hands relaxed and he moved his head so he could see her face.

Her eyes fluttered open, her green orbs soft, and filled with hope and confusion. He pressed his lips to her forehead. "Should I apologize?" he questioned.

"No, if you do, I may have to do something physical and hurt you," she breathed out a deep sigh. "I'm not trying to be a tease" her voice wobbled and she broke eye contact, as her eyes filled with tears. His arms tightened, pulling her into his chest.

"I didn't think that, and I wouldn't. We were both active participants," his chin settled on top of her head. The floral scent of her shampoo was wrapping itself around him and he wanted nothing more than to nuzzle her neck.

He swallowed hard. "You could accuse me of teasing you, as well, or worse, trying to get in your pants," he pointed out. "And on Monday, you tell Jason, he challenges me to pistols at dawn, and then Nicole winds up a widow and you hate me for life," he deadpanned, getting her to giggle.

"Never know, she might not wind up a widow," she returned.

"Trust me, I've gone shooting with Jason," he frowned down at her. She stuck her tongue out at him and he groaned.

"Lady, the things I want to tell you to do with your tongue."

She gasped and her cheeks flushed.

"Christ, I'm sorry Bayleigh! I shouldn't have said that." Heat rushed to his own face. What the hell was wrong with him?

She cleared her throat and stepped back. His arms dropped, allowing her to step away. "So, I guess I'll meet you at your place around, say, five o'clock? To go to dinner?" she fidgeted with her car keys, the jingling sound grated on his nerves.

Nerves that were calming down as her words sunk into his overstimulated brain. She wasn't running away.

"Yes. I'll be home by five o'clock. Oh the spare key for the back door is under the gnome on the ledge. Call me if you get into any kind of trouble. Did you charge your cell phone last night?"

"Yes, I found my charger. It had shifted and slid inside of a shoe. My phone has a full battery today." She headed for the door. "I'll see you at five, then," smiling over her shoulder, she stepped outside. Her footsteps tapped out a steady beat down the steps before fading.

Her car's engine revved in the parking lot and he

moved to the window in time to see her pull out of the lot. *Shit. Should have gotten her number.*

He stood there, the clock ticking off the passing seconds, and he wondered if Jason would give him her cell phone number. Without asking any probing questions. Somehow, he didn't think so. And not a can of worms worth opening. Glancing at his watch, he set an alarm for 3:30 pm and headed for his office. No way was he going to be late for his date tonight. Now to get through the next six hours, without reliving the last twenty minutes in his fantasies all day.

CHAPTER 6

ollowing the directions he'd written out for her, Bayleigh found herself in the town square within minutes of leaving Jack's office. She wandered around the square for a bit, doing some window shopping, getting a feel for the town. The wind had picked up, the strong gusts bringing the promise of the cold front. She was glad she'd grabbed her wool coat before leaving London. Too bad she hadn't grabbed a few dresses. A simple jade dress in one window caught her eye. She entered the store and was able to locate the dress, and the salesclerk walked over to her as she was studying it on the hanger.

"We have a dressing room in the back, if you'd like to try it on."

"Oh...thanks," Bayleigh looked up from the price tag. "Do you sell shoes, as well?"

"Oh, yes, we sell everything!" the clerk laughed. "I don't recognize you, are you new to town?"

"Sort of. I mean, I'm just visiting my brother." She followed the clerk back to the shoes.

"Sorry. I don't mean to be nosy. But I've lived here every one of my fifty-eight years, and my parents lived here their entire lives, and their parents. Well, you get the picture. I may not know all the names, but I remember faces." She studied Bayleigh's. "And you do look familiar. Who's your brother?"

"Jason Morrow." Bayleigh bit back a smile. Typical small towns. She wondered how long it would be before everyone in town knew she was here now.

"Oh, how wonderful you came to visit! Are you staying with Nicole's family until they get back, then?"

"Mm-hmm" she made a noncommittal sound. Hadn't Jack said he and Nicole were like family? She wasn't sure he'd want the whole town knowing she was staying at his place. Not that anything was going on between them, well, not yet. WHOA...where had that thought come from? She sat down on a bench with a thump.

"Honey, you ok?" The clerk's concerned voice broke through her fog and she shook her head.

"I'm fine." Smiling, she held up the shoe she still had in her hand. "I like this one." The clerk ushered her into a dressing room and within minutes, she'd tried on the dress and shoes, deciding in an instant to buy both. The clerk was able to talk her into buy into buying a wrap to go over the dress, reminding her of the dropping temperatures outside. Blocking out the endless chatter of the clerk, Bayleigh looked around the shop while everything was boxed up.

Only two hours after leaving his office, she was parking her car in front of his house. Alone. She found the spare key he'd told her about and let herself inside. She giggled as she lifted the gnome to remove the key. Jack did not strike her as the garden gnome kind of guy.

Carrying her bags into the living room, she shut the door, relocking it. The silence unnerved her. Even from here, she could hear the hum of the refrigerator.

She made her way over to the stereo system and studied it. With a push of the button she had it on and the music blaring. Better. Smiling, she recognized the music. So Jack liked country music. She would have pegged him as a classical kind of guy.

The framed photographs on the bookshelf next to the stereo snagged her attention. Jack in a tux, with her brother, and that must be Nicole. She picked up the frame and studied the woman. She was radiant, Jason's arms around her, her head thrown back, laughing. Setting the frame back down, her gaze roamed over the remaining pictures. Startled, she realized most of them were of Jack and Nicole.

Frowning, she moved away and grabbed her bags, heading for her room. She pulled out the purchases she'd made, hanging the dress on the closet door. Should she still wear it? What was up between him and Nicole? Did she trust him? How well did she know him? What if he...

"STOP!" She screamed it at the top of her lungs. Thank God he wasn't home yet. She buried her face in her hands. What had that stupid therapist told her to do? Deep breaths? Check. Not helping much, but she was doing it.

Trying to get her thoughts under control, she pulled her backpack over to her and dug her journal and a pen out. She pressed her lips together as she flipped to an empty page and then started writing out the very questions that had just been running through her mind.

It was one of the coping techniques that had been suggested to her. Write it out, then cross out the ones that you may already know the answer to, or that may not really matter. Sometimes, it helped. Sometimes, it triggered a bigger attack. But it was one of the few that helped get it her thoughts in order.

She wrote for a long time. Her fingers were cramped by the time she was done, and with a gasp, she realized she had about a little over ninety minutes before Jack was due home.

Tossing her book and pen aside, she rushed into the bathroom. She hadn't wanted to put any effort into looking good for a guy in almost three months. Tonight, that was changing.

She was just finishing with her hair when she heard a knock on the bedroom door. Butterflies were taking flight in her stomach. Crossing over to the bedroom door, she swung it open with a smile. "Hey. I didn't hear you come home."

His eyes raked over her. "With the music as loud as you had it, not surprising." A wink told her he teasing. "And you were in the shower."

"Oops. I forgot about the music. It's a good thing you don't have neighbors." Her lips tilted up as she her own eyes skimmed over him in his navy slacks and light blue button down dress shirt. His hair was still damp from his own shower. "You look nice."

"You look amazing. You ready to go?" He held his hand out to her and without hesitating, she put hers in it and walked down the hall with him. She felt the warmth in her cheeks as he helped her with her wrap, his hands lingering on her shoulders. She closed her eyes and breathed in his scent.

He dropped his hands from her shoulders offered her his arm with a slight bow. "Your chariot awaits, my lady." She giggled and shook her head, allowing him to lead her to his truck.

"So I didn't get any frantic phone calls begging me to come save you. I take it you found the square without any problems?"

"I did. You have a nice town. Everyone was very outgoing and helpful. Oh!" She made a face, shifting to face him. "By the way, I wasn't sure if, well, uh, one of the ladies started talking and I told her who my brother is. I guess she knew Jason and Nicole are out of town and she asked if I was staying with Nicole's family. I sort of said yes, but didn't say it was you."

Jack laughed. "Welcome to small town living, where everybody knows your name and personal business." He reached over and patted her leg. "Don't worry about it. I forgot to mention that Pop, uh, that's what I call my uncle, stopped by today. He knows you're here."

"You call your uncle 'Pop'?"

"Uncle Steve got to be too formal, but he's not my dad. When we came up with the name, I still had hopes someday I'd find who my dad was."

"And your aunt?"

"For some reason, I never had an issue calling her 'Ma'." He shrugged, but his hands clenched on the steering wheel.

Not even realizing she was doing it, she slid her hand across the seat and placed it on his arm. "So, this restaurant, is it a chain or something local?"

He glanced between the road, her hand on his arm and her face and she loosened her hold, drawing back. Right hand still on the wheel, he reached over with his left and trapped hers. "I like it there," he told her, his voice huskier than normal.

"It might cramp my arm, having to hold it up like this."

"Can't have that, can we?" he switched to driving with his left hand, snagged her hand with his right, and laid their joined hands down on his thigh. She smiled over at him, a faint blush on her cheeks.

"And here's the restaurant. I wouldn't say it's a chain, but there are a few locations around the Hill Country."

He squeezed her fingers before releasing her hand as he parked the truck and opened his door. "Stay there!" He ordered, laughing as she tossed a mock salute his way. But she stayed in the truck this time until he came around and opened her door.

She was still laughing as he helped her down. He brushed back a strand of hair from her face, his fingers caressing her cheek. "Your eyes could light up a room when you laugh." Her laughter faded at his murmured words, and her heart started racing.

Her gaze danced away from his, taking in her surroundings and she licked her lips. He cupped her cheek and she stared at him. "It's ok. It's just me," he kept his voice low, even. "If I'm making you uncomfortable, in any way, tell me."

"No. It's not you," she choked out a laugh. "God, how clichéd can I get? 'It's not you, it's me,'" she drew in a ragged breath. "I'm ok. I just need a second," a few more deep breaths with her eyes closed. The rough pad of his thumb was stroking over her cheek in a gentle caress. She turned her head into his palm, nuzzling it, and his other hand tightened against her waist. She peeked up at him, biting her lip.

"There's no pressure here. This is a simple dinner between us." He tucked her hair behind her ear. "Let's go inside before the wind gets any colder." With his arm wrapped around her shoulders, he turned towards the restaurant's entrance.

The hostess greeted them and showed them to a table, and within minutes, had water, fresh bread and their wine on the table. Bayleigh's eyes scanned her menu before drifting to Jack. She'd known what she'd wanted as soon as they walked through the door. A juicy steak and baked potato, with everything they offered topping it. With a sigh, she closed it and set it aside.

"Decide already?" He looked over at her with a smile, closing his own and setting it on top of hers. He motioned to the waitress and they placed their orders.

"How long do you think you'll stay in Waketon?" he asked after the waitress walked away.

Small talk. She could do small talk, couldn't she? "I'm not sure, yet. I don't want to wear out any welcomes," she reached for the bread. "You said you grew up here?" Maybe she could get him to talk, then she wouldn't have to.

"I did. I was born in San Antonio, my birth mother came home for a few months, but one morning, Pop got up, found a note on the kitchen table and Ma found me still in my crib."

"Did she ever...?"

"Once a year or so she'd show up," he cut off her question. "She never stuck around long. During one visit, Pop had her sign the legal documents giving up her rights to me. The visits spaced out after that. Last I heard, she was in Arizona."

"I'm sorry." Not knowing what else to say, that was all she could offer.

"Trust me, I know I'm better off without her. Ma and Pop treated me like their own son. It was my own insecurities that caused any problems with it, but we're long past that." He assured her.

The waitress brought their salads and refilled the water glasses.

"So what was it like growing up here?" Bayleigh forked up a bite of the crisp lettuce. *Food. I can keep my mouth full, not have to talk.*

"Pretty much same as it is now, I guess. Everyone gets into your business. The whole town will know I was out on a date with you by midnight."

"Date?" The lettuce got stuck halfway down her throat and she coughed. She grabbed her water glass to wash it down. *Oh God, he wants this to be a date. I can't do this.* She forced herself to take another bite, the dressing leaving a sour taste in her mouth.

"Isn't that what you'd call this? Two adults, having dinner and I'm paying by the way," he winked at her.

"What? Oh, never mind." *He's teasing me. I need to get a grip.* "Did you play sports?"

"This is Texas. Playing football is like part of the by-laws of the state or something. And I also played basketball." His gaze caught and held hers. "Do I get to ask questions, too?"

"I'm sorry, I'm not good at this."

"What, eating dinner?"

"Small talk, being on a date," her fingers tightened around her fork at the word. "I haven't done this in a very long time."

"I see," he pushed his salad plate aside and stretched his arm out. His hand rested inches from hers. She glanced down. With one finger, he stroked the back of her hand. Her stomach flipped over and her pulse picked up a few extra beats.

"We won't call it a date," he whispered, for her ears alone.

The waitress was approaching with their main entrees. She swallowed hard. *How does he get it when I'm not even sure I do?*

Jack let the conversation drop. She picked up her fork and knife, and took a deep breath. Just the smell of the food had her appetite returning. She cut off a small bite and chewed. Amazing. A prime cut of beef, cooked the way she liked it: medium well.

The flavors of the marinade burst on her tongue. The baked potato, still wrapped in the aluminum foil was split right in the middle. Steam rising off of it, the butter melting and mixing with all the other toppings and running down the sides. Absolute perfection.

"So tell me a little about you? How'd you go from being a computer science major to being a backup singer in a band?"

"I did the computer thing as a concession for my mom. She didn't want me to major in music. I figured by majoring in computer science, I could learn how to use a computer to help me write my music."

"So you never wanted to be in a band?"

"Every teenager wants to be in a band. But my love of music is in writing it. I don't need to be the person in front of the mic." She paused to take a few bites of her food before continuing. "Becoming a backup singer, well, I did it for Will. I mean, I know all of their songs, forwards, backwards. And I thought, once upon a time, that he was it for me. It made sense at the time."

"What are you going to do now?"

"I don't know. I can always sell my music. I have folders full of music that never fit Will's style."

"Why'd you become a lawyer?" she asked after a brief lull in the conversation.

"The law intrigues me. There are so many levels to it. And everyone thinks they have the right answer and knows which law will apply. But then someone else will come along with a counter-argument and a different law."

"But you don't practice criminal law?" She seemed to remember her brother telling her that at some point.

"No, well, not really. I mean, I take things the court assigns me, like DUIs and shoplifting. But for the most part, I do things like estate planning and law related to being a rancher. Even in today's world, people argue about property lines, water rights, and if you've entered into a contract for breeding purposes, there's always a good fight to be had there. And this is Texas. We have to know all about mineral rights and oil rights, fun stuff like that."

"Then why'd you join the military?"

"A few reasons. There's the grandiose statement of 'I

wanted to serve my country,' which did apply. And of course, the whole September 11th thing was going on. I was in my freshman year at A&M when that happened. Granted, I was already in ROTC classes at that point, but I was still at a point I could have quit had I wanted to. But I can still remember being in class and the instructor walking in, his face white as a ghost and his hands shaking. He couldn't even get the words out, just turned on a television and we all sat there, dead silence in the room. I knew there and then, I'd never quit. My family and I, we didn't lose anyone in the terrorist attacks that day. But I felt I owed it to those families that did."

"How long were you in for before your own injuries?"

"Almost five years. My initial commitment was up and I had stayed in. I knew I would be going back for my law degree at some point, but I still had things in the military I wanted to accomplish. I wish I could have stayed in longer, done more, but a greater force decided it was time for me to move on." Jack grew silent as they both finished their meals. The waitress came by to offer dessert but they both declined. Jack studied Bayleigh from across the table, her head bent, avoiding looking back at him. He frowned.

"What's bothering you tonight?"

Her gaze flew to his. "What?"

"You're quiet, tense, and your fingers are rolling the corner of the napkin between them," he leaned forward. "You can talk to me."

She glanced down, and sure enough, she had the edge of the linen napkin between her thumb and finger. She grimaced, masking it as their waitress approached with their check.

"So, talk. What's wrong?" The waitress was walking away to run his card.

"It's nothing," she huffed out a breath and then straightened her spine and drew her shoulders back. "Can I ask you something?"

"Sure," he had buttered another roll that had been left on the table and was lifting it to his mouth.

"Why do you have so many pictures of you and Nicole in your home?"

Startled, he choked. He took a long drink of water, his eyes never leaving her face. "Because she's my best friend."

"I've never framed that many pictures of my best friend before."

"Did you look around the room any, or just the one bookshelf?" Jack pursed his lips, and leaned back, his entire focus on her. "Because, yes, the one bookshelf has a lot of pictures of just Nicole and myself. But the shelf below it has pictures of myself, Mitch and Nicole. And another shelf has pictures of my aunt and uncle." Brow furrowed, he cocked his head to the side. "What are you accusing me of?"

"I'm not, I just don't want to see my brother hurt!" she stopped talking, feeling her face getting hot, and refused to look at Jack.

"What the hell? Where is this coming from, Bayleigh?"

She forced herself to meet his gaze. "I don't want to see my brother hurt," she repeated, proud of herself for keeping her voice low and calm. Reaching for her water glass again, she was even prouder to note her hand wasn't shaking.

"You've told me yourself, and your brother has told me, how little you two talk. So you come into my home, look at a few pictures, and jump to the conclusion that Nicole and I were once together, or maybe are still screwing around behind your brother's back?" His voice was just as low and calm as hers had been, but there was a hardness in his eyes now.

The waitress approached and he sat back. He scrawled his name across the credit card draft, slid his card back in his wallet and pushed back from the table. "You ready to go?"

She stood up and removed her wrap from the chair beside her. Ever the gentleman, he took it from her and held it open for her. Swallowing hard as he helped her with it, she peered up at him through her lashes. His face was set in stone and he didn't say a word, wouldn't even look her in the eye. He placed a hand low on her back and guided her out of the restaurant.

The temperature had dropped dramatically since they'd arrived, and it was starting to rain. Jack hurried her across the parking lot. He settled her into her seat and slammed her door. Tears filled her eyes. She should have kept her mouth shut, waited until Monday.

She averted her head as he climbed into the cab and closed his own door. "You're jealous," he commented.

"No, I'm not!" she denied.

"Yeah, you are. Or are you going to try and tell me you kiss every guy like you kissed me today?" His hands clenched on the steering wheel.

Her face was flaming hot. He was right and she knew it. Her jaw was clenched so tight, she was afraid her teeth would shatter.

"Nicole and I are best friends. That is all we've ever

been, all we'll ever be." She chanced a look his way after he said that. He was staring out the front window.

"Nicole will probably cut my...Nicole's mother held Nicole up to some standard of perfection no one could ever hope to attain. She had her convinced that every problem in life was because a man held a woman back. Nicole was petrified to ever falling in love." He glanced at her. "When she kicked your brother to the curb back when they were in college that was why. Plain and simple, she got spooked. Mitch, Carly and I spent years picking up the pieces and trying to find out what had happened between them. Neither one of them would talk about it. But never, not once, did I ever try anything with her, or on her, or her on me for that matter. Christ, we were raised more like brother and sister than anything," he shuddered.

The rain and wind picked up, beating out its harsh melody. She swallowed hard. She needed to fix this.

"There's something I..." she stopped. How much did she want him to know? Talk about being petrified. "Will and I broke up ages ago because he has a wandering eye and I'm pretty sure he cheated on me. But I had nowhere else to go, so I stayed with the band. Which meant he thought I was there because of him...so we'd hook up every so often, try it again, but he'd fall back into his old habits and we'd break up again. Last fall, I decided I'd been stupid long enough, and I called things off for good. But I couldn't leave England yet, so I was stuck there." She allowed herself to look at him and found him facing her. "I came back to Texas because I didn't know where else to go." She'd had to raise her voice to be heard over the rain. She glanced outside as a strong burst of wind caused the truck to rock.

Jack reached over and put a hand on her arm. "One thing I've learned in this life, the 'why' isn't important. What is important is that you learned from it."

Nodding, Bayleigh blinked back the tears that were filling her eyes. "Can we just go now?"

He removed his hand from her arm and put the truck in gear. The pelting rain and the *swish-swish, swish-swish* of the wiper blades filled the silence between them. The decibel level swelled and her pulse ramped up in answer. She looked over, noticing Jack's face was grim.

"Sleet?" She wasn't sure he could even hear her.

"Yup. Is your seatbelt on?" He didn't take his eyes off the road.

"Of course." But she double-checked to make sure. "How much farther?"

"We'll be fine. Roads aren't bad yet." His cell phone rang, making her jump. He slipped his Bluetooth on and answered it. "Hello? Hey, Sweetie. What's up?" He listened for a minute. "Where's Mitch?" More listening. "Carly, calm down. We're on our way. We'll be there in ten minutes. Just stay calm, and keep the phone nearby." He clicked his cell phone off.

"Something wrong?" Bayleigh asked as Jack checked his rearview mirror before pulling off onto the shoulder. He checked in both directions and then pulled back onto the road, headed in the direction they'd just come from. The tires slid on the wet pavement. Her fingers dug into the armrest of the door.

"My cousin's wife is having contractions and she's home

alone. Mitch had to go up to Waco and the storm that is dumping this crap on us" he motioned out the window at the now-freezing rain, "has him stuck there. Ma and Pop left for a weekend in San Antonio this morning. She's home alone and panicking because of the ice," he turned off of the main road and onto the dirt road leading to his cousin's house.

"How far along is she?"

"She's not due for a couple of more weeks, which isn't helping the panicking any." Jack replied as they pulled up in front of his family's home. He jumped out of the cab.

She had her door open and was stepping down when he reached her side. "Ground is already getting icy in places. Be careful." Taking hold of her arm to help her up the icy steps, he led the way. Carly met them at the door.

"I'm sorry, Jack. I didn't know who else to call. I called my doctor earlier and he said to just monitor the contractions, I wasn't in active labor. But now, I'm scared," Carly gave him a hug, noticing Bayleigh for the first time. "You should have told me you were on a date."

"I wasn't," he gave Bayleigh a wink as he turned to her to introduce the two women. "Carly, this is Bayleigh Morrow, Jason's sister," he said as he tucked an arm around Carly and started to lead her down the hallway to the living room, shrugging out of his coat as he walked. "Now, tell me what's going on?"

"I started having contractions and—"Carly's voice trailed off and she put both hands on her protruding stomach. "Oh, God!" They all glanced down at the sudden gush of water.

The look on Jack's face almost had Bayleigh in hysterics. "Ever done this before?" she moved to Carly's other side and put a hand on her lower back and gripped her elbow.

"Horses, cows, yes...Humans, never, not once," Jack confirmed, his eyes wide at the weird breathing techniques Carly was using, his face a little green as he looked at the mess on the floor.

"OK. Go get some towels," Bayleigh instructed her. "Is there a downstairs bedroom in this place?"

Carly nodded and stood up as straight as she could. "This way." Carly accepted Bayleigh's help and they headed down the hallway to a bedroom. Bayleigh helped her onto the bed. "How far apart are the contractions?"

"About eight minutes now." Carly rubbed at her stomach. "What am I going to do?" Her eyes were wide, a few tears present, and her hands shook. Jack's footsteps sounded down the hall and he paused at the doorway.

"You're going to stay calm and do what we tell you. Okay?" Bayleigh placed pillows behind Carly's back to support her.

Carly released a ragged breath and nodded. "Thank you."

"Now what?" Jack moved to stand beside Bayleigh. He still looked a little green.

"Well, you call 9-1-1 and see how soon they can get a crew out here, and I'll coach our little momma through any more contractions."

"You've done this before?" Jack dialed the phone and waited for the call to go through.

"Yeah. A friend of mine asked me to be her coach a

couple of years ago." Bayleigh smiled at Carly. "How long have you been feeling the contractions?"

"All day. But I thought they were those Braxton-Hicks ones," Carly's breath hitched. "I tried to call my mom in town, but it's her bridge night. She's pretty notorious for forgetting to take her cell phone with her when she leaves the house." Tears filled her eyes. "Mitch is supposed to be here for this."

"Carly, stay calm," she laid a hand on Carly's stomach. "You're having another contraction. You need to breathe through it." Together they breathed through the contraction. "Did you do any kind of child birth class?" Carly nodded and Bayleigh reached down and squeezed her hand.

"Good. So, we're just going to do the breathing techniques, and stay focused and relaxed," she kept up the chatter, waiting for Jack to hang up the phone and tell her that the paramedics were on the way. She glanced over at him, catching the frown on his face.

"Now what?" she pitched her voice low.

"The weather caused a huge pile up on the interstate. All ambulances and paramedics are being routed there. They'll try to divert someone to us, but it could be awhile. They said to call back if the birth was imminent."

"How far is the hospital from here?"

"Maybe twenty minutes," Jack grimaced. "Think we have time?"

"Unless you want to deliver the baby here, I say we make a run for it," Bayleigh told him with a grin, her words causing his face to go pasty white.

"What do you say, Carly? I hear they have good pain meds at the hospital!"

"You said the magic words," Carly moved to stand up. Jack was at her side to help in an instant.

"So, you're Jason's sister?" she looked over at Bayleigh as they led her down the hallway. "Oh, dear. I forgot about the floor," she paused and looked over at where Jack had thrown a couple of towels.

"Don't worry about it. We'll get you to the hospital and I'll come back later and clean it all up," Jack promised her, glancing at his watch as he grabbed her coat out of the closet.

"Are you okay?" Carly stared at him as he zipped his own coat up. "You don't look so great."

"I'm fine. Just don't ask me to look...don't ask me to deliver the baby, okay?" Jack muttered as he jerked open the door. "It's a little slippery. Hold onto my arm and I'll get you down the steps.

"I thought the weather was supposed to start getting bad *tomorrow*." Bayleigh muttered as he helped her up into the cab.

"Yeah, well, welcome back to Texas," he muttered back as he climbed in after her.

Jack drove as fast as he could in the deteriorating weather conditions. His shoulders rose, tensing every time Carly moaned with a contraction. If she was sure of where she stood with him right now, Bayleigh would have laughed. With the three of them crammed into the cab of his truck, Bayleigh's leg was pressed against Jack's. Every time his foot shifted, his muscles flexed until she was hyper-aware of him. Even through her layers of clothes, his warmth soaked through. This close the clean scent of his skin tempted her.

Carly gripped her hand again and she refocused on the issues in front of her.

"How much further?" Bayleigh murmured to Jack.

"Almost there," Jack pointed out the window. In the darkness around them, the lights from the hospital were like a beacon. "Where should I go?"

"ER. They can get her up to Labor and delivery a lot faster than we can," Bayleigh told him. Jack nodded and pulled into the ambulance bay.

A security guard stepped out of the doorway and approached the vehicle. Jack lowered the window. "I've got a lady in labor!"

The guard nodded and grabbed a wheelchair. He was yelling over his shoulder to the nurses' station.

"Don't leave me!" Carly' eyes were wide, her breathing fast and choppy. Bayleigh was pretty sure most of the bones in her right hand were crushed.

"I'll stay with you. Jack can go park the truck," Bayleigh slid out of the truck as the nurses helped Carly into the wheelchair. Carly smiled her relief as they wheeled her into the ER, Bayleigh following. The truck roared and drove out of the ambulance bay to park it somewhere else.

Heck of a first date. She followed the parade of nurses and techs.

She paused in the hallway, the sounds and smells of the hospital overwhelming. Frantic footsteps hurrying down a hallway in those rubber-soled shoes everyone in a hospital seemed to wear. Constant beeps and bells going off. Nurses, doctors, techs, and everyone calling out instructions to each other. And that smell that is unique to a hospital...the antiseptic, medicine smell.

Her stomach dropped. What was she thinking? She couldn't do this. She needed to get out of here.

"Ma'am, are you Bayleigh? Mrs. Williams is asking for you," a young girl in a set of maroon scrubs came out of the room.

"I'll be there in a minute." *Control. Get it under control*, she willed herself.

Brisk footsteps sounded behind her and a hand touched her shoulder. "You ok?"

She looked up into Jack's concerned face. "No," she whispered. "Hospital...I can't."

He turned her to face him. "Yes, you can, Bay. I'm here with you. We need to help Carly." He looked down at his feet, his fingers were rubbing in small circles along her collar bones. "And, uh, I don't do well in these situations."

"Meaning what?" her gaze narrowed on him.

"What you're feeling right now—panicky, closed in, super sensitive to every sound and smell in this place, is the same way I'm feeling," he gave her a grin. "You can kiss me, take my mind off of it."

"Oh, whatever," she stepped away from him but returned his grin. "Let's go see what your cousin needs." Together they walked into the room where Carly had been taken.

"All I know is, Mitch owes me big time for this one," he told her under his breath, earning a chuckle. "Big," he repeated, as Carly clutched her stomach and screamed.

CHAPTER 7

"Hey, big guy. How's the head?" Bayleigh moved over to stand beside his hospital bed when she noticed his eyes were open. Jack groaned as he pushed himself upright.

"You're enjoying this, aren't you?" he asked with a glare in her direction.

"Hey, it's not every day you get to see a big, strong man faint," Bayleigh told him with a laugh. "Carly fell asleep about an hour ago and they took the baby back to the nursery for a little bit and I figured it was time to check on you. I thought you might like to head down to the cafeteria and see what they have to offer?"

"What time is it?" Jack asked, trying to focus on his watch.

"Five fifteen," Bayleigh stepped back as Jack stood up. "I've talked to your cousin Mitch and he's trying to figure out how to get back here. The news is reporting that most of the interstate between here and Waco is shut down due to the ice. I also talked to Jason and Nicole. They're going to come back on an earlier flight tomorrow, or rather today, if they can arrange it."

"What about Ma and Pop?"

"Carly was awake when they called back, so I didn't talk to them," she explained as she led the way down the hallway to the elevator. It had been a long night and she was still riding high on adrenaline. "She also got in touch with her mother. I think she's trying to figure out how to drive on the icy roads as we speak."

"Thanks for staying with Carly," he told her, grimacing as his fingers probed at the knot on the back of his head.

"No problem."

He followed her out of the elevator and down the hallway to the cafeteria. "I take it you've been out exploring while I was incapacitated?"

"Only to find coffee." Bayleigh handed him a tray and headed for the serving line. "The nurses assured me they have a great breakfast here. Which is a good thing, that little storm last night created a nice little covering of ice at least an inch thick. The news guys say it'll get above freezing once the sun comes out, though."

Jack grabbed a tray and moved over to the grill line, ordering enough food to feed a small army. Bayleigh added the two large cups of coffee she'd grabbed and they headed for the cashier. Jack paid and then they moved to corner table in the near-empty dining room.

"Did you get any sleep?" Jack asked after they'd sat down and started eating. He'd filled his plate with eggs, bacon and toast and she helped herself to a small serving of the eggs and bacon.

"Are you kidding me? I was too busy enjoying holding

the baby." Bayleigh didn't want as much to eat as he did, so she finished her meal sooner than him. She cradled the cup of coffee in her hands. She glanced over at him and gave him a mischievous smile.

"So, you're not big on needles, I take it?"

"Good God, did you see the size of that thing? It was at least as long as my arm!" he shuddered as he glanced down at his arm, causing Bayleigh to laugh.

"It wasn't that long! It was a normal needle. You missed the one they used in her back. Now *that* one was at least as long as your arm," she told him with a straight face.

"Getting woozy here," Jack warned with a glare in her direction. "All I'm going to say is that men do not need to be in the delivery room when a baby is born. It's unnatural," he shot back, finishing his coffee and standing up. Bayleigh laughed again and stood up with him, walking with him back to the elevators.

"By the way" he stopped at the elevator and stood there, looking at her.

"Yes?" Bayleigh reached over and hit the button, then met his gaze, waiting for him to finish his thought.

"Thanks for staying with Carly through the delivery," he leaned over and kissed her soft lips. "I owe you one."

Bayleigh stared at him, surprised by the action. As far as kisses went, it had to rank right up there as the most unromantic one she'd ever had. So why were her lips tingling?

Jack stepped forward as the elevator arrived, the doors opening with a "swoosh". Jack took her hand and pulled her into the elevator with him, hitting the button for the maternity floor. As soon as the elevator arrived on their floor and the doors opened up, Bayleigh led the way down to Carly's room.

"There you are! I was beginning to wonder where you two had wandered off to," Carly greeted them as they stepped back into her room. Bayleigh tensed as she realized Carly was no longer alone. An older woman and another man, who looked to be close to Jack's age, were sitting on the couch in the room.

Jack paused when he realized she'd stopped just inside the door before realizing why. "Bayleigh, this is Cindy, Carly's mom. And this big doofus is her cousin, Paul. He's the chief of police here."

"Bayleigh! Thank you so much for staying with Carly all night. She tells me you are an excellent labor coach." Cindy stood up and walked over to Bayleigh, giving her a hug.

"She did the hard part. I just stood there and held her hand." Bayleigh looked over at Jack. He could still see the wariness there, but it wasn't as apparent as it had been when they'd first walked into the room.

"You kept me from panicking a few times." Carly told her. "I don't know what I would have done if you hadn't been here."

"What am I, chopped liver? I'm the one who got you here, in the middle of an ice storm, after all." Jack reminded her, giving Bayleigh a wink.

"And promptly hit the floor when they started putting needles in me!" Carly shot back.

"Yes, we heard all about how you braved the icy roads and got Carly all tucked in safe and sound in labor and delivery, and then checked yourself into the ER." Paul stood up and moved over next to Jack, clapping him on the shoulder.

"Who'd you hear that from?" Jack glanced over at Bayleigh, noticing for the first time she'd moved back over to stand by the door, almost as if she was planning to duck out it at first opportunity. He held his hand out to her and with a slight hesitation, she took it, allowing him to draw her into the group.

"Janine. She couldn't wait to tell me about the big bad war hero who passed out when the nurses approached the pregnant lady with a needle." Paul laughed, moving to sit back down. "Janine's my sister. She's a nurse down in the ER and she couldn't wait to tell me about it," he supplied for Bayleigh.

"Doesn't HIPPA apply here?"

"She was calling to inform Aunt Cindy that Carly was in labor. And also to see if we knew who to call since you'd knocked yourself out. She told me as an officer of the court and a concerned family member," Paul informed him.

"Right. You might want to come up with a better story. That one won't stand up in court," Jack advised, as the nurse walked in pushing the bassinet.

The nurse gave Carly some instructions on when to feed him and how to contact her if she needed any help and then excused herself, allowing the family members to crowd around Carly and the baby to admire him.

Bayleigh waited a few minutes and then nudged Jack's arm with her elbow. "I'm guessing Carly would like to breastfeed in private," she whispered to him.

"Paul, how about I buy you and Bayleigh a cup of coffee and we can go check out the driving conditions?" he suggested to his friend. Carly gave Bayleigh a smile of gratitude and then turned her attention back to her son.

"How is it you know so much about childbirth and babies?" Paul asked as they moved towards the elevator.

"I had a friend whose boyfriend didn't want to be a daddy. I agreed to be the coach when the time came," Bayleigh explained. "It was before the band went to Europe, right after I graduated from college."

"Lucky us," Jack murmured as they exited the elevator and made their way to the coffee stand. Paul excused himself when his cell phone rang, moving off to the side to answer it. Jack ordered the three cups of coffee and Paul joined them as they sat down at a table.

"Good news and bad news." Paul announced, sitting down across from Bayleigh. "The state highway patrol has shut down most of the roads leading out of town; the bridges are iced over and presenting too much of a risk, unless it's an emergency." He paused to take a sip of his coffee.

"So we're stuck here?" Bayleigh glanced around the cafeteria. She'd managed to avoid the panic attack last night, but she wasn't sure how much longer she could hold herself together. The euphoria from watching a baby being born was fading fast.

Paul gave a slight shake of his head. "Not necessarily." He looked over at Jack. "With your truck, you should be able to make it out to your place, or your uncle's. I just wouldn't try to make it back into town once you're out there."

Jack nodded in understanding and turned to Bayleigh.

"It's up to you. I've got plenty of food and supplies back at the house," he told her.

"I think I'd prefer to head back to your place, if you don't mind driving us there," Bayleigh told him. "I've kind of had enough of hospitals to last me a lifetime, to tell the truth."

Jack reached under the table and gave her hand a quick squeeze. "Then that is where we will go," he promised her, his eyes full of understanding.

"Give me a call when you get out there, then, so I know you made it." Paul instructed as he stood back up and stretched. "I'm heading over to the office but my cell will be on."

"Will do." Jack promised, watching his friend walk to the elevator before turning back to Bayleigh. He reached over with a finger and pushed a lock of hair back away from her face. He could see the exhaustion that was creeping into her eyes. "We just need to head back upstairs, tell Carly where we're going. Then I'll take you home," he told her. Bayleigh gave him a brief smile, but he could see the appreciation in her eyes.

"I almost forgot about Carly. We can stay here if you want to be near her," Bayleigh offered but Jack cut her off.

"Her mother is here, as well as a whole hospital full of doctors and nurses. She'll be ok." He stood up and held his hand out to Bayleigh. "Besides, my head is killing me. I just want to go home to my own bed." With a grateful smile, Bayleigh took his offered hand. They stopped in Carly's room to check on her and let her know what the plan was, and Jack promised to call her later. Within minutes, they were headed out to the parking lot.

. . .

"MAYBE WE SHOULD JUST STAY HERE," Bayleigh suggested as Jack managed to chip the ice away from the passenger side door and open it.

"Nah, we'll be fine. Let me climb in and slide over so I can start the engine. That way the defrosters can do most of the work." He stepped up into the cab of the truck and then reached a hand down to help her up. Sliding over under the wheel, he got the engine started and waited for the air coming out of the vents to warm up before he turned the windshield defroster on.

"I'll wait a few minutes, let it get the ice melting, and then I'll go out and chip it off."

"Do you want help?"

"Nope, you stay in here where it's warm," he grinned at her. He reached behind the seat and found his ice scraper. "I'll be back."

Bayleigh watched him from the warmth of the truck as he scraped the ice off the windshields. Once the heat kicked in and started the melting process, he only had to get a small area cleared before he could get the edge of the scraper under it and get huge chunks cleared out of the way. It took him a few minutes to get the windows cleared off before he was back inside the cab with her.

"Man, it's cold out there!" He pulled his gloves off, turning the heater on high and holding his hands over the defroster. "Once I get feeling back in my hands and feet, we can head home," he looked over at her. "You doing ok?"

"I'm fine," she looked over her shoulder at the hospital. "Thank you for agreeing to head back to your place."

Jack reached over and gave her hand a quick squeeze. "I told you before, I don't like hospitals either. I'm just as happy as you are to leave this place behind." He dropped her hand and placed his back on the steering wheel. "Ok, let's go, then."

Driving much slower than he had on the way to the hospital the night before, Jack headed home. It took forever, and more than once he felt his tires lose traction. He was the only one stupid enough to be out on the roads right now though. If it weren't for the near-panic attack he'd seen Bayleigh have last night, he would have tried to convince her to stay in the hospital for a while. At least until the temperatures climbed to above the freezing mark and this shit started to melt.

Almost ninety minutes after leaving the hospital, they both heaved sighs of relief as he parked the truck near his porch steps. "Stay here until I come around for you. I don't want a repeat of the other day. I'm not sure I could carry you inside this time," he told her with a quick wink as he opened his door and slid out.

Giving him a mock glare, Bayleigh did as she was told, waiting until he had her door open and offered his hand to her to help her down. The ice wasn't bad up near his porch, and they made their way up the steps and inside without incidence.

"More coffee?" he asked as they shed their coats, hanging them on the backs of kitchen chairs.

"No, I think if I have any more coffee this morning, my stomach will burn a hole in itself. I think I'm just going to take a shower and then climb into bed." She narrowed her gaze as she looked at him. "Are you ok? You're looking pretty pale all of a sudden."

"I'm fine. Now that we're home and I can relax, my head is pounding. I think I'm going to take something for it, call Paul to let him know we made it home without winding up in a ditch, and then I'm climbing into my bed. My shower can wait until later," Jack tried to give her a reassuring smile, but could tell from the frown on her face he wasn't succeeding. "I promise, Bayleigh. I'm fine. But I am going to be taking some of my heavy-duty pain killers and not just ibuprofen. Don't worry if I sleep for a long time."

Bayleigh nodded, but waited until he'd taken his medicine and headed for his own room before she walked down the hallway to hers. Walking into the bathroom, she groaned at her reflection in the mirror. Most of her make-up had worn off and her mascara ringed her eyes, making her look like a raccoon, and her hair was a mess. With a sigh, she grabbed a washcloth and started washing the makeup off. She turned the shower on full blast and stepped under the spray as soon as the water had heated up. She was so exhausted, she barely took the time to condition her hair and make sure all the soap was rinsed off before she turned the water back off. Drying off, she pulled some leggings and a long t-shirt on, before she tiptoed down the hallway to listen at Jack's door to make sure he was okay. She could hear him moving around behind the closed door, so she made her way back to her own room, leaving her door open so she could hear him if he called out at all. She climbed under the covers and was asleep almost as soon as her head hit the pillow.

. . .

JACK DECIDED to take that shower once he got back to his room. He stood under the hot spray, letting the force of it hit his neck and shoulders, easing some of the kinks out of his muscles. After pulling on sweatpants and a t-shirt, he stepped back into the hallway to check the thermostat. He continued out to the kitchen to grab a bottle of water. He did a double take as he passed by Bayleigh's room and realized she'd left her door open. Stopping, he stood in the doorway and watched her sleep for a few moments.

She was beautiful, in so many ways, and not just on the outside. Her kind and gentle nature. Her compassion for others. Surviving her attack added to her strength. He hoped she could see that.

Realizing he was standing there staring at her, he hurried out to the kitchen and then back to his room. He stretched out on his bed, groaning as the knot on the back of his head touched the pillow. It took a few tries before he found a position he was comfortable in, that didn't cause his head to hurt even more, and then, like Bayleigh, he fell asleep.

CHAPTER 8

RACK!
    CRASH!

With a muffled curse, Jack shot out of bed, his hand reaching for the sidearm he always set on the footlocker next to his cot, coming up empty. Cursing louder, he swung his legs off the cot, coming fully awake when his feet connected with the rug by his bed.

Rug. Bed. No side arm next to him.

He wasn't in Afghanistan. He was home, in Texas. And there was freezing rain coming through a huge hole in his window. And the force of the wind was blowing it far enough into the room to get his bed wet. His eyes strayed to the clock; just past noon. He had been asleep for a couple of hours.

"Jack? Are you ok? What happened?" Bayleigh ran into the room, her face white.

"I'm thinking one of the trees near my window just lost a limb," he gestured towards his window. "I'm fine, but I need to get some plastic over that window. Can you go out to the kitchen and grab the black garbage bags out of the pantry? I think if I put a couple of those up over the window, it'll at least keep the rain out. I need to go find my hammer and nails," he moved past her on the way out to his garage.

When he rejoined her in the bedroom, he had his hammer, some nails and a piece of plywood. "I forgot I had this," he explained as he set it against the wall. "It won't cover the whole window but maybe it'll keep the worst of the rain out. Can you help me hold it in place?"

Bayleigh nodded and stepped up beside him, shivering as the freezing rain and sleet blew through the broken window panes. Jack hammered in a couple of nails to hold the plywood in place and then turned to her.

"Why don't you go change into dryer clothes? I'll finish getting this up and then clean up the glass."

He looked at the mess and shook his head. In the time it had taken them to get the plywood nailed up, the rain and sleet had made a mess of his bed. "Looks like I'm sleeping on the couch," he glanced over at her as he said it.

"Oh," was all she said before turning away. He heard her door close down the hall, and he went to work, cleaning up the mess. The blankets on the bed were bunched up and tossed in the bathtub. Once the rain stopped and everything thawed out, he'd take them outside and shake them out, make sure all the glass was off of them, as well. Satisfied he'd done all he could for the moment, he headed out to the living room.

Bayleigh's door was open again and he paused to check on her. She looked up when the floorboards creaked. Her face was pale and even from across the room, he could see the rapid rise and fall of her chest.

"You ok?" he asked, glancing around the room.

"I'm fine."

"Then why are you struggling to catch your breath?" his eyebrows drew together as he frowned at her.

"Loud, sudden noises are one of my triggers. Breaking glass is a huge one for me," her fingers plucked at the quilt on her bed.

"Yeah, me too. Well, the loud sudden noises part, at least," Jack glanced over his shoulder towards his room. "So are you really ok?"

"I think so," she took a deep breath and nodded. "The jitters always last a while, but I can breathe without feeling like a rock is sitting on my chest." She tilted her head to the side and studied him. "Are *you* ok?"

"I can think of nicer ways to be woken up out of a sound sleep," he glanced at his watch.

A short laugh escaped her. "Yeah, I can, too." She pressed her lips together and glanced away. "I feel bad about you sleeping on the couch. If I hadn't shown up without calling Jason first, you'd be able to sleep in here."

"A few hours on the couch won't kill me, Bay. I can run out in a few hours, after the ice melts off, and buy the glass to put in the window," he held up his hand, anticipating her next comment. "And no, you are not giving up the bed for me."

"Well, in that case, why don't we share it?" her own eyes went wide as she realized what she just said, but she didn't retract the offer.

"Bayleigh, I would love nothing more than to share a

bed with you, even if it's just to sleep. But I am not going to do it if it's going to send you into another panic attack. I can handle the couch."

Bayleigh's gaze was unwavering as she answered, "I can handle sharing a bed with you."

Jack sucked in a breath at her words. With slow and deliberate movements, he moved to the bed, stretching out on his side next to her, facing her. "If you change your mind, at any time, I'll move to the couch," he assured her.

"I know," and for the first time, made the effort to reach out and touch him. Her hand slid across the space between them and touched his. He turned his hand and intertwined their fingers.

"Now go back to sleep," he whispered with a smile.

THE RINGING of her cell phone had Bayleigh jerking awake. Without opening her eyes, she reached for it, managing to swipe the screen and answer it. These rude awakenings needed to stop.

"'lo," she mumbled. She was so not a morning person.

"Hey, Leigh. I saw on the news Texas is in the middle of the worst ice storm in the history of ice storms. I hadn't heard from you since you left England, so I decided I'd better check on you." Only one person on Earth called her 'Leigh'.

"Oh, crap, Maddie! I am so sorry. I meant to call the other day but things have been a little screwy," Bayleigh apologized to her best friend. She tried to roll over, but there was a large pile of blankets piled up behind her and a heavy weight across her abdomen and she couldn't move.

"How'd it go with your brother?"

"He's not here. He and his wife are up in Dallas for a long weekend. I'm staying with his best friend," Bayleigh explained. The weight across her stomach tightened and the events of the previous night rushed back at her and she realized it wasn't a bunch of blankets behind her, but Jack. She must have moved closer to him during the night.

"Wait, his best friend? I'm assuming that would be another guy, right? Are you doing okay?"

"I'm fine, Maddie. I've had a couple of panic attacks, but I've managed to sleep through the night the last couple of nights. Oh, and I even walked into a hospital the other night."

"Hospital? You said you were okay!"

"Jack's cousin went into labor and with the ice storm, we had to take her to the hospital. I wound up in the delivery room with her because Jack," his arm tightened around her waist again, warning her against telling tales on him. "Jack decided to wait in another room."

"Wow. I should have talked you into going to Texas sooner."

"I wasn't ready."

"So, this Jack guy. Is he hot?"

"I'm not going to answer that right now." Bayleigh shifted so she could at least turn her head to check on Jack. She knew he was awake but he had his eyes closed. His lips twitched as he listened to her side of the conversation.

"Is he there? You sounded like I woke you up. Did you sleep with him?"

"Stop, Maddie! We're in the middle of that ice storm,

remember? A tree limb crashed through one of the windows and we had to bunk together. That's all!"

"So you did sleep with him!" her friend teased.

"Jesus, yes, sleep being the operative word! Now stop it!" she hissed as Jack opened his eyes and winked at her.

"Okay, Okay, I'm sorry. It's just, well, I've been worried about you."

"I know, Maddie. I promise, I'm doing fine here. I may even start writing ballads again."

"Wow, you are feeling better! Call me later, when Mr. Hottie isn't around." Maddie hung up the phone before Bayleigh could respond.

Turning her screen off, Bayleigh chanced a look over her shoulder at Jack. His eyes were open and he was laughing. "Mr. Hottie?"

"You heard that?"

"I could hear everything," he nodded as his fingers stroked her stomach, causing all kinds of strange sensations to riot through her body. "So, how'd you sleep?"

"Amazingly well. How about you?" she turned the question back to him as she rolled over so they were face to face. Her movements forced the blankets to slide down to her waist and she shivered at the freezing temperature in the room. She yanked them back up, burrowing back into their warmth. She could still hear the steady *ping* as the ice hit the windows of her room.

"Better than if I had slept on that couch. Thank you for sharing the bed with me." His voice was still husky from sleep and his hair was sticking up in all directions. Bayleigh hated to think what her own hair looked like.

"Who was that on the phone?"

"My best friend Maddie. She owns a bar near Nashville. Her former fiancé was in the Army and she followed him to his duty station near there somewhere."

"Ft. Campbell," Jack supplied.

"That sounds right. Anyway, it didn't work out and she grew up around bars, so she took over running one there and when the owner retired a couple of years ago, he left it to her. She happened to be in England when I hurt my knee and I broke down and told her the whole story. She made me promise to come home as soon as I could travel."

"I think I like Maddie. And not just because she's smart enough to know I'm hot," he teased.

"I swear, I haven't talked to her or emailed her since I met you! She came up with that all on her own!" Bayleigh felt her face growing warm.

"Are you saying you don't think I'm hot?" he teased as he brought his hand up and cupped her face, his thumb caressing her cheek.

"Can I plead the fifth on that?"

"I'll just take it as a yes, you think I'm hot," his thumb continued the gentle stroking.

Bayleigh cleared her throat, restless and looking anywhere but at him. "Is it getting warm in here to you?"

"Afraid to answer me?"

Bayleigh stopped fidgeting and looked back at him. "You scare the crap out of me, Jack Williams."

Startled, he stopped stroking her cheek. "Why?"

"You are the first man I can spend time with, alone, without going into a full-blown panic attack, since everything that happened last year. Six months ago, hell, six *weeks* ago, it wouldn't have mattered if the closest hotel was three days away. I would have chosen that drive over staying here, alone, with a man. It wouldn't have mattered who vouched for you."

"And that's a problem?"

"I don't know what it is! I'm just saying it's not my normal, or what has passed for normal for a long time! And being this off-balanced is a little bit scary!"

Jack smiled and slid his hand along her cheek, pushing a few strands of hair back behind her ear and resting his fingers on her scalp. He pushed a few strands of hair back behind her ear. "What would you like to eat?"

"What?"

"It's after three pm, so I figured we could get up and make something to eat and take a look at the weather reports," he slid his hand away from her face. "And then, if you're up to it, we can talk."

Bemused, Bayleigh watched as Jack tossed back the covers and left the bed. With a smile on her face, Bayleigh sat up and pushed the covers back, shivering as her feet touched the cold floor. Grabbing clothes out of the dresser, she stepped into the bathroom to change. She had a thermal shirt on under her t-shirt, jeans and two pairs of socks, and still felt the cold. Adding a second long-sleeved shirt to the layers, she headed out to the kitchen where Jack had already made the coffee.

Deciding on sandwiches, they made a plateful, and Jack grabbed chips out of the pantry. With their hands full, they headed for the living room so they could turn on the T.V. and figure out what was going on with the weather. Jack flipped through the channels until he found the local weather and turned the volume up.

"...crazy storm front that moved into the Hill Country over night. Usually with this weather pattern, we get that layer of ice during the night and then by noon the next day, it's all melted away." The meteorologist clicked through some viewer pictures that had been sent in through the day. "But as you can see, this storm stalled out and the temperatures never made it above freezing today. Combine that with the fact that the freezing precipitation has continued all day and it looks like it'll continue for at least one more night, the state police are advising everyone to stay inside, stay home, and stay safe. Most of the major roadways have been closed, including Interstate 35 from Waco to San Antonio. We should get relief as this warm mass of air here moves across the state, pushing this storm out of the way, sometime tomorrow afternoon..."

"Well, that sucks," Jack muttered as he turned the volume down.

"So now what?" Bayleigh tossed her napkin on her plate and set it on the coffee table.

"Now, I'm going to go outside and see if there was any other damage from that tree branch falling earlier, before I lose what's left of the daylight. And I need to make sure I have enough firewood stacked on the porch."

"Firewood?" she looked over at the fireplace. She'd noticed yesterday there was a fire laid in the grate, but hadn't given much thought to it.

"I'm surprised we haven't lost power yet. Being so far out from town, I tend to lose power a lot during ice storms or heavy thunderstorms." Jack got up off the couch and walked over to the window, looking out into the approaching night.

"You're not going to expect me to cook over a fire, are you?"

He chuckled. "No, the stove is gas. And for the record, I won't expect you to cook unless you want to do it. I have a generator that will kick in if the power does go out. But I only have certain things wired to it, like the refrigerator. I didn't think I'd ever need one big enough to have to worry about powering the whole house. And usually I only need it for a couple of hours, at most. We won't have any heat other than the fire. So we should bunk down in here, where I can light a fire in the fireplace." He turned to stare at her as he said the last part.

"Are you expecting me to panic over that?"

"I'm not sure what I expect. I do want to make sure you're okay with all of it, though," he stepped away from the window, moving back over to stand near the couch.

"I think I'm okay with all of this, Jack. We've already shared a bed and I managed to avoid screaming the house down."

"Honey, you can scream the house down all you want when we're in bed together, as long as it's my name you're screaming. And for the right reasons."

Her face flamed as he winked at her as he walked past the couch. "I'll be outside if you need anything."

"I think I'll go run around in the ice storm to cool off," Bayleigh muttered, watching as he walked out of the room.

"Heard that!" he called back over his shoulder.

"Of course you did. Ears like a bat, too," Bayleigh muttered as she gathered up the leftovers from their late lunch and headed for the kitchen. As she glanced out the kitchen window, she realized that the sleet had stopped for the moment. Well, she couldn't hear it hitting the window anymore, at least. Of course, with the layer of ice that was covering the window, she wasn't sure she'd be able to hear it anyway.

Making sure everything was cleaned up and put away, she was in the process of making a fresh pot when she heard her cell phone down the hall. If they did lose power, she wanted one last hit of caffeine. The phone could wait.

She hit start on the coffee maker and then headed down the hall to her bedroom to retrieve her cell phone. Swiping her finger across the screen, a frown crossed her face when she saw that she'd missed several calls from her brother. And he'd left a couple of messages, too.

Retreating to the kitchen, she put in her code and pulled up her voicemail, listening to her messages. He was just checking on her and Jack, and since neither of them were answering their phones, he was more than just a little worried.

With a soft laugh, Bayleigh hit the call back button and waited for her brother to answer.

"Bayleigh, is that you?"

"Yes. It's me. We're okay."

"Weather channel makes it look pretty bad. And all the flights to Austin are cancelled." Jason sighed. "We were hoping to make it back there, but I-35 is closed from Waco to south of Austin, so we can't even drive it."

"We saw that on the news. The roads were bad when we were driving home this morning, so I'm guessing they're beyond horrible now. Jack drove on the shoulder most of the way, even across a field or two." Bayleigh smiled at the memory.

"I'm surprised he didn't make you guys stay at the hospital. Carly said her mom was staying with her, and they'd offered the two of you beds as well."

"Jack said he doesn't like hospitals."

"True, but he hates driving in bad weather even more. I'm just glad you two made it home. Is everything okay there?"

Bayleigh massaged her temple as she answered. "I guess. He's bringing in wood for the fireplace. We haven't lost power yet, but he seems to think it's only a matter of time. Oh, and he lost a bedroom window to a tree branch. He said he was going to look and make sure there wasn't any other damage to the house."

"Well, at least you're not alone, I guess."

"You got a problem with this, Jason?" Bayleigh's eyes narrowed.

"Christ, no. I had a problem with you and that asshole Will. Jack is not an issue," Jason paused. "Well, one thing you do need to know about him, if you're going to be sleeping with, I mean, sleeping in the same room as him." Jason corrected himself, causing Bayleigh to giggle.

"Bayleigh...." Jason's voice had that 'much older brother' warning tone to it now.

"Okay, I'm sorry. Continue. What do I need to know if I'm sleeping with Jack?"

"Jesus, Bayleigh. Those words do not ever need to come out of your mouth again. I do not need any type of mental images here. Got it?"

Bayleigh almost doubled over with laughter and tears were running down her face. "Okay, Okay. I'm sorry. What do you need to tell me?"

"Jack has PTSD. I've never known him to be violent, but I know he has nightmares and doesn't sleep well. Don't approach him if he's having a nightmare until you're sure he's awake and with you, if you know what I mean."

"Yes, I know what you mean."

"Has something happened?" Now she could hear the suspicion in his tone.

"No, no, nothing like that. I, uh, have some experience with this, but not with Jack," Bayleigh rushed to assure her brother. "Look, Jason, we're doing fine here. But I do need to talk to you when you get back to town. One on one time."

"Is it about the estate? You know what Mom's terms were."

"Yes, in a way, it's about the estate. And yes, I know the terms. But there's more to it. And I don't want to go into it right now. Please, just trust me on this?"

There was silence from the other end for a few seconds. Bayleigh could just imagine her brother staring off into space, trying to figure out what she was up to this time. Will had been livid when he found out her mother hadn't out right left her inheritance to her, instead making Jason in charge of it until she reached the respectable, mature age of thirty. Any decision regarding her trust fund had to go through Jason, and certain criteria had to be met. Bayleigh simply could not access the money herself.

"All right, Bayleigh. I'll trust you. I'll call you tomorrow to check in with you. Love you, sis."

"Love you, too, big brother." Bayleigh whispered as she hung up the phone. A sound behind her had her whirling around to find Jack standing there.

"Oh, uh, hi. How long have you been standing there?" she raised a hand to her cheek. She knew it was red, she could feel the heat in her face.

"Not long. I carried a bunch of wood up onto the front porch so we'd have plenty on hand if we need it. And then I walked around to the back of the house to make sure there wasn't any other damage from that tree branch." Jack stepped over to the sink and started to wash his hands. "Don't worry, I didn't hear you just tell your brother who just happens to be my best friend we're sleeping together," he winked at her.

"I didn't mean...I mean...Oh, hell. Jason was flustered about saying it first and I was teasing him!" she threw her hands up in the air when he started laughing.

"I can just imagine your brother's face the second he realized what he'd said," still chuckling, Jack poured himself a cup of coffee. "Thanks for making a fresh pot. So what warnings was big brother giving you about me?"

Bayleigh moved over to refill her coffee cup as well. "That you have PTSD, but I'd already assumed you did."

"That's the only warning he gave you?"

"Should he have warned me about something else?" Bayleigh raised her eyebrows as she turned to face him.

"I don't know. What do big brothers usually warn their baby sisters about when it comes to guys?"

"Jason has always been silent when it came to my private life except when I moved to England with Will. He told me then he didn't think I should. Shows how much I should listen to him, I guess," she cocked her head to the side. "With you and Nicole so close, didn't you ever warn her about who she dated?"

"Nicole didn't date when she grew up here. She met your brother in Austin, when I was in College Station, and anybody else she dated didn't last very long." He glanced over as the wind rattled the windows. "I guess we should start getting stuff together in case the power does go out."

"Tell me what you need me to do, then."

"I've got extra pillows and blankets in the closet in the bedroom next to yours. Grab some of those and bring them out to the living room. I've got some foam pads and sleeping bags in the storage area we can use to cushion the floor."

Bayleigh nodded and moved off down the hallway to the bedroom he'd indicated. She opened the door to a large walk-in closet. The shelves on one side held folded up quilts, fleece blankets and pillows. Grabbing an armful of the blankets and piling the pillows on top, she headed for the living room. She dropped everything on one end of the couch, sinking down beside the stack and waiting for Jack. She stretched her leg out in front of her and massaged the area just above her knee.

Jack walked in with the foam pads and sleeping bags, looking over and taking in her actions. "You ok?"

"I'm fine, just the residual ache," she glanced at the rolled up foam pads he was carrying under his arm. "Those are going to cushion the floor?" she gave him a dubious look.

"They'll provide a layer of insulation between you and the hardwood floor. If we spread the sleeping bags over the pads, we'll have some cushion. It won't be as soft as a mattress, but it won't be the hard floor, either," he tossed his pile onto the floor next to the couch and moved over to the fireplace. "I'll get the fire started."

Bayleigh watched as he added more kindling to the fire already laid out and checked the flue to make sure it was open. She pushed herself to her feet and moved to the mound of gear in the middle of the floor. Unrolling the two mats, she started work on creating a bed of sorts.

Jack struck a match and held it to the kindling, making sure it caught before settling the screen in its place. He set the matches on the mantle and turned to watch her as she spread the first sleeping bag over the two mats. He noticed she'd laid the two mats next to each other and was making up a single sleeping area. That had been his hope when he brought everything in from the storage area but he wouldn't have been surprised if she'd chosen separate sleeping spaces. He hadn't missed the slight wheeze in her breath earlier, before he'd gone outside. The idea of sharing sleeping quarters with him wasn't as easy for her as she'd like him to believe.

"Here, let me help," he offered, stepping over and picking up the second sleeping bag. "If we use both of these as part of the mattress, we should be good. I have plenty of quilts and other blankets we can use as we need them."

"Thanks," Bayleigh sat back on her heels as he unrolled the second sleeping bag and helped her settle it on top of the first one. Just as they finished making up their 'bed', the lights flickered and went out.

"So much for watching a movie," Jack commented as he tossed the pillows towards the end of the bed. "I need to grab some water and ibuprofen. Do you need anything while I'm out there?"

"Something to drink would be great. What time is it, anyway?"

"A little after five," Jack told her as he glanced at his watch. He stretched his hand out and offered it to her, helping her to her feet.

"I think I'll go change into something a little more comfortable than jeans to lounge around in," Bayleigh told him as she moved off down the hallway.

Jack headed for the kitchen and took the ibuprofen he needed for his headache. The pain wasn't as bad as it had been earlier in the day but it was still there. Remembering how Bayleigh had been rubbing her leg earlier, he decided to take the bottle back into the living room with him. Grabbing a couple of drinks out of the fridge, he headed back for the living room. The temperature in the rest of the house was already dropping.

Bayleigh had already returned and had settled herself onto the couch with her leg stretched out in front of her. Jack stood in the doorway and studied her in the light from the fire. She'd changed into yoga pants, and she'd taken off the sweatshirt she'd been wearing earlier. And he was pretty sure she wasn't wearing a bra.

Clearing his throat to get her attention, he held out her drink for her. "I also grabbed the bottle of ibuprofen," he told her, holding it up for her to see.

"Thanks," she held her hand out and took both bottles from him, opening the medicine bottle and shaking a few pills into her hand. "How'd you know I needed these?"

"You were shifting weight off your leg again earlier in the kitchen when I came in from outside and just now you were massaging it," he waited for her to swallow her pills then reached over and took her hand in his, pulling her to her feet. With a reassuring smile, he led her over to the sleeping bags. "Lie down on your back. I'm going to see if I can help those muscles relax in your leg."

"Jack, I don't know about this..." Bayleigh tugged at her hand, trying to pull away.

"Trust me, Bayleigh. I'm not going to hurt you," Jack told her, his voice soft. "And I promise if you need me to stop, at any point, all you have to do is say so."

Bayleigh's shoulders rose and fell with her rapid breaths but she didn't pull try to pull away again. Jack dropped her hand and she lowered herself onto the makeshift bed, positioning herself as he'd indicated.

"I'm just going to massage your leg for you, through your clothing. Only your leg, nothing else. Okay?" Jack knelt down in front of her, his eyes on hers. He waited for her to nod and felt her tense and jerk as he placed his hand on her lower leg, bending her knee so he could reach her calf. In a perfect world, he'd have her lie on her stomach but he knew that would make her feel too vulnerable and open to a full-on panic attack. As it was, he could feel the tension radiating off of her so he just kept his hands in place for a moment, letting her body adjust to his touch.

Her cotton yoga pants fit her like a second layer of skin and he could feel the tight muscles underneath the fabric. With a gentle touch, he began to massage her calf in an attempt to get the muscles to relax. He could feel the muscles soften under his hands the longer he manipulated them. As the tension began to ease, he worked his way up the leg to her thigh, his fingers finding the knots and the areas causing her all the trouble.

Glancing at her face, he caught the occasional grimace as he would press in deeper with his thumbs on the stubborn knots, but she didn't complain or draw back from his touch.

"Where'd you learn to do this?" she asked after a few minutes.

"Self-preservation, for the most part. When I started law school, I was too stubborn to let anyone else touch my leg. But with all the walking I had to do, my leg would get these unbelievable cramps. My schedule didn't allow for much time to get to regular physical therapy appointments. Add to that the issues I had with the nerve damage, so if I went to the wrong therapist, they could wind up doing more damage than good. So I either had to learn to give myself a massage or let someone else do it. I chose to learn."

"Lucky for me," Bayleigh sucked in a breath as his thumbs dug into a sensitive spot. He backed off, his eyes going to her face.

"You okay?"

"Just a sore spot there," she tilted her head back, focusing on a spot on the ceiling.

"Do you need me to stop?"

"No, just talk to me and get my mind off of the pain," she instructed.

"You were talking to Jason earlier. How are he and Nicole doing?" Jack asked after a slight pause.

"They're a little antsy, I think, wanting to be back here and not able to make it. He was worried about us. I've missed several calls from him and he said he'd tried your phone, too."

"I'll have to check it later. I'm sure Nicole is going crazy not being able to see Carly and the baby. I should check in with the rest of the family, too."

"You told me Carly is her best friend, cousin by marriage. Are they her only family?"

"As far as we know. The man who raised her as his daughter didn't have any family. We didn't know until last summer that he wasn't her biological father, so there's the possibility that she has a whole bunch of siblings out there somewhere."

"Does she want to know who her father is, or was, or whatever?"

"She's trying to find him. She has her mother's journals and her mother named a few guys in them from around the time Nicole would have been conceived. She's hired a PI firm to track them all down, see if any of them will admit to having had a one night stand with her mom. If they even remember her." Her muscle had relaxed as much as he thought it was going to in one session, so he dropped his hands, moving away from her to sit with his back against the couch. Bayleigh sighed and sat up as well, reclining against the mound of pillows that had been tossed on the floor.

"What about you?"

"Me?"

"I was just wondering if you've ever tried to find out who your father is. You had said the other night that you started calling your uncle 'Pop' because at the time you thought you might someday find your own father." Bayleigh's eyes dropped to her lap. "Sorry, I guess I'm getting a little personal."

"It's okay, Bayleigh. I'd just forgotten I'd mentioned it." Jack stared into the fire for a moment before answering.

"I don't even have a name to start with. I've always

suspected that my mother had no clue which guy she was sleeping with donated his sperm to my creation. And I don't think she cared. My grandfather didn't cut her off, he just cut her out of the will. That's when she left me here and signed over her parental rights to Steve and Helen, when Granddad died. As a kid, I always had my fantasies that he was some football hero or something like that, but I have a feeling he was just some cowboy that passed through, working our ranch or one of the other local ones. Or maybe one of the rodeo cowboys," Jack shrugged his shoulders. "Ma and Pop raised me as their own. I owe them everything I am."

"I'm sure they're proud of you."

"They are. They never hesitate to show it. And they never hesitate to knock me down a peg when I need it, either. They've been there for the highest of my highs and the lowest of my lows."

"Your injury?" her eyes roamed over his chest, as if she could see through his shirt to the scars on his ribs and abdomen.

"That, and when my ex left me," he admitted quietly.

"Your ex? Ex-wife?" her eyebrows shot up.

"Never made it to the alter," he shook his head. "I'd proposed before leaving for the desert and we were going to get married when I got back. Instead, I was injured and she didn't want to be saddled with someone who couldn't function as a whole person. So she left."

"Couldn't function as a whole person? What the hell does that mean?"

"At the time, I had a lot of issues. I was depressed, I wasn't sleeping, and I was in a lot of pain and taking a butt

121

KELLI HENEGHAN

load of prescription drugs, and struggling to make it into law school. Hell, I would have left myself if I could have," he bit off a laugh.

"Did she even try?"

"Try what?"

"Try to help you, try to understand, try to get through it, try anything!" Bayleigh pushed up into an upright position to face Jack.

"I was shutting her out, Bayleigh. I wouldn't talk to her." Jack didn't know why he felt like he had to defend his ex to Bayleigh.

"So? That's when you try harder. That's when you go to counseling together and find out what you can do to help the one you love. You don't just leave him alone to deal with it by her...I mean himself."

"Is that what happened to you? Did Will leave you alone to deal with everything?"

Bayleigh swallowed hard, her gaze moving around the room before returning to Jack's. "Will and I were on the path to being over before it happened, but yes. Will blamed me for the attack. Correction, he didn't blame me for the attack itself, he blamed me for everything that happened *after* it. He thought I should have just let Andrew do whatever he wanted to do with me, so that the bar wouldn't have closed and we wouldn't have lost our gig."

"The fucker thought you should have been *raped?*" Jack's voice had gone soft.

"I don't think that's how Will thought of it, but yes, that's what it boils down to. That's why I left the band. He was making the other members choose between loyalty to me or to the band itself. I don't need the band and I don't want to make my life as a singer, so I stepped down. Once my injuries had healed enough that the doctors said I could travel home on my own, I left England." Bayleigh hadn't realized she was crying until a tear fell unto her hand. "At that point, I just wanted to come home. I threw what I knew I would need into my bags and booked my flight."

"You do know that no matter what you did or said to that guy Andrew, he never had any right to try and touch you in any way. Tell me you know that."

"I know that," she repeated, her voice soft, but firm.

"Tell me you know that Will was wrong," he instructed her.

"I know that, too," she repeated.

Jack sat up and reached for her hands, tugging on them and pulling her across the makeshift bed until she was sitting next to him with her back against the couch, tucking her up against his side. He grabbed one of the fleece blankets and wrapped it around them, snuggling up with her, his arm wrapped around her. "Tell me your story."

"You know my story," she looked at him in puzzlement.

"No, I know bits and pieces. I want to know how you got from here to there and back to here. Talk to me. We have all night, nowhere to go and no distractions."

Bayleigh stared into the fire for moment and Jack gave her the time to gather her thoughts. "I was a music major and my mom thought I'd use the degree to teach. But I've always wanted to write my own music. I have the minor in computer science as a backup because technology is never going to go away. I figured it was good to have a back-up, you know?" she glanced up in time to see his nod.

"I met Will at an open mic night where I was messing

around with one of my songs. He liked my song, invited me to hear his band, and then I started following his band around to local bars. He started using some of my stuff and then I started singing back up for him and we just sort of fell into dating each other. It was a gradual kind of thing, over a period of several months. But once I started dating him, I was all about him. I thought he was it for me. My mom didn't like him, tried to talk me out of seeing him. Jason couldn't stand him, either. I just thought it was because Will wasn't in college and was the 'starving musician'. I figured with time, they'd come around. Then mom got sick and died and Will was there when I needed him. I thought it was true love and we'd always be together."

"How long did that last?"

"Until we got to England. He's got a wandering eye and a little thing like a relationship doesn't mean he can't sample what else is there. We were probably broken up more than we were together, if you want the truth of the matter. But I didn't want to admit to Jason that I'd made such a colossal mistake in following him to England, so I stayed with the band. Besides, I was gaining the experience I wanted and needed with writing music."

"What happened last summer?" he felt her shoulders tense against him when he asked the question. He heard her heavy sigh and then she dropped her head on his shoulder.

"The owner of the pub where we had our contract became obsessed with me. And I was the clueless idiot. I had no idea he'd been stalking me. When the police went to his house, he had a wall of photos of me. He even had pictures of me backstage changing." She paused and glanced towards Jack.

"I wouldn't say you were the clueless idiot. Had there been signs you were being stalked?"

"Not that anyone could ever come up with. I mean, Andrew was around a lot but he was the owner of the pub. He gave me a weird vibe, but to be honest, I got weird vibes from a lot of the guys over there."

"What happened that night?"

"Andrew overheard a fight between me and Will. I had threatened to leave England and come home, so Andrew followed me back to my apartment. I heard him break the window and went to investigate. He slammed me up against the wall, wanting to 'talk'," she swallowed hard, but Jack still didn't see any of her normal tells of an approaching panic attack.

"Then what?"

"I tried to talk him into leaving. He slapped me around a bit. At one point I tried to scream and he knocked me to the floor."

"Jesus, Bayleigh..."

"It was what I needed him to do, though. It put me in reach of one of Will's electric guitars. I swung that sucker like a Louisville Slugger, caught him right in the side of the head."

"Good for you!" he gave her shoulders a squeeze.

"My neighbors had heard all the noise and called the cops. They were breaking in the front door at that point. So compared to what it could have been, I was lucky."

"Your injury to your leg didn't happen at the same time though, did it?"

"Ah, my leg," Bayleigh moved her leg underneath the blanket. "So, this is the really stupid part. For a while, after it happened, I was afraid to leave the apartment. At all. Then one of my neighbors talked me into going to a couple of kickboxing classes with her. Her reasoning was if I knew how to fight, I wouldn't have to destroy another guitar, if I ever needed to defend myself again."

"You took a bad hit in kickboxing?" Jack guessed.

"Oh no, I hated kickboxing and quit after a couple of classes. But I realized how out of shape I was, so I started running. The problem was, I would hear sounds or see someone who resembled Andrew and I'd slide into a panic attack. Sometimes, it was more of a flashback. During one episode, I took off down some stairs and fell. That's when I did all the damage to my leg."

"How much of this does Jason know?"

"I'm not sure. I never told him any of it. I was too ashamed," she admitted. "I know none of it's my fault and I'm not to blame, but at the same time, if I'd never gone to England, none of it would have happened. What if Jason throws that in my face?"

"He won't," Jack assured her.

"I hope not."

"Something in your brother's voice the other day when he was talking to me tells me that he knows about the attack. I would guess he did what I did and Googled your name. But I know your brother. He is not going to turn his back on you. He'll be upset you didn't call him when it happened, but he's going to be more upset with the fucker who did this to you."

"Thank you for that," she whispered against his shoulder and he pressed a kiss to the top of her head.

"So what did happen to that asshole?"

"He committed suicide when he found out he was going to lose his bar. Turns out I wasn't the only singer he'd been stalking and once the story broke a few of the others came forward to press charges."

"Can't say I'm sorry." They sat together for a few moments, the only sounds in the room the crackling of the wood as the fire burned, its warmth reaching across the room to them.

"So now that you're on the road to recovery and no longer part of the band, what do you want to do now?"

"Write songs. I've had a real mental block since last summer but I think now that I'm away from the constant reminders of all of that, I want to get back to it." She pushed at the blanket. Now that the room was warming up, the fleece was getting to be too heavy for her.

"What will you do with them?"

"Sell them. I never pursued it before because of a sense of loyalty to Will and the band. He liked being able to say my stuff was exclusive," she grimaced. "I never realized what a controlling bastard he is."

"Now you know. So how do you sell them, do you know?"

"That won't be a problem. I've had some other bands and people show interest in the past. If the word gets out that my stuff is on the open market, it'll sell. Once I get settled somewhere, I'll find a studio so I can do demos, too."

"Sounds like you already have it all planned out."

"The basics, maybe," she shrugged her shoulders. "I

need to bounce a few ideas off of some of my friends here in the States. The nice thing about being a writer is you can pretty much do it anywhere. It helps to be near the center of the industry to make your contacts, but I've already done that, thanks to Will."

"So you could live and work anywhere?"

"Within reason, I guess so. I mean, I'd want to be somewhere there's a lot of traffic in the industry, like New York, LA, Nashville. Or even Austin would work."

She glanced over to the windows as the ice started pelting them again. "Sounds like the storm is picking back up."

"Looks like it," he agreed, glancing towards the windows. "I need to call the rest of my family and check in.

"I'm think I'm going to call my brother again. I think maybe I owe him a long over-due conversation."

"Why don't you stay in here where it's warmer? I'll go out to the kitchen, give you some privacy, if you want."

"I, uh, I'm not sure, to be honest."

He gave her shoulders another squeeze and then withdrew his arm before standing up. Stretching his back, he reached down and held his hand out to her, helping her to her feet. "Why don't I go out to the kitchen, make my calls, and you check in with Jason? I'll come back in here when I'm done and if you don't want me in here, you can tell me to leave." She nodded and he paused and then lowered his head and gave her a brief kiss. "It'll be okay, Bayleigh. You made it to the other side. You do realize that, right?"

"I think I'm beginning to believe that," she gave him a soft smile. "Go call your family."

Jack gave her hand a squeeze and headed for the

kitchen, grabbing his phone off the end table where he'd laid it earlier. He called his uncle first to check in with them, make sure they were still okay in San Antonio and didn't need him to do anything around the ranch. He checked in with Mitch, Paul, and Carly as well. He gave Bayleigh as much time as he could as he could stand in the freezing kitchen, but even turning on the gas stove to use the 'old-fashioned' coffee percolator he had didn't help warm things up much.

He headed back to the living room with two cups of coffee, pausing in the doorway, his eyes scanning the darkened room, finding her curled up in the corner of the sofa, the phone clutched in her hand.

"Bayleigh?" he spoke her name gently as he stepped into the room and she raised her face to him. Even from across the room he could see the tear streaks down her face. If he had been wrong about Jason, he would kill his friend with his bare hands. Better yet, he'd skin alive him with a scalpel. Much more painful that way.

He set the coffee down on the table and moved over to the couch and sat down beside her. "What happened? What did he say?" he wrapped an arm around her shoulders and pulled her against him to comfort her.

Bayleigh laid her head on his shoulder as she sighed. "It's fine, Jack. Don't go all caveman protector on me against my own brother."

"That obvious?"

"A little," she sniffled as she reached up to wipe a few remaining tears away.

"So, what did he say?"

"He lectured me for not calling him last summer, and

again when I got hurt. And again when I decided to fly across the Atlantic by myself."

Jack chuckled, earning himself a soft smack from her. He caught her hand and held it against his chest. "What else did he say?"

"He threatened to dismember Will for not protecting me better. He seems to think Will may have known Andrew was stalking me and may have, uh, 'pimped' me out, for lack of a better term."

"It wouldn't surprise me, if Will always put the band and his career first," Jack agreed. "And if Jason needs help, I'll be first in line."

"Will's not worth either of you winding up in jail."

"Sweetheart, you're in Texas, and we have an 'in' with the law in this town, remember?" he nudged her with his shoulder and he felt the smile against his shoulder.

"So, what else did he say?"

"We'll figure it all out once he and Nicole get back but he's going to give me more access to my trust fund so I can pay for some demos for the songs I've written, help me find some studio space."

"That's awesome, Bayleigh."

"It's a start, at least," she agreed, as her finger traced circles on his chest. "It was good to hear him say he was on my side."

"I told you he would be."

"I know. And I should have never have doubted him. But when you hit rock bottom, your mind just goes to worst case scenarios, you know?"

"I do know," he agreed in a quiet voice.

"Did you doubt your family would understand you?"

"There are times I still doubt they understand. No one else has seen combat, so they can't fully comprehend what I go through. Paul was active duty and was stationed overseas for a year but was lucky and never saw combat, but he had the stress of the deployment." Jack paused and stared into the fire, collecting his thoughts. "But they are there for me when I need them, day or night. Any of them. Or all of them. Just like Jason and Nicole will be there for you, if you give them that chance."

"I know," she repeated, her voice soft. "I just had to find myself again first, you know? I think somewhere between my dad dying and my mom getting sick so soon after, I lost myself. I didn't have a chance to figure things out before my mom died and then we had the offer to move to England. I didn't feel like Jason was being all that supportive of me at the time, and Will was, so I went."

"And now?"

"I've grown up," she said, sitting up to look at him. "I may want my brother's approval but I don't plan on moving half-way across the world just because we disagree on something again."

"Sounds like a good idea," he nodded. "So, what do you want to do now?"

"Now?"

"Yeah. It's six o'clock. And while I could take you to bed and spend hours entertaining you there, I don't think that's what you had in mind for tonight," he told her with a wink.

"You'd have a heart attack if I agreed to that, though."

"Maybe," he grinned. "We could play cards."

"Poker?"

"You play poker?"

"Of course I play poker. You got a deck of cards and chips?"

"What are we playing for?" Jack stood up and headed over to the entertainment center and the shelves underneath it. He withdrew the poker chips and the deck of cards he kept there and brought them back to the coffee table. Bayleigh cleared off the table while he sorted out the chips and shuffled the cards. She cut the deck and he dealt.

"I don't know. What would you suggest?" she asked as she reached for her cards.

"You have to dedicate your next song to me if you win."

"Uh, okay. And if you win?"

"I get to kiss you."

Bayleigh's eyes flew to his and her hands paused in the act of picking up her cards.

"Stakes too high?"

"Not at all," she whispered.

"So it's a deal?"

"It's a deal." The question was, how fast could she lose?

CHAPTER 9

"That's it. I'm done." Bayleigh tossed the cards on the table. "That's at least five hands I've lost to you."

"I thought you said you knew how to play poker."

"I guess I'm out of practice."

Jack gave her a knowing glance as he gathered up the cards and put them back into the box, but she was busy restacking the chips in the tray and missed it. "Are you out of practice with your guitar, too?"

"No, why?"

"I thought maybe you could play something for me." He stood up to put the poker chips and deck of cards away. And to hide his smile. He had known as soon as they started playing that she was doing everything she could to lose the game. So he kept challenging her and not cashing in on their bet. He was enjoying this little game.

"It's all still a little rough. I don't have anything that's finished," she hedged.

"So, use me as a sounding board," he suggested.

"Well, if you're sure you don't mind. I would like some feedback on a couple of them. I'll go get my guitar and be right back," she pushed herself to her feet and left the room. He grabbed the empty coffee cups and carried them out to the kitchen and set them in the sink to wash later. He walked into the living room just as Bayleigh was sitting down on the couch with her guitar, checking the tuning. He stood in the doorway watching her for a moment and then walked over and stretched out on their makeshift bed, making himself comfortable.

Seeing him there, Bayleigh gave him a soft smile. "This is one I've been working on for a while. It's too 'soft' for Will, but it would work for a solo female artist, I think." She started strumming the chords, her eyes closed as she focused on the music. He focused on her.

"I think you need a second a bridge at the end," he told her as her voice faded away. Her eyes blinked open and by the way she looked at him, he thought she forgot he was even there.

"That might work," she strummed the chords again, working through the song. "It still needs something, though."

"What else you got in your arsenal?" he put his hands behind his head and waited for her to continue. She thought for a moment and then launched into another song. All of them were her softer, more romantic songs, songs she had never even played for Will, knowing he would have shot every single one of them down. But Jack helped critique them. He had an ear for music. He could tell where she was getting hung up without her even telling him, whether it was the chords or the lyrics.

"Yeah, I can see why you don't think you'll have any issues selling these," Jack told her as she put her guitar back in its case.

"Once I get an agent and get my name out there, I'm sure I'll get interest. And I just need to let Maddie know I want an agent. She'll make it happen." Bayleigh yawned and Jack glanced at his watched, surprised to see it was almost ten o'clock.

"Why don't I bank the fire and we can go ahead and get to bed? We've had a long couple of days." He took her hand and drew her closer and he saw her breath hitch. He knew she thought he was going to collect on that bet now, but he had plans for that bet, and he was going to leave her waiting for just a little bit longer. The anticipation had to be killing her before he was going to cash in on that bet. But he could tease her until then. Leaning in he brushed his lips over hers, feeling her sigh.

"Go ahead and climb under the covers. The temperature will drop some when I bank the fire. I don't want you to get a chill."

He could see the disappointment in her eyes as he stepped away from her but she was quick to mask it. He turned to the fireplace and he heard the blankets rustle as she did as she was told. As he turned from the fireplace he heard a sniffle.

"Bayleigh?"

"I'm fine."

He crawled across the sleeping bags and leaned over her as she tried to hide her face in the pillows. "No, you're not. Why are you crying?"

"Just leave it alone, Jack."

"Babe..." he was at a loss.

"I'm not your 'babe'!" she spat at him.

He sat back on his heels and stared at her. "Okay. Bayleigh," he tried again. "Talk to me, here. I just want to help. Why are you crying?"

She rolled over onto her back, staring up at him, tears streaming down her cheeks. With an annoyed motion, she reached up with one hand and wiped the tears away. "You bet me a kiss and I lost. I lost five fucking hands of poker to you. On purpose. Do you know how often I lose in poker? And I lost five straight hands tonight. And all I got was a peck on the lips as you told me to get into bed so I didn't get 'a chill.' Like I'm a child. So don't call me babe. You made it as clear as you can that you're not into me. I get it."

Jack stared at her, his eyes wide with disbelief and then he laughed. Even as her eyes narrowed in anger, he laughed. As she sat up and pulled her fist back, though, he sobered. "No, none of that," he cautioned, catching her fist in his hand, pulling her up against him. "You really think I'm not interested in you, Bayleigh? Does that feel as if I'm 'not into you'?" he positioned her against him so that she could feel how into her he was. Every single hard inch of him.

"Oh," was the only thing she could manage.

"Yeah, 'oh' is right," he shook his head, with a mock glare pushing her back down onto the sleeping bags, and laying down beside her, propping himself up on an elbow and leaning over her. "I was trying to tease you, Bayleigh. Build the anticipation. I guess it back fired on me."

"You think?" she muttered. "So, you do want to kiss me, then, right?"

"Yes, Bayleigh. I want to kiss you. Among other things."

"I-I want that, too," she whispered, seeing the desire flare in his eyes.

He moved closer, leaning in and pressing his lips to hers. He teased her lips open with the tip of his tongue, playing a game of cat and mouse as he would meet and stroke her tongue with his and then retreat, forcing her to seek him out if she wanted more. He smiled against her lips as she mimicked his movements. He felt her hands come up and slide around his neck, as he slid his fingers through her silky hair.

He pressed kisses to her jaw and then down her throat, tracing the neckline of her shirt with his tongue, causing her to angle her head back and arch towards him. Kissing his way back up to her mouth, he brought one hand between them, pushing her shirt up, laying his hand on her stomach.

Leaning back so he could see her face, he smiled as he took in her flushed features as she opened her eyes. "Doing okay?" he questioned as he stroked her stomach with his thumb.

"I'd be doing better if you'd keep kissing me," she tugged on his neck, pulling him back down to her.

With a chuckle his mouth closed over hers again as he slid his hand a little higher, his thumb stroking the underside of her breast. He'd been right; no bra.

She shifted so that she was lying on her back. As he moved with her, he positioned himself between her legs, pressing against her and releasing a groan as she rubbed herself against him. His hand slid up and over her breast, teasing the nipple into a hard peak, pushing her two shirts up and out of his way.

With a muffled curse, he grabbed the hem of the shirts and pulled them over her head, tossing them to the side of the sleeping bags. Kissing his way down her neck to her breasts, he drew a nipple into his mouth. Arching her back, she moaned, her hands tugging on his own shirt, pulling it out of his jeans and out of her way.

"God, you taste so sweet," Jack murmured as he kissed his way between her breasts. "I want to be inside of you, baby."

In an instant, Bayleigh was transported back to that night in England, when Andrew had broken into her apartment. She could hear his voice, as clear as a bell. *I know you'll taste as sweet as honey. You were made to fit me. You know you want me. Stop teasing me!* She was trapped in that room with him and she knew what was going to happen to her if she couldn't get free. She had to get out; she had to fight.

Bayleigh was crying and pushing against Jack's shoulders. "Oh, God, stop! Please, no, stop!" Her hands fisted and she swung at Jack's face but he pulled away from her in time.

Jack sat up and grabbed one of the blankets he'd pushed aside moments ago. Dodging her flailing arms as she fought her demons, he wrapped her up and pulled her against him, tucking her head against his shoulder. Rubbing her back in soothing circles, he waited for whatever memory had grabbed her to let go.

When her sobs quieted a few minutes later, he relaxed his arms and chanced a look at her face. "You with me again?" he questioned, his voice soft. They were the first words he'd spoken since she'd started with the flashback.

"I'm sorry, Jack," she sniffed and fought to free a hand from the blanket. Jack used the edge of the fleece blanket to wipe the tears from her face, leaning in to give her a warm kiss.

"Don't ever apologize for having a flashback, Bayleigh. It's not something you can help, or control, or even prevent, most of the time," Jack told her, his voice firm. "Can I ask what triggered it though, I mean besides the obvious?"

Bayleigh cleared her throat and looked away from him. "Your words," she whispered. "Andrew said something that night very similar to what you said. Once I heard it, it was like I was back in that room with him, trying to talk my way out of there. He told me what he was going to do to me, in great detail."

Jack's arms tightened around her but he had to ask. Before he did anything else God-awful stupid, he had to know. "You said he knocked you around a bit that night. But did he touch you?"

Bayleigh swallowed hard before shaking her head. "He tried. But that's when I started screaming and fighting back. When I knew I couldn't talk my way out of that room, that he wasn't going to leave until he'd raped me, I started fighting."

"That's my girl," Jack pressed a kiss to her temple and Bayleigh sighed, her head dropping onto his shoulder.

"How is it that you can know me for a couple of days and know what I need and Will, who has known me and even loved me at one time, couldn't stand to be in the same room with me after the attack?"

Jack clenched his teeth to keep from saying the first thought that popped into his head—*"Because that guy's a fucking jackass and you're better off without him."*

"Part of it is just having been done this road, to some extent, myself. As much as my family tried to be there for me after the IED explosion, they had no clue how to help me. I became friends with a few other veterans during rehab for no other reason than we'd survived the war and whatever had sent us to rehab," he shared, instead.

"Do you still have flashbacks?"

"Not so much flashbacks. I'll have nightmares, sometimes. Like earlier, when the window broke. The ice hitting the windows sounds remarkably like the sand hitting windows and our B-huts. I wasn't having a nightmare but I was dreaming about being back there. And when the branch came through the window, I woke up reaching for my weapons."

"So it'll get be better?"

"We all hope that it gets better," he pulled her against him even more. "Not everyone makes it through to the other side. Some do, only to slide backwards. Hopefully, they have friends and family who, if nothing else, will be there to extend the hand to help pull them back and help them find whatever else they need. That's what Nicole did for me in California, and when I moved back here to Austin for law school, Mitch stepped in and checked on me a lot, especially when it became clear that the fiancé was going to become the ex-fiancé."

"The panic attacks are the worst for me. This was the first flashback I've had in a while. I still get nightmares a lot, although I haven't had one since leaving England," she sighed and pushed back from him. "I'm sorry about, well, all of this," she waved her hand in front of herself. "You shouldn't have to deal with such a mess, and one who can't even say 'yes' and then carry through with it."

"Oh, Bayleigh," Jack shook his head and leaned in to give her another quick kiss. "No man is worth his weight in gold if he holds what you've been through against you. Remember that." He pushed himself to his feet and then leaned over to grab one of the pillows and a blanket.

"What are you doing?"

"I'll sleep on the couch," he waved a hand towards it as Bayleigh stood up and grabbed the pillow from him.

"Why?"

"Because I don't want to trigger anymore flashbacks, nightmares, or panic attacks tonight. I'd offer to sleep in another room but I'd freeze to death by morning," he tried to pull the pillow back from her.

"I don't want you to sleep in another room or on the couch!" Bayleigh tossed the pillow to the floor and then tugged the blanket out of his hand. "Please, Jack?" she pleaded.

Jack swallowed back his groan. He was still hard as a rock and wouldn't get any sleep if she were pressed up against him all night. Who was he kidding? Even if he slept on the couch, he wouldn't be sleeping.

"Alright, babe. Get yourself comfortable under the covers. I'm going to go down the hall and find a pair of shorts I can sleep in for the night."

"Shorts?"

"Well, I tend to sleep in the buff. I haven't been the last couple of nights because you're here. But I can't sleep in jeans," he gave her a wink and left the room, headed for his bedroom. With any luck, the freezing temperature in his bedroom would kill his hard-on and he'd be able to at least get back into the room and under the covers before his cock decided to help pitch tents in his living room.

CHAPTER 10

*H*ours later, jack was on his back, staring up at the ceiling. Bayleigh was curled up beside him, her head on his shoulder and an arm across his chest. She'd already been under the covers and on the far side of the pallet and half asleep when he'd returned from his bedroom. She'd murmured a soft 'thank you' when he slid into their make-shift bed. It hadn't taken long for her to fall asleep, but he couldn't relax enough. The sound of that glass breaking had sent his mind back to a time he wanted to forget.

He'd almost managed to fall asleep himself when he heard the first whimpers. Pushing himself up on his elbow, he'd looked over at her. In the firelight, he could just make out the crease in between her eyebrows. She was starting to thrash around, her movements hindered by the blanket she'd wrapped around herself.

"Shh, babe. It's okay. You're safe," he whispered, leaning over and smoothing a few strands of hair back off of her face. At his touch, the crease disappeared and her movements settled. "Go back to sleep, sweetheart. I'm here."

She'd turned onto her side, facing him, and drifted back into a deeper slumber, only to reawaken him less than an hour later, this time with a scream. "Bayleigh, it's okay. I'm right here," he reached over and cupped her cheek, his hand slipping down to her shoulder. "Wake up, Bay!" He'd had to repeat himself a few times before her eyes blinked open. Even then, they didn't focus on him but darted around the room, looking into the dark corners, searching for something.

"You're safe, Bayleigh. You're with me, in my home. Remember?" he let his hand slip off her shoulder, not wanting to add to the terror he could see in her eyes as they continued to look around the room.

"Jack?" her voice husky from sleep but still filled with fear from whatever nightmare he'd woken her from.

"Yes, babe. I'm here," Jack soothed.

"What time is it?"

"Close to midnight," he squinted to see the numbers on his watch. "Why, you got somewhere else to be?" he teased.

"I was hoping it was later and I could just get up now," she admitted, rubbing at her eyes. "How many times have I woken you up already?"

"That was the first time."

"Really? 'Cause I swear I remember you telling me to go back to sleep earlier, too."

"Well, I wasn't asleep yet that time. And you were just moving around a lot. I'm not sure if you were having a nightmare or what."

"Can I ask a favor? A huge one?" her voice had a slight quiver to it.

"Of course."

"Will you hold me, just until I go back to sleep?"

Jack had stretched out and Bayleigh had scooted across the sleeping bags until her head was on his shoulder. He'd curved his arm around her, holding her close, breathing in the fruity smell of her shampoo. Bayleigh shifted around and then sighed. "You make me feel so safe," she whispered, her breath warm against his neck. He tightened his hold on her and listened to her breathing even out as she drifted back to sleep.

And so now here he was, two hours later, wide awake, trying to figure out what he was going to do with this girl. Ever since returning from the desert and being dumped by his fiancé, he'd stuck with women who were looking for a good time, in bed and out of it, for the short term. And the shorter the better, as far as he was concerned.

But here was a woman who needed more than just a quick lay. Bayleigh was going to need patience and understanding and lots of time to get past what had happened to her. But he was so out of practice with anything beyond what Nicole called his "flavor of the month club" that it wasn't even funny.

Jack brought his free hand up and scrubbed at his face. Bayleigh moved in her sleep, bringing a leg up and settling her thigh across his leg, her knee brushing his still-hard-as-a-rock member. Suppressing his groan, he shifted, trying to put a few inches in between her knee and his pecker. Damn thing didn't need any more reminders that she was in bed with him, wrapped up in his arms.

She'd called him 'safe'. Good lord, Nicole and Jason both would bust a gut if they'd heard that one. Jason used to just shake his head when they'd head out for drinks and he'd have a pocketful of numbers from women within the first thirty minutes.

"Jack?" Bayleigh pushed up onto an elbow, blinking the sleep out of her eyes.

"I'm still here," he smoothed his hand up her back. "You ok?"

"Yeah, but your arm was squeezing the life out of me. Are *you* ok?"

"Sorry, just lost in thought I guess," he reached up and pushed her hair back out of her face. Even in the dim light from the fire, he could see the wariness in her eyes.

"About what a mess I am?"

"You're no more of a mess than I am, Bayleigh," he assured her, urging her to lay back down beside him, her head back on his shoulder. Her hand rested on his chest, over his heart.

"I didn't see you falling to pieces at any time in the last few days. You said earlier that you were even dreaming about the desert when the tree branch broke your window and you were still all calm and cool."

Jack drew in a deep breath, releasing it slowly as her hand started smoothing over his chest. "Yeah, calm and cool. That's me, all right," he managed to answer, gritting his teeth as his cock twitched.

"Then what's wrong?"

"It's nothing, Bayleigh. We should just try to get some more sleep."

Her hand stilled on his chest and then she levered

herself up on her elbow again. "You don't have to play babysitter anymore, Jack. I can sleep on the couch."

JACK SLID both arms around her waist and held her still as she made the move to slide out from their pallet of sleeping bags and blankets. "No way, babe. First of all, if anyone sleeps on the damn couch, it will be me. Second of all, and you need to listen very close to what I'm saying here," he paused and waited for her eyes to meet his.

"I am not babysitting you. I have been lying here all night harder than I can remember ever being, and trying to control my caveman instincts. If you hadn't been attacked and threatened with rape, and if you weren't still trapped in nightmares, flashbacks, and panic attacks, I'd be pulling out all the stops right now. I want nothing more than to roll you over and burying myself so deep inside of you, you feel me there for a week."

Bayleigh swallowed hard. "Oh," she whispered.

"So, yeah, I've been holding you for the last two hours, trying to convince Mr. Happy here the ending he wants is not gonna happen."

Bayleigh pressed her lips together before letting her head drop to his chest. He felt her shoulders shaking and wrapped his arms around her. "Oh, baby, I didn't mean to make you cry."

She picked her head up and he could see her biting her lip to keep from laughing. "Oh, you're laughing at me, now, are you?"

"Mr. Happy?"

"Well, I didn't think 'Willy the one-eyed wonder-worm', was appropriate here," he winked at her.

"Please tell me you don't actually call your, uh, that is, you haven't named *it*, have you?" Even in the firelight, he could see the blush creeping over her features.

"All men name *it*. When you're allowing someone else to make decisions for you, you like to know their name, right?"

"Oh my God," she muttered, closing her eyes and dropping her head back down to his chest. "That was awful."

"I was quite proud of it, myself." He shifted her off of his shoulder, turning so they were each lying on their sides and facing each other. "So, back to the issues we're both having here tonight—I want to ask you something personal. It stays between us, I promise," he slid his hand under her chin and tilted her head back so he could look in her eyes.

"Nothing good is ever preceded with 'it stays between us'," Bayleigh closed her eyes for a couple of seconds, before opening them and looking into Jack's concerned face. "Okay."

"Have you tried having sex since the attack? Before tonight, I mean?"

Bayleigh took a deep breath and shifted away from Jack, rolling onto her back. Pulling the blankets up to her shoulders for her, he laid his arm across her stomach.

"I'm just trying to find some kind of solid ground for us, Bayleigh," he whispered, coming up on an elbow so he could still see her face. She turned her head towards him and gave him a small smile.

"I know," she laid her hand over his on her stomach. "So, the short answer there is 'no'. Will made his moves on me a couple of times after the attack and I just...couldn't. But I never had flashbacks with him, though. Panic attacks, yes. He couldn't handle those at all. He'd just tell me to snap out of it and walk away."

Jack shook his head at the other man's stupidity. "His loss," he muttered.

"And your gain?"

"I can hope, can't I?" he smiled at her. "He never tried to force you or anything, though, did he?"

"No, he wasn't quite that stupid." Bayleigh turned her head on her pillow so that she could look into his eyes. "The thing is, Jack, I didn't care one way or the other about Will. Not by the time all of this was happening. I just wanted to know that I'm still able to, you know?"

His hand came up to cup her face and he stroked her cheek with his thumb. "You can't force it, Bayleigh, and certainly not with a guy who isn't going to take his time and take care of you, on all levels. You have to be ready."

"What if I never make it back? What if I'm never ready?"

Jack could see the shimmer of tears in her eyes and he leaned forward enough to press a chaste kiss to her mouth. "Baby, the way you respond to me...you'll get there. Just give yourself some more time." He smiled at her. "Still want to sleep on the couch?"

"No, I'm pretty comfortable where I am," she slid her arm around his neck, pulling his face down to hers again for another kiss, this one a little longer and deeper.

"Ahh, Bay. This isn't going to help matters," he groaned against her lips.

"Are you saying you don't want me to kiss you anymore?" she arched an eyebrow at him.

"I'm saying we need to stop kissing and try to get some sleep," he pressed his lips to hers in a chaste kiss. "So go to sleep!" he ordered, causing her to giggle.

She snuggled in against him, earning another groan as she moved closer, her head once again finding a place to rest against his chest. Within in minutes, he could tell by the steady rise and fall of her shoulders against him that she was falling asleep. With a contented sigh, he closed his eyes, willing himself to follow.

CHAPTER 11

*T*he sun streaming through THE uncovered windows woke Bayleigh up just a few hours later. Her head was now pillowed on Jack's chest, her arm across his stomach, and his arm curled around her, holding her to him. She laid there for a few minutes, listening to his slow, steady heartbeat.

She still couldn't wrap her brain around how safe and secure she felt with him, after only knowing him for a couple of days. She'd known Will for years now and had never felt like this with him. Will had made the token effort of being supportive when the attack happened but he expected her to just shake it off and keep going.

With Jack, he knew there were steps to take, even knew what those steps were. She was mortified that she'd had that flashback last night, and then the dreams afterward. But Jack's calm and no-nonsense approach, his support through all of it the last few days. A smile touched her lips as she remembered his reaction to finding her on the couch yesterday after speaking with Jason. She had known from

151

the look on his face that he thought Jason had let her down and he was ready to battle his best friend over it.

But Jack had been right. Jason wasn't upset with her, at least not over the attack or anything that had happened to her. He had offered unconditional love and support, even over the phone.

No, he was upset that she hadn't called him when it had happened. Another thing Jack had been right about. But he would be there for her now, no doubt about it. And she'd heard Nicole in the background while they were on the phone offering her support, as well.

Jason and Nicole had both been excited to hear she wanted to stay close, maybe not in Waketon, but close enough to visit often. Jason told her to scope out what she needed for both a living space and a recording studio and he'd release the funds from her account.

"Good morning," Jack whispered, breaking into her thoughts. "Sleep well?"

"How'd you know I was awake?"

"This," he told her, grabbing her hand on his abdomen and stopping its movements. "It's going to get a reaction I'm not sure you want right now."

Only then did she realize she'd been caressing his muscles through his shirt. She felt the heat rush to her cheeks.

"I am so sorry!" she tried to push away from him but he wrapped both arms around her and held her close.

"Remember the other day when I offered to apologize for kissing you and you told me not to, because you didn't want to hurt me?"

Bayleigh laughed and nodded her head.

"Well, same thing applies here. You can touch me all you want, honey. Just know that I am not unaffected and I am not made of steel." His arms loosened from around her and she slid her hand up to his chest, laying it over his heart.

"Maybe if we just push past my fears," she whispered.

"You mean, me ignore you when you start having a flashback?"

"I'd know it was you, and I know you won't hurt me. We could try it," she insisted.

"No, we couldn't." he shifted so that he could roll her over onto her back and he leaned over her. "You're so tense right now, Bayleigh, that if I try and move you, you'll snap in half," his hand came up and she flinched. With a heavy sigh he dropped his hand before touching her. Her hands moved back to his chest and gripped the front of his t-shirt, fisting in the material.

"I know you won't hurt me," she insisted, her eyes wide as they searched his.

"In here you know that," he tapped her chest in between her breasts. "But up here, you're not so sure."

"Yes, I am!"

"Bay, it's okay. There's a reason it's called Post-traumatic stress disorder. You suffered a traumatic experience, and as much as you want to move on, you just can't. I get it. Believe me, I get it," he brought his hand back up and cupped her cheek. "But I will not ignore the signs of a flashback or a panic attack. That could potentially do so much damage to your psyche."

"I just want to feel *normal*. I want to be *me*, again."

"I didn't know you before but I think you'll find your-self again, Bayleigh."

"How can you be so sure?" she whispered, her voice quivering, as she blinked back tears.

"Because the woman I see in front of me right now is a fighter," he told her, leaning in and pressing a kiss to her forehead. He glanced over his shoulder at the fireplace. "I need to add some wood to the fire before the embers completely go out." Tossing the blanket off, he pushed himself to his feet with a groan and stretched his back, glancing at the windows as he did so.

"Did it stop sleeting or is the layer of ice so thick we just can't hear it?" Bayleigh asked, following his gaze.

"I think it stopped," he answered, as he moved to the fireplace and added more logs and kindling to the fire, stoking it until the flames flared back up.

"Do you want me to make us some breakfast?" she asked, sitting up.

"Not yet. You stay in here where it's warm. I'll go turn the oven on, get the kitchen warmed up."

"How long do you think it'll be before they get the power back on?"

"Depends on how much of the town is out and what caused it," Jack shrugged. "And of course, how long the temperature stays below freezing. Hopefully those weather guys get it right today and the temperature comes up above freezing." He picked up his phone from the edge of the coffee table as it buzzed with an incoming message. Looking at the message, he smiled and glanced over at her. "Carly sent a picture of her and the baby and a message for you," he handed the phone over to her.

"Aww, he's so adorable," Bayleigh gushed, looking at the picture before reading what Carly had written. With a gasp, her eyes went to Jack. "She wants me to name him?"

"His middle name, yes. She said she wouldn't have gotten through labor without you. Guess I'm still chopped liver," he muttered with a wink, taking his phone back. "So, what's it going to be?"

"I've never named a baby before, I don't even know what to suggest! Did she say what his first name is?"

"Robert, after her dad."

Bayleigh nodded and pushed the covers off of herself, standing up and stretching, much like Jack had done moments before. Jack watched as her shirt pulled tight across her breasts and he swallowed.

"I think I'm going to head into the kitchen. Why don't you stay in here for a bit?" *and let me cool off.*

"You sure you don't want me to help start breakfast?" she asked, turning towards him but he'd already started to walk out of the room.

"Nope. I'll be fine," he answered over his shoulder.

BAYLEIGH FOLDED up their blankets and stacked them on the seat of the armchair. She rolled up the foam mats and stacked those along with the pillows next to the chair. Checking the screen in front of the fireplace to make sure it was in place, she headed for the kitchen.

Jack had used the percolator and brewed a fresh pot of coffee and was scrambling eggs when she walked into the room. It was cooler than the other room, but the stove and oven were heating it up so it was at least comfortable.

"Can I do anything to help?" she asked, stopping at the edge of the counter.

"I've got it under control, but thanks," he smiled at her over his shoulder. "Coffee's ready, if you want some."

Bayleigh nodded and moved over to the stove, reaching for the percolator on the back burner. Jack had already set a cup next to the stove for her, and seeing his half-empty cup, she filled his back up.

"I called Paul, he said most of the town is without power right now. Crews are working on it, but he said to be prepared to be without for a day or two. Then I called my uncle's foreman. He's been checking on Jason's place; they still have power over there and at my uncle's, and the contractor was able to fix that broken pipe at Jason's before the storm hit yesterday," he dished up the scrambled eggs and bacon and motioned to the pot holder next to her hand. "Hand me that and I'll get the biscuits out of the oven. I figured we'd dish it all up in here and eat back by the fire, where it's warmer," pulling the pan out of the oven, he placed a couple of biscuits on each plate and picked them up. "Can you grab the coffee mugs?"

They headed back to the living room and settled on the couch. "So, do you want to head over to your uncle's or to Jason's?" Bayleigh asked as they ate.

"We can try. We could take the back road to my uncle's. Jason's place would be a bit trickier to get to, if the roads are still icy."

"Or we could stay here, right?"

"If you don't mind roughing it," he set his plate down and watched her finish eating. "Have you thought of any names?"

"Chandler," she set her own plate aside and picked up her coffee mug, cradling it between her palms.

"Family name?"

"No, a friend of mine lost her baby at 27 weeks a few years ago. She was going to name him Chandler. And I like how it sounds with Robert."

Jack nodded and took his phone out of his pocket. "I can text Carly, let her know."

"Thanks. But please tell her she doesn't have to use it if she doesn't like it. I don't want her stuck with a name she hates."

"Trust me, Carly and Mitch don't do anything they don't want to do. But I'll tell her, if it makes you feel better." He sent the text and then tossed the phone aside. "So, if we're going to try to wait out the storm, what would you like to do to pass the time?"

"I have a few ideas for songs I want to work on, if you don't mind me strumming on my guitar."

"Nope. I have some legal papers I need to review. Will it bother you if I stay in here?"

Bayleigh shook her head and stood up. "I'll take these to the kitchen and clean up, since you cooked," she told him, heading for the doorway. It didn't take her long in the kitchen, since he'd only used the one pan to make everything, other than the biscuits.

Heading for her bedroom, she grabbed a pen and one of her other notebooks and headed back to the living room. Jack had refilled both coffee cups and had claimed one end of the sofa to work from. He already had his papers spread out around him.

Bayleigh settled herself on the opposite end of the sofa

and opened a notebook, looking over the lyrics she'd written down months ago. Emotionally, she hadn't been in a place where she could write love songs; but today, the words were pounding inside of her head, desperate to get written down before she forgot them. Taking a sip of her coffee, she got to work.

From his vantage point at the end of the sofa, Jack watched as she began tapping out a beat with one hand against her thigh, wrote a few words down, scratched others out and wrote more. He gave her a smile when she looked over with a raised eyebrow.

"Am I too distracting?"

It took a second for him to realize she meant with her work, not just her. "Sorry, no. I just find it fascinating how you do that," he told her, shuffling the papers in his hand and trying to focus on them. "I like the rhythm you've got going."

"Thanks," she gave him a small smile before turning back to her notebook. She tried to block him out as she returned to working out the rhythm and the lyrics. It was how she worked. Rhythm and lyrics first, then the notes. She wished Jack had a piano; she'd love to do some layering on this with the guitar and piano. This song had to be perfect. It was the one she wanted to send to Maddie. The one she wanted to launch her career as a full-fledged songwriter.

GIVING up on his own work, Jack leaned back and just watched as the song came to life in front of him. He knew she'd forgotten he was even there, as she hadn't glanced over at him in at least an hour. And he knew that because for the first twenty minutes they'd been in the room together, she'd glanced at him out of the corner of her eye every twenty seconds. He knew *that* because he'd been watching her. And timed it.

She laid her pen aside and picked up the guitar, glancing at her notebook as she started to strum a few chords. The haunting melody she had going was tugging at his own heartstrings, making him wonder what the lyrics were going to be.

Just then, she glanced over at him. "You've stopped working," she noted.

"It was just updating a will. Those don't take long," he told her. "Need a break?"

"Yes. I think my leg went to sleep," she muttered, her hand rubbing at her injured thigh.

"Do you need more coffee? I was going to refill my cup, I can get you some as well," he offered, standing up. She handed her cup over and went back to massaging her leg.

"You ok?" he indicated her leg as he walked back in with the two cups of fresh coffee. Handing one over to her, he resumed his seat at the far end of the couch.

"Yeah, it's just the residual ache. It's pretty much always there." Bayleigh took a sip of the coffee. "So, what do you think?" she indicated the guitar and notebook.

"I can't wait to hear the lyrics that go with that melody."

"I'm not ready to share those yet," Bayleigh shook her head. "Have you checked the weather reports?"

"No, but I did check the thermometer outside the kitchen window. Temperature is hovering right at thirty degrees now. If it holds, and doesn't start raining again, we might be able to head to my uncle's or to Jason's."

"I really don't mind staying here, Jack."

"Well, we'll see what happens."

"You know, if you're tired of having me here, you can just go ahead and take me over to Jason's. I know he won't care if I stay there."

Jack turned towards her so fast she was afraid he was going to spill his coffee in his lap. "Where'd that come from?"

"You've been distant since we got up this morning. I thought maybe, I don't know, that you'd changed your mind and didn't want me around anymore," she leaned over and set her coffee on the side table. "It's okay if you don't. I just don't want to wear out my welcome."

"Christ, Bayleigh," Jack huffed out a breath and leaned his head back against the sofa cushions. "I've been distant because all I can think about is that heavy make-out session we had last night. I'm thirty-four years old and you have me as horny as a teenage boy with his first girlfriend. I'm keeping my distance so that I don't do something so fucking stupid, I trigger more flashbacks, panic attacks, and nightmares!"

"Oh," Bayleigh swallowed hard before turning to look at him. "You do realize that I haven't had any panic attacks since we got here that first day, right? And the nightmares stopped as soon as you started holding me last night?"

"I triggered the flashback, which in turn triggered the nightmares!"

"Okay, yes, your actions triggered a flashback. And Jack, whether it's with you, or the next guy, or hell, ten guys from now, those flashbacks and nightmares are bound to happen. You told me yourself you woke up thinking you were back in the desert the other day when the window broke!"

Jack sighed heavily, turning his head to stare into the fire. It was on the tip of his tongue to tell her she wasn't going to have to worry about the next guy, but he squelched it. No way was he bringing up long-term at this point.

"We've been over all of this, Bayleigh. I won't force you past a point you aren't one-hundred percent ready for."

"What if it's not forcing?"

"Bayleigh..."

"No, I mean it. What if we, I don't know, experiment for lack of a better word," she rushed to cut him off before he could say anything else.

He stood up and walked over to the fireplace setting his coffee on the mantle before adding another log to the grate. Dusting off his hands, he turned to look at her.

"I'm listening," he finally said.

Hands clasped tightly together to minimize the trembling, she forced herself to keep her eyes locked on his. "We experiment and see how far we get before my mind takes over and you stop us. Last night, it was something you said. Maybe if I tell you everything he said and did to me in that room, we can avoid any triggers."

Jack walked over and sat down beside her. Wrapping his arm around her shoulders, he pulled her against his side. "Bayleigh, I know what talking about my experience did to me. Are you sure you want to do this? And are you sure you want to do this *with me?*"

She wrapped her arm around his waist, hugging him closer. "Yes."

"You trust me that much?"

She nodded and placed her head on his shoulder. "I do, Jack." She felt him turn his head and press a kiss to the top of hers. "I know I'm completely safe when I'm with you." His arm tightened around her shoulders before he released her, easing away so he could look at her.

"I have some serious reservations about this, Bayleigh. I'm not a counselor. We could be doing major damage here."

"Or we could be helping me to take a giant step forward, Jack!" Bayleigh reached across and took his large hand into her much smaller one. "I just want to feel something again, something other than fear."

Not breaking eye contact, he brought her hand to his mouth, placing a kiss in her palm. "I get that, Bayleigh, I do. I just want to make sure we're doing the right thing, for both of us."

She smiled at him. "And that's another reason why you have my trust. You think about me, about both of us, not just you," she whispered, leaning in to place a soft kiss against his lips. "I know I'm still going to have issues, there's no magic wand or magician's spell that can be said. But we'll never know unless we try, right?"

Jack shook his head, his grip tightening on her hands. "I want you to have a safe word, though."

"You're not going to tie me up or use handcuffs, are you?" she looked up at him, apprehension showing in her eyes.

"Not unless you ask me to," he gave her one of his

winks. "No, I just want to make sure you have an out, in case I miss something or it gets too heavy too fast for you."

Bayleigh nodded, her lips pressed together as she considered what he said. "How about Oreos?"

"Oreos?"

"It's not something I would normally say during sex and I'm assuming not something you'd hear during sex," she told him with a smile.

"Fine, Oreos it is," he leaned forward and returned her kiss. "I'm still not sure this is the best idea."

"Would you rather I go get drunk in a bar and let some stranger..."

"Hell, no!" Jack cut off her question. "But I'm not going to just jump in the sack with you, either, Bayleigh."

"So, where does that leave us, Jack?"

"We do something I haven't done in a very long time, Bayleigh...we date, we get to know each other. The attraction is there, and when you're comfortable with it, we'll act on it. But not until then."

"Date?" she stared at him like he'd grown a third eye. "You haven't dated in a long time?"

"Not exclusively, no. And not with the intention of getting to know them," Jack squirmed as he realized how shallow that made him sound. "After the end of my engagement, I had no desire to relive that experience. I kept my relationships brief."

"I'm not sure I'd call them relationships then," Bayleigh muttered, narrowing her eyes. "How long are you willing to be, uh, 'exclusive' with me?"

"If we're going to try and be intimate, then for as long as

the relationship lasts. I don't sleep around, Bayleigh and I'm not a man-whore."

Bayleigh laughed and Jack smiled at her. "So, are you sure? Once this ice storm is over, you want to try to continue a relationship?" he asked, tugging on her hands until she slid over to sit next to him and he could wrap his arms around her.

"Yes, Jack. I'm sure," she laid her head on his chest with a contented sigh. Jack smiled and adjusted their positions so they could stretch out on the couch, side by side, arms around each other, enjoying the moment.

CHAPTER 12

*T*hey spent a lazy day just cuddled up on the couch, Jack only getting up to add more wood to the fireplace. The temperature outside continued to hover at the thirty degree mark, meaning everyone else in the family was still stranded throughout Texas.

Mid-afternoon, Jack's cell phone rang. "Hey, Mitch," he answered, his hand rubbing circles on Bayleigh's back. With her head on his chest, she could hear both sides of the conversation. Poor Mitch was going crazy, stuck in Waco, with his wife and newborn son in the hospital in Waketon.

"Shit!" Bayleigh sat up and reached for the phone. "Let me talk to him, please!"

"Hold on, Mitch. Bayleigh wants to talk to you about something," perplexed, Jack handed the phone over to her.

"Hi, Mitch, sorry to interrupt, but I just realized I know someone who might be able to help. Where exactly in Waco are you?" she asked him.

"The Hilton."

"Okay. Let me make a few calls and I'll have Jack call

you back," she disconnected the phone and scrambled off the couch. "Where's my phone?" her eyes scanned the room.

"Here," Jack picked it up off the coffee table and held it out to her but didn't let go when she reached for it. "Take a breath and talk to me. What's going on?"

"Maddie, my friend? Her brother Brian owns a security firm, private investigation team, something along those lines. Honestly, I'm not sure exactly what they do, but he and his friend Rick are both pilots, and they can fly helicopters as well as jets." She paused and caught his eye, a slight smile on her lips. "They paid Will a visit after I hurt my leg, let him know that if he had anything to do with it, they'd make him pay. I think if a line forms behind you and Jason, you can start with them."

"They interested in you?" he tugged on the phone, pulling her up against him.

"Interested? Not at all. I'm just Maddie's friend, who was there when she needed someone to lean on. Brian has his own troubles with the opposite sex. Some girl back home in Virginia. And Rick has it bad for Maddie," Bayleigh wrapped her arms around him. "Jealous?"

"Just checking," he tucked his head and kissed her. Hard. Bayleigh melted against him for a moment before pulling away. "Hold that thought. If one of them is willing to fly into Waco and pick up Mitch, maybe we can have him home tonight."

"They'd do that for you?"

"Yes. I told you, I was there for Maddie when she needed a friend," she held up her finger as her phone made the connection but she didn't move away from him.

"Hey, Maddie, it's me. I need a favor from Brian or Rick. How can I get in touch with them?"

"Brian's actually here with me this weekend. You okay?" Jack could hear Maddie's worried voice over the speaker.

"I'm fine, Maddie. We're still iced in. I need to see if Brian can help a friend, though. It involves flying."

"Oh, well, let me go find him."

A moment later, a deep voice came on the line. "Hey, Bayleigh. Maddie says you need help?"

"Hi, Brian. Well, a favor is a better description. My brother's best friend had a baby, but he's in Waco and the wife and baby are here in Waketon. No one can get anywhere because of this damn ice storm..."

"And you want me to come save the day." Brian finished for her on a chuckle.

"Yeah, pretty much. Can you?"

"Let me check the weather reports. You said this guy is in Waco?"

"Yes. And then you'd need to fly him to Waketon. You'd have to talk to him and Jack to figure out where all to land."

"Who the hell is Jack?" Brian muttered.

"Not important right now," Bayleigh told him, feeling her cheeks growing warm as Jack chest shook with suppressed laughter. "Maddie can fill you in, if you're that interested."

"Fine. Give me twenty minutes to check weather reports and I'll call you back," Brian hung up and Bayleigh tossed her phone on the couch.

"He'll call back in twenty minutes."

"I heard him," Jack's arms wrapped around her. "So these guys will really just drop everything to help you out?"

"Like I said, I was there for Maddie when she needed me," Bayleigh laid her head on his chest. "It was back when I was in college and she was engaged to that guy in the Army. She'd gotten pregnant and he decided he wasn't cut out to be a daddy, so he left her. Brian was overseas at the time and she wouldn't talk to Rick. And then she went into premature labor and lost the baby."

"Chandler," Jack whispered, his arms tightening around her.

"Chandler," Bayleigh took a ragged breath. "Hardest thing I ever did, watch my best friend go through hours of labor just to hold her baby that was already dead."

"Jesus, Bayleigh. That poor girl."

"That wasn't even the worst of it. Her ex found out she'd miscarried and showed back up on her doorstep, almost as soon as she got home from the hospital, wanting to 'reconcile'."

"You have got to be kidding me," Jack pulled back and stared down at her.

"I wish I was. Maddie was too weak and out of it at the time to do anything about him, but I wasn't. I laid into him, full force. And when he wouldn't leave, I may have 'accidently' thrown a paperweight at his head. It may have hit him. Police reports are vague on that."

"Wait…*WHAT*?" Jack's eyes had gone wide.

"I refuse to say anymore as I can't recall if there's still a gag order, or statute of limitations or anything like that still in effect," Bayleigh pressed her lips together.

"Are you serious?"

"Ask Brian when he calls back. He helped bury it for me."

"Jesus. Remind me never to piss you off. Paperweights and guitars," he muttered, eyes narrowed as he considered her. She waggled her eyebrows at him and smiled as her phone rang. She wiggled out of his arms and snagged her phone off of the couch.

"That wasn't twenty minutes."

"It didn't take that long to pull up the weather," Brian replied. "Is this guy Jack nearby, can I talk to him to get some details? I've got a short window of time to do this before the next front moves in."

Jack took the phone from her with a grin. "This is Jack Williams."

"Hi, Jack. Brian Tucker here, your pilot-du-jour. This is going to take some fancy coordination. I'm going to head to Waco in the company jet. I have a friend who lives near Waco who owns a helicopter and he owes me a favor, and his private airfield isn't iced in, he said. So I can land there. He's going to meet me there with the helicopter, fully fueled and ready to go. So, who am I picking up and where?"

"My cousin Mitch. He's in Waco, staying at the Hilton. I'll get you his number and you and he can coordinate that part. As for drop off, if you're coming in by helicopter, I'm going to get you clearance to drop off at the police department here in Waketon. The chief here is the cousin of his wife. He'll make sure Mitch gets to the hospital from there." Jack's hand reached for Bayleigh's and gave it a squeeze. "I can't tell you how much we appreciate this."

"Bayleigh's like a sister to me. Anything she ever needs,

she's going to get. She knows it, too." Brian laughed. "I'll be wheels up in about an hour. Text me your cousin's number and I'll call him from the road so I can have Rick file the flight plan for me. Can I talk to Bayleigh for a minute?"

Jack handed the phone over to Bayleigh. "Brian, thank you so much for this."

"Don't go there, kid. You doing okay? Maddie caught me up on the highlights."

"I'm fine. I'm still working through it all but I have a lot of support now." She looked over at Jack and felt her cheeks grow warm, knowing he could hear both sides of the conversation still.

"Yeah, Maddie was pretty sure about that, too." Brian laughed in her ear. "You always have our support if you need it. Take it easy and I'll call you when I land there."

"Fly safe, Bri."

"Always do, 'Leigh. I always do."

Bayleigh hung up the phone again and looked over at Jack. "Did you text Mitch?"

"Yup. He's going to call in a few minutes so you can give him Brian's number. You're amazing, you know that?"

"I'm not..."

"Yes, you are. You stepped up the other night and helped Carly, even though you almost went into a panic attack when we hit the hospital. And now, knowing about your friend Maddie and what you helped her through, it couldn't have been as easy as you made it look. Plus everything else you've gone through over the last year. And now, you're pulling in favors for my friends. You. Are. Amazing." He leaned over and kissed her as he enunciated each word.

"I'm just being me, Jack," she dropped her forehead to his chest.

"I know. That's what makes you even more amazing," he rubbed his hands up and down her back. "Mitch should be calling any second now. Why don't you go make some coffee for us and I can give him your friend's contact information?"

Bayleigh nodded, and after pulling up Brian's contact information on her phone, handed it over to Jack, just as his own phone rang. She smiled at him and headed for the kitchen, hearing him greet his cousin.

Standing in the kitchen, she stared out the window at the frozen landscape, lost in thought, waiting for the coffee to perk. She was glad Mitch was going to get to make it back to Waketon and see his son finally. She should have asked Brian if he'd stop in Dallas and pick up Jason and Nicole, but he wasn't running a taxi service. And she wasn't going to abuse their friendship. The ice would melt. Someday.

"You okay, babe?" Jack's arms came around her waist, making her jump.

"Other than heart attack you just gave me, I'm fine," she leaned back against him.

"Sorry. I thought you heard me walk into the room."

"I was lost in thought. Everything squared away with Mitch?"

"Yes. And I called Paul with the information so he could get it going on this end for when they're ready to land here. If all goes well, he'll be at Carly's side in less than four hours."

"I'm glad I could help."

"He asked me to tell you 'thanks' and said I should give you a kiss, too."

"Oh, he did, did he?"

"Yup. And he is my older and wiser cousin. I should listen to him, don't you think?" Jack asked as he turned her around in his arms.

Bayleigh hands went to his chest in a reflexive motion, fisting in the soft cotton of his shirt. She wanted the kiss, and her body even wanted what kissing could lead to; it was her *head* that had her tensing up.

"Relax, sweetheart. You get to set the pace and the rules. Remember?" Jack kept his hands loose on her waist.

"I can't help it," she whispered.

"I know, baby. I know," he pressed a soft kiss to her temple, drawing her closer.

Bayleigh gave a full body sigh, pressing herself closer, drawing strength from him. "That's what makes all of this so much harder," she muttered.

"What's that?" his hands stroked over her back, his touch both soothing and stroking fires to life at the same time.

"You're so damn understanding about everything. An hour ago, I was curled up against you on the couch, kissing you, and now, here in the kitchen, I'm so tense you could break me in half. And you act like it's no big deal!"

Jack leaned back and used his finger to tilt her head so that he could look in her eyes. He wanted to make sure she could see the sincerity in his own eyes as he said what was on his mind; after all, he was a guy and he was bound to screw it up somehow.

"Bayleigh, it's not a big deal. Not when you look at the big picture. You've got almost a year's worth of walls to break down. Take it from me. It won't happen overnight. Besides, we've already agreed that we're going to take it slow and get to know it each other," he paused and smiled at her. "Hell, woman, we've known each other, what, three days now? Now, I'm not saying that I'm ready to stand up and declare undying love and devotion to you from the tallest mountain because I don't believe in love at first sight. But I am saying I feel something for you a lot deeper than just lust. And I don't want to rush into it and screw it up." He took a deep breath, watching as his words sank in and registered. He saw her swallow hard and she nodded.

"I don't want...I don't want to screw it up and push you away, Jack," she whispered.

"You're not pushing me away. There's a difference between pushing me away because you're too scared to try, and pushing me away because you're locked in a flashback or panic attack. As long as we continue to know the difference between the two, and can talk about them, I can deal with it. Okay?" he pulled her back against his chest, kissing the top of her head. He felt her sigh and he wrapped his arms around her tighter. Yup, she had managed to lodge a place in his heart. No turning back now.

CHAPTER 13

A few hours later, jack walked into his living room and leaned against the doorframe as he watched Bayleigh work on her song some more, lost in her own world. He cleared his throat to gain her attention.

"Oh, how long have you been standing there?" she asked, setting her guitar down and stretching her arms above her head.

"Not long," he answered, trying hard not to ogle her as her breasts pushed out against her shirt. "Uh, my uncle called and said the foreman was reporting a couple of problems and he wanted to see if I could go check on things. I wondered if you might want to take a ride with me, get out of here for a while."

"I thought the roads were still icy," she glanced at the windows.

"That's the beauty of my land connecting to my uncle's. We can use all the dirt roads and fields. And the temperature actually did get up to above freezing for a short amount of time today, so right now, it'll just be slushy, not icy."

"I'd love to get out of here and take a ride with you."

"Why don't you pack an overnight bag, too, just in case this takes a little while to fix? That way, we can stay over there if we need to. Or if we just decide we like having central heat and real beds again," Jack suggested as she walked over to him.

Bayleigh stopped in front of him and studied his face. "You're not just trying to get rid of me, are you?"

"I swear, Bayleigh, I won't leave you over there if you don't want to stay," Jack told her, his hand coming up to cup her face. "The choice will be yours though. And I'm packing a bag, too."

She nodded and then stood on her tiptoes to press a quick kiss to his lips. "I'm sorry I keep questioning you,"

"Don't be sorry. You've been through a lot. Besides, it keeps me honest," he gave her a wink. As she moved to step away from him, his hands shot out and he pulled her against him. "Doesn't mean I don't want more, though," he whispered as he gave her a deeper kiss than she'd given him. One that had her toes curling and her fingers digging into his biceps.

"Now, go pack that bag. We'll head over when you're ready," he told her, setting her back on her feet. Dazed, Bayleigh nodded and watched him walk away. It took her a few seconds before she could get her legs to carry her down the hallway to her room to pack an overnight bag.

"You about ready?" Jack tapped on the door.

"Almost. I want to bring my guitar. Is that okay?"

"Sure. Why don't you go grab it from the living room

and I'll go ahead and take these bags out to the truck? I went out a few minutes ago and turned it on so it'd warm up for you."

Bayleigh nodded and handed her backpack over that she used to pack a few essentials into. Grabbing her guitar case, she headed for the living room and secured her guitar inside, along with the notebook and pen.

"All set?" Jack asked, coming into the room.

"I think so," she glanced at the fireplace. "What do we do about that?"

"I made sure it'll die down and go out and the screen is in place. We're good to go," he held her coat out to her. Shrugging herself into it, she zipped it up and pulled on a pair of gloves he held out to her.

"I put salt on the steps, but be careful. There's still some icy spots here and there," he told her, as he took her hand in his and then turned to pick up her guitar. Leading her through the kitchen and out the back door, he didn't let go of her hand until they'd reached his truck and he'd helped her up into the cab.

"So, how far is it to your uncle's?"

"Just a few miles, actually, but going across the back fields and at low speeds, it'll take probably at least fifteen minutes or so," he answered, turning the heater fan down and shifting the truck into gear.

"Have you heard from Mitch or Brian yet?" she glanced at the clock on the dashboard. "Shouldn't they be close to arriving soon, too?"

"I know Brian made it to Waco and they took off from there. Mitch is probably too engrossed with seeing his son for the first time to think about calling anyone. And I'm sure Brian's trying to beat the weather back to Waco or Dallas. Wherever it was he was planning on getting back to tonight," Jack drove down his driveway and towards the back of his property where he could pick up the backroad to his uncle's place.

"Oh, I was really hoping I'd get to see him," Bayleigh sighed. "I've missed him, Rick, and Maddie."

"Maybe they just haven't landed yet, and he'll still call you," Jack soothed as they approached a gate. "So, here's the downside of driving across the land. We have to stop, open all the gates and then close them."

"Oh, do you want me to do it?"

"No, you stay in here where it's warm," he told her as he shifted into park and opened his door. He unlatched the gate, swung it open, got back into the truck, pulled through and repeated the process in reverse.

As they approached the next gate, Bayleigh stopped him with a hand on his arm. "This is ridiculous. Either let me do it, or let me drive your truck through. Otherwise, it's going to take forever to get there!"

Pausing, he considered what she said and then nodded. "Fine, I'll get out and open the gate. You pull the truck through and I'll close it behind us. Just please don't scratch my truck up!"

"You line this baby up right and it won't get hurt," Bayleigh shook her head at him as he jumped out of the truck and she slid under the wheel. As soon as he had the gate open, she shifted into drive and pulled forward, stopping as soon as she'd cleared the gate.

"Happy?" she asked, as he slid back behind the wheel.

"That my truck is still in one piece? We still have a few

of those to get through," he teased. Bayleigh smiled at him and they moved on, repeating the process at the next few gates as they made their way to his uncle's house.

"There it is," he pointed as they turned a bend and the house came into view. As he approached, he tapped the horn twice. "Just letting them know we've arrived," he told her, when she gave him a questioning look.

"Them? Who's them?"

He pointed at the front porch as the door opened. Bayleigh gasped beside him and she turned to him with wide eyes.

"How'd...that's Jason and Brian...when'd...what...?" she couldn't even form a full question.

Jack laughed and released the wheel to reach over and give her hand a squeeze. "Jason figured out how to get to Waco in time to catch a ride. He and Brian asked me not to tell you. They wanted to surprise you." He stopped the truck, shifted into 'park' and unlocked the doors. "Go say hi," he whispered.

"Oh my God, Jack. Thank you so much. I love you for this!" she threw her arms around his neck and kissed him. Full on contact, tongue-meet-tongue, toe-curling, let's get it on, kiss. She wasn't holding back.

The first time she'd initiated contact with him, other than a chaste kiss or two maybe, and it was in front of her brother. Hopefully the shock of the cold air would extinguish any residual flames and evidence before Jason got a good look at him. And did she just say she loved him?

With a groan, Jack pulled back, resting his forehead against hers, noting her breathing was just as ragged as his own. "Go say hi before you get us both into trouble," he whispered, giving her a gentle kiss. "I'll grab our bags and meet you inside,"

She gave him a smile and slid across the seat, opening her door and heading for the porch. Jason, Brian, and Nicole met her at the foot of the steps and she launched herself at her brother with a high pitched squeal that would put any two year old to shame. Jack grinned and took his time getting out of the truck. He'd grab the bags later, if Bayleigh decided to stay here, but for now he'd at least grab her guitar. He wasn't sure what the freezing temperatures would do to the instrument and now wasn't a good time to find out.

Nicole saw Jack approaching and broke away from Jason, who was still hugging his sister. "Hey, Jack. How's my computer system?" Nicole greeted him with a smirk.

"It survived your absence. Partly due to your sister-in-law there knowing how to save it," Jack told her, giving her a hug. "Find what you need in Dallas?"

"No, he wasn't the one, either. But this guy remembered Mom and gave us some names of guys in his unit who he thinks she might have talked to and hung around with, but he couldn't say if any of them would have slept with her," she shrugged her shoulders. "I may never know for sure who my birth father is but at least I can say I tried to find him."

"We will contact every name she wrote down in those journals. If he is one of them, we'll find him," Jason told his wife as he joined them, wrapping an arm around her waist and placing a kiss on her forehead. "Cole, this is my sister, Bayleigh. Bayleigh, this is Nicole."

"So nice to finally meet you Bayleigh. Jason has told me

so much about you!" Nicole stepped up and wrapped Bayleigh in a warm hug. "And Jack says you prevented him from killing my computer?"

"He just managed to input a wrong code and had it locked up. Once I deleted the code, it was fine," Bayleigh winked at Jack. "It takes a special kind of talent to lock up the system you have."

"That's what I keep telling him! Hard to believe he was at the top of his class," Nicole commented.

Jack rolled his eyes and held a hand out to Brian. "You must be Brian."

"That's me. Nice to meet you, Jack," Brian shook his hand and then wrapped an arm around Bayleigh's shoulders. "You ready to go inside? I was told you two have been without power since the ice storm hit," he kept a hand on her elbow to help her up the steps. Jack watched them walk away, his teeth clenched together.

"So it's like that already, is it?" Nicole asked him, keeping her voice low as she walked between him and her husband.

"What?"

"Better not be," Jason muttered, shooting his best friend a dark look.

"Are you kidding me, after that kiss they just shared?" Nicole laughed.

Jack scrubbed a hand over his face, checking to make sure Bayleigh and Brian were far enough ahead they couldn't overhear. "It's not like that, Jason...not exactly. So back off with the big brother routine. I know what she's been through in the last year, more than you do right now," he held up his hand. "I'm not trying to start anything. She chose to hold back from you until now. I just happened to be here this week, and we connected over the whole PTSD thing, which is its own kind of screwed up. Do we have more in common than that? Who knows, but I'd sure as hell like to find out."

Nicole and Jason stared at their friend in shock. "Okay, where is the real Jack Williams?" Nicole whispered, looking between Jack and her husband. "This man is scaring me."

"Oh, shut up," Jack hissed, starting to walk off.

"Jack, wait," Jason grabbed his buddy's arm. "You've got to give us a minute here, dude. I mean, you're the 'love them and leave them' original, you know what I mean? And this time, we're talking about my sister, and you may not want to leave her. It's going to take a few minutes to wrap my head around that," Jason shook his head. "I'm not saying I don't approve, not that either of you asked for my opinion or anything. I'm just saying it's going to take a minute for me to adjust to thinking that way about you and Bayleigh," he dropped his hand from his friend's arm. "But did you have to kiss her like that in front of me, man?"

"First of all, she kissed me. Second of all, remember all those times you and Nicole have made out in front of me? Payback's a bitch," Jack chuckled as he walked up the steps and into the house, Nicole's laughter and Jason's muttered curses following him.

CHAPTER 14

"*A*re we back to this?" Bayleigh asked, stepping up next to him as he finished adding wood to the fire.

Dusting his hands off, he glanced over at her. "Back to what?"

"You making me think that you don't want to be around me. You're being all cold and distant again," she kept her gaze locked on his.

Jack glanced around the room with a sigh. Jason and Nicole were cuddled up on one of the sofas, talking to Brian, who was watching him and Bayleigh through narrowed eyes.

"So you and Brian are just friends, never more than that?" he asked, his voice pitched low so it wouldn't carry across the room.

"Just friends, never more. Like you and Nicole," she tilted her chin up in a slight challenge.

"Point taken," he muttered. "Then why is he watching us like that?"

Bayleigh turned her head, her own eyes narrowing as she took in Brian's gaze. Realizing he'd been caught, Brian gave her a grin and turned his attention back to Jason and Nicole.

"I would rather imagine he feels like you used to with Nicole, a protector of sorts," Bayleigh shrugged her shoulders, turning her attention back to Jack.

"Ah, but the difference is, Nicole didn't have any big brothers to watch out for her. Yours is sitting right there," Jack jerked his chin towards Jason.

"But Brian knows that there's been a distance between me and Jason, and I don't mean in just miles," Bayleigh returned, cocking her head to the side. "Look, Jack, I've been with a guy who didn't trust me, yet if I asked where he was, I was expected to trust him one hundred percent, no matter what. Even when I found random phone numbers and articles of clothing I knew weren't mine," Bayleigh closed her eyes and sighed. "I won't live like that again. Tell me now whether or not you can trust me, because if it's not..."

"I trust you, Bay. In the short amount of time we've known each other, I think you rate right up there with the rest of my family," Jack interrupted her.

"So if it's not trust, what is it?"

Jack sighed, and reached out a hand to clasp one of hers, pulling her out of the room and down the hall to Mitch's office. He closed the door behind them and backed her up against it, caging her in with his arms on either side of her. Her eyes were wide with surprise, but not fright, he noted.

"That kiss you laid on me outside, when we first pulled

up? You rocked my world, without even meaning to, which makes it even more amazing. And you did it in front of all of them," he leaned in to kiss her lips. "But then, you jumped out of my truck and ran into his arms, let him help you up the steps, and stayed by his side for the last thirty-nine minutes."

Bayleigh stared at him in shock. "You've been keeping track of how long we've been here, and how much of that time I've spent talking to Brian?"

Jack groaned and leaned his forehead against hers. "It sounds a lot creepier when you put it like that."

"You're jealous," she murmured as she slid her hands up his chest and resting them on his shoulders.

"I have never in my life been jealous of another man, so I don't know what the hell I am," he grumbled, pulling her against him. "I just know I didn't like the feeling I had of watching you, seeing you completely comfortable around someone else, knowing that if I make one wrong move, I send you into hysterics."

Bayleigh dropped her head onto his shoulder, wrapping her arms around his waist. "You don't send me into hysterics, Jack. And I feel just as safe with you as I do with Brian. Who's to say I wouldn't become tense and panicky if Brian did make a wrong move around me?"

Jack wrapped his own arms around her and buried his face in her neck, inhaling her scent. "Can we leave that out of our little experiment? I don't need to know how other guys make you react."

Bayleigh laughed, agreeing, "I am fine with only exploring how you make me react."

"Should we explore a little now?" Jack asked, trailing kisses up her neck to her ear and biting her earlobe. He felt her jerk in his arms at the bite, but she hadn't pulled away and her hands weren't pushing him away.

"Uh, Jason and Nicole..." her voice trailed away as his tongue licked a path along her jawline.

"They won't bother us. Not if Jason values his life," Jack muttered, pressing a line of kisses down her neck. "But you're right. I am not making out with you in my cousin's office, with your brother down the hall," he pressed one last kiss to her lips and stepped back. "But later tonight, we're can do some exploring and find out exactly what you desire," he promised, as he took her hand in his and reached to open the office door.

Bayleigh pulled on his hand, stopping him before he could open the door. As he turned to look at her, she stepped in closer to him. "I want it noted that *you* halted our exploring session this time, not me, not a panic attack or a flashback, or anything else," she told him.

"Your point?"

"You don't always make the wrong move. And I can already tell you what I desire," she side-stepped him and opened the door, stepping into the hallway. "You," she said over her shoulder with a wink.

Jack gave a short laugh and shook his head before following her back to the living room. She waited outside of the living room for him to join her and then took his hand, leading him over to the couch to sit down with the others.

They all hung out in the living room for a short period of time before Jason decided he was hungry and wanted to raid the refrigerator. Nicole discovered a stash of her aunt's homemade spaghetti sauce in the freezer, so she and Bayleigh set out to make spaghetti with homemade sauce and garlic bread. It didn't take long to get the dinner ready and on the table. Brian, Jack, and Jason took care of cleaning up the kitchen afterwards. Nicole and Bayleigh sat at the kitchen table drinking coffee, getting to know each other.

"Well, if I'm going to be flying again tomorrow, I should hit the sack," Brian told them as he handed off the last dish he'd dried to Jack. Jack glanced at the clock on the stove, surprised to see it was already after eight p.m.

"Are you guys staying here tonight or heading back home?" Jason asked Jack as he walked over to the table and held his hand out to Nicole to pull her to her feet.

"I'm getting a little used to the central heat. I think we'll go ahead and stay here." Jack answered, stepping over next to Bayleigh and resting his arm around her waist. "Is that okay with you?"

"I'm fine, either way, but yes, if there's enough room, I wouldn't mind staying here," Bayleigh answered.

"There's plenty of room. Aunt Helen and Uncle Steve built this house hoping Jack and Mitch would never leave," Nicole smiled at her. "They've remodeled a bit over the years, but the upstairs now has what amounts to two master bedroom suites, and three spare bedrooms. Plus there's the guest suite downstairs. Granted, a couple of those bedrooms are small, but they work when we all want to crash here," Nicole explained.

"Then we'll stay here," Jack squeezed her waist. "I'm

just going to run out and get the bags out of the truck," he told her. "Nicole, which rooms should we take?"

"Take your old room for yourself and give Bayleigh Mitch's old room. At least Carly has made it into more of a guest room and it's not a shrine to his glory days," Nicole told him, following him to the front door. "I gave Brian the downstairs guest room and Jason and I will have my old room," she gave him a knowing grin.

"And managed to pretty much put me and Bayleigh on the complete opposite side of the house from everyone else."

"She happened to mention that both of you have been having trouble sleeping. This way, you can keep each other company and not worry about the rest of us," she winked at him. "The beds in both rooms should be made. If not, you know where everything is. I'll see you in the morning," she gave him a hug and then headed to the stairs, where her husband was waiting for her. Jack shook his head at her antics and then grabbed his coat out of the closet, pulling it on even as he went out the door to get their bags out of the truck.

Walking back inside the house, he found Bayleigh waiting for him at the foot of the stairs. "You okay?" he asked, after he hung up his coat and walked over to her.

"I'm fine. Brian and I were just talking for a minute after you all left the kitchen, and when I walked out here, I realized I have no idea where I'm sleeping tonight," Bayleigh told him as she tried to smother a yawn.

"Come on, sleepyhead. I'll show you to our rooms," Jack chuckled and took her hand in his, leading her up the stairs. "Jason and Nicole are in her old room down that hallway, last bedroom on the right. The set of double doors are to Mitch's and Carly's suite. Nicole is probably going to lose her old room to the nursery, once Carly agrees that the baby doesn't need to be in their room."

"And down this hallway are where mine and Mitch's bedrooms were. Ma and Pop's room is right across the hall. I think Ma knew she needed to keep a closer eye on us than she did on Nicole," he winked at her as he opened one of the doors. "This was my old room," he explained, pulling her inside.

"I heard Nicole say to put me in Mitch's old room..." she started to say.

"That's the beauty of Nicole's plan," Jack interrupted, walking over to a door. "Our bedrooms connected through the bathroom," he explained, opening the door. "Your room is through there. Or you can stay in here with me. Your choice," Jack watched her face, looking for any signs of hesitancy or fear.

"Wow, I think my entire apartment in England could fit inside of these rooms," Bayleigh whispered, stepping into the room and looking around. Her eyes met Jack's and she smiled. "Who gets the bathroom first?"

"You go right ahead," he set her bag down on the end of the bed. "I'm going to go downstairs and grab a drink."

"Liquid courage?" she asked with a raised eyebrow.

"Water. I'm getting water to drink, smartass. Do you want anything?"

"I'm fine, but thanks," she laughed, grabbing her bag off the bed. "If you're disappearing to give me some room, I'll be out of the bathroom in twenty minutes."

"Take your time," he called over his shoulder as he

walked out of the room, making sure the door closed behind him. He could only hope everyone else had gone to bed; imagining her in the shower had not done him any favors. Maybe he could think of something he needed out of his truck? The weather would kill his libido in a second. He debated it as he headed for the kitchen.

CHAPTER 15

*J*ack stayed downstairs for as long as he dared, giving Bayleigh the time she'd requested. He headed back upstairs and walked into his old room to find her propped up against the headboard, already under the covers. The tight tank top she was wearing to sleep in cupped her breasts, leaving nothing to the imagination. She had a book on her lap but he forced himself to keep his gaze on her face. If he glanced down again, he would lose it.

"Are you warm enough?" he asked, grabbing his own bag off the floor where he'd set it earlier.

"I'm fine. Just looking through your old yearbooks," she held the book up and he groaned.

"Keep in mind my freshman year was my awkward year," he told her, heading for the bathroom.

"I'm more interested in all these things people said to you," she waggled her eyebrows at him. "Sounds like you were quite the ladies' man in high school."

Jack stopped and looked over his shoulder. "High

school was a long time ago," he muttered, stepping in the bathroom and shutting the door. The room was still a little steamy from her shower, so she must've taken longer than she'd said she was. The aroma of her soap still lingered in the air, toying with his senses as he took his own shower and toweled off. The floral scent made him think of fields of wildflowers and picnics. And making love in the Texas sun. Muttering a curse, he turned the hot water off and stood under the freezing cold spray. God, he hated cold showers.

After getting his raging hormones under control yet again, he toweled off and reentered the bedroom, dressed only in his shorts. He was going to take advantage of having central heat and Bayleigh in his bed. Even if they didn't do anything but sleep tonight, he wanted to feel her against his chest. Bayleigh looked up from his yearbook and grinned at him.

"Which year are you looking at?" he asked, going around to the far side of the bed and climbing in under the covers beside her.

"Your senior year. I love all of the candid shots of you and your friends," she tapped one of them and he shook his head.

"That was the year Nicole was one of the editors and she had it out for me because of who I was dating," Jack tried to take the book out of her hands.

"And who were you dating?"

"The Varsity Cheerleading squad. Maybe a few from the JV squad. I can't remember anymore. They aren't important," he tugged on the book again, this time succeeding in pulling it out of her grasp.

"Why would Nicole be upset that you dated a few

cheerleaders?"

"It probably had something to do with the fact I was dating all of them at the same time and a couple of them were her friends," Jack told her, setting the yearbook down on the nightstand.

"No way!" her eyes went wide and she stared at him.

"I was sixteen, I think, and as we discussed before, the hometown football hero. I was a god!"

"You were a horn dog!" she shot back, laughing. "All of them, as in all of the cheerleaders?"

"Yeah, the whole squad. I'm not sure who was more upset, the cheerleaders or Nicole."

"You're lucky they let you live!"

"You know, I was just trying to be the good guy. All of those girls liked me and wanted me and I didn't want to disappoint any of them."

"Uh-huh. How many dates did you have after that?"

"I decided after that I needed to keep my mind on my studies for a while. And then when I rejoined the dating world, the girls made sure they posted it on the school's website whenever someone had a date with me. The counselor and the principal weren't too thrilled with my behavior, either, now that I think back," Jack told her with a smile, as he stretched out on his back, hands folded behind his head. "So who did you date in high school?"

"I didn't date in high school," Bayleigh muttered.

"Oh, come on. A hot chick like yourself?"

She reached over and slapped his chest, and he caught her hand, holding it, his thumb stroking over the pulse point in her wrist, feeling it speed up at his touch. "I didn't," she insisted, turning her head to look at him. "I mean, I dated some but just guys that I considered friends. I never dated as in 'boyfriend-girlfriend' dating."

"Okay, so what kinds of guys did you hang out with?" he asked, tugging on her hand until she slid over in the bed and laid her head on his shoulder.

"Nerdy, bookish boys. I wasn't cool enough to date a jock, such as yourself."

"Not even in college?"

"I met Will. He was the first hot guy that ever looked twice at me," her fingers were tracing patterns on his skin.

"I think you're selling yourself short," Jack turned slightly so that she was on her back and he could lean over her. "I'm betting you were like some of the girls in our high school—the hot guys looked but the girls always had their nose buried in a book and didn't notice," he leaned in to kiss her, his tongue tracing the edge of her bottom lip, teasing her. She moaned and brought her hand up to the back of his head, holding him to her so she could deepen the kiss.

Jack drew back and studied her. "What are we doing here, Bayleigh?"

"You're kissing me. I'm touching you," she stroked his chest, eliciting a deep groan from him. "I think this may be called foreplay," she waggled her eyebrows.

"Two can play at that game, sweetheart," he warned, lowering his head to kiss her as his own hand swept down over her chest. A teasing touch, that's what it was meant to be. He could feel her nipples through the thin tank top, pressing into the hand he settled over her breast. Using his fingertips, he teased the nipples into hard points, switching back and forth between both breasts, teasing, stroking, and pinching. Her hands were mimicking his motions on his chest, driving both of them wild.

She broke the kiss, her breathing ragged. Keeping her eyes locked on him, she reached for the hem of her tank top, ripping it off over her head. "I think I like this game," she whispered as she watched his eyes glaze over with desire as he brought his hand back up to cup her breast.

"We're playing with fire, you know," he whispered, his thumb stoking across her nipple, causing her to moan and arch her back, thrusting her breasts towards him. "Hold onto me, sweetheart," he muttered, lowering his head to take her nipple into his mouth. He felt her hands on his head, the scrape of her nails on his scalp, the feeling more erotic than he'd ever remembered feeling before. He lapped at her nipple, drawing back to blow on it, watching the goosebumps break out on her skin, before he sucked it back into his mouth, rolling it between his teeth, giving it a gentle bite, before switching to the other one.

Bayleigh moaned again, as her hands slid up to his shoulders, her fingernails digging in, trying to pull him closer. Her legs parted, her left leg wrapping around him, pressing the lower half of her body up against his. Jack could feel the heat of her arousal through her pajama bottoms and his shorts. He stroked a hand down her side, his fingers skimming along the edge of her cotton pants, finding the tie in front and tugging on it, sliding his hands inside to cup her ass and pull her against him, letting her feel his erection through their clothes.

With a sharp inhale, Bayleigh's fingers clutched his hips and even through his shorts, he was pretty sure her nails had pierced his skin. Her whole body had become tense. He released her nipple with a 'pop' and leaned back to look at her.

"Bayleigh? You with me?" he whispered, his hand coming up to stroke over her hair, pushing it back away from her face.

Swallowing hard, she opened her eyes and looked at him. "I can't," she whispered and then started sobbing.

Jack swore under his breath, reaching over and grabbing the tank top she'd pulled off of herself. He sat her up and pulled it over her head, and then made her lay back down, pulling the blankets over her. He slid out of bed, grabbing a t-shirt out of his bag and turning off the bedside light before joining her in the bed again.

Settling in beside her, he pulled her into his arms, making sure the blankets stayed tucked around her. She settled her head on his shoulder and although the sobs had stopped, he could feel her tears soaking into the t-shirt. "It's okay, Bayleigh," he murmured against her hair. "I'm just going to hold you tonight. That's all," he reassured her.

"I'm sorry, Jack. I really thought I could do it tonight," Bayleigh released a heavy sigh, tipping her head back to try and see his face. "Please don't leave me," her voice broke on the plea.

Jack's arms tightened around her. "I won't leave if you don't want me to, I'll hold you all night if that's what you need. But please, baby, don't push yourself past your limits because you think it's what I want, Bayleigh," he shifted her slightly so he could press a light kiss to her lips. "Go to sleep. We'll talk tomorrow, okay?" Jack shifted his hips away from her as she burrowed in closer to him. It didn't take long before he felt the tension ease out of her muscles as sleep claimed her. He laid awake, holding her to him, for hours, keeping the nightmares away, for both of them.

CHAPTER 16

*T*he next morning, the weather had cleared at last and the temperature was already above thirty-two degrees before Bayleigh had even made it downstairs. Brian was already making arrangements with the airfield to get the helicopter ready so he could fly back to Waco and switch it out with his friend for his small jet. Jason and Nicole had offered to drive him to the airfield and then they were going to head to the hospital to see the Carly and the baby.

Jack and Bayleigh were cleaning up the kitchen while the others all got ready to leave. Jack finished loading the dishwasher and watched Bayleigh wipe down the countertop and table.

"You okay this morning?" he asked, taking the rag from her hands and tossing it into the sink before sliding his arms around her waist and pulling her up against him.

"I'm just tired," she tried to smile at him.

He shook his head and bent to kiss her softly on the lips. "Don't ever lie to me, Bay," he whispered as he pulled back. "You can tell me to buzz off or it's none of my business, but please don't lie, to me or yourself."

Bayleigh took a deep breath, glancing over his shoulder towards the doorway, making sure no one was lingering there to listen in on what she was about to say. "I don't want to tell you to buzz off, and I would say you have a vested interest in what's going on with me right now," she pressed her lips together briefly, struggling to find the right words. "But right now, Jack, I'm not sure how I'm doing. I want to be okay, I want to be back to my normal self, but every time I think I gain a few steps, I realize I'm right back where I started, if not even further behind!"

Jack nodded, taking a step back from her, but holding her hands tightly in his. "I think you're trying too hard, at least where I'm concerned," he squeezed her hands when she opened her mouth to interrupt. "Don't get me wrong, I find you hot as hell, and I want you in my bed and I want to find out if what we have is as explosive as I think it's going to be. But we can't force it. *You* can't force it, Bayleigh," he reached up and cupped her face with his palm. "We need to take a few steps backwards together, this time. When we leave this morning, we're going to go back to my place and get all your stuff. We'll pack it up and take it and your car over to Jason's, and then I'll drive us to the hospital."

"What if that's not what *I* want?" Bayleigh asked, turning her head just enough to press a kiss to his palm.

"It's not what either of us *want*, baby. But I do believe it's what you need. At least right now," he pulled her up against his chest and gave her one of his scorching kisses. Bayleigh moaned as he lifted his head and he gave her a half-grin. "Don't worry. We're going to start dating and getting to know each other, just like we talked about the other night. And while we're doing that, you can figure out what you want from all of this, too. But for both of our sakes, we can't keep playing with fire, like we did last night."

"I still say it's you," she whispered as he took a step back.

"God, I hope so," he muttered with a wink. "Now, you go find your friend Brian and tell him good-bye. He was shooting daggers at me this morning. You need to assure him that I'm the good guy here!" he gave her a gentle push in the direction of the door.

Bayleigh made her way to Mitch's home office, tapping on the door when she saw Brian standing by the windows. "Is everything okay?"

"What?" Brian's head shot up and he turned towards her. "Oh, yeah, it's fine, just can't get in touch with Kaitlyn."

"Kaitlyn? Isn't she the young woman...?"

"Yeah, she's the one," Brian glanced at her and scrutinized her face. "You and Jack working it out?"

"There's nothing to work out. Right now, we're just working on it," Bayleigh shook her head, rolling her eyes. "I found a guy that doesn't care what happened last year, well, he cares, but he cares because of what it's done to me. He doesn't care that it happened. I mean, oh shit, I don't know what I mean," she sat down on the couch in the room and buried her face in her hands. "The man has me so tied up in knots right now, Brian, I don't know what to do!"

"But you've told him what happened, right? All of it?"

"Yes, he knows all about it now. I kind of had to tell him

most of it when I started having panic attacks moments after meeting him," she gave him a rueful grin.

"Yeah, well you tried to deny anything was wrong when I saw you have one, so let's not delve too deeply into what that means, shall we?" he grinned at her as he watched the blush creep over her cheeks. "And you're going to tell Jason all of it now, too, right? I can hand over my big brother card to him?"

Bayleigh laughed and hugged him. "Yes, go back to being just Maddie's big brother. I'm going to work on all of my relationships for a while, so tell Maddie to be ready for a long visit once I finish my songs."

"So you are serious about that?"

"My songwriting? You better believe it. I was never meant to be the one up on stage singing. And after what happened last year, well, that just clinched it. Someone else can have that fame and glory. I'll stay backstage and just bask in the knowledge that I created the beauty my way," she kissed his cheek and stood up. "Promise to message me when you land in Tennessee?"

"I promise either Maddie or I will let you know I got home," he stood up and gave her a hug. "Take care of yourself, 'Leigh."

"You take care of yourself, too, Bri," Bayleigh hugged him tight and stepped back. "I'll talk to you soon, then."

Jason was in the foyer when she stepped out of the office, and he glanced up when he heard her footsteps. "Jack says you want to come stay with us. Is everything okay?"

Bayleigh stepped up to her brother and hugged him

tight. "I'm getting there, Jason. I'm not there yet, but I promise, I'm getting there."

Jason drew back and studied his sister. "You're going to stop talking in circles and clue me in, right?"

Bayleigh nodded, hugging him again, "I promise, later today, after we've had our fill of newborns and family members, you and I will have a long talk. I didn't mean to keep you in the dark for so long, and I want to fix it."

"We are 'fixed,' little sister. The moment you booked your flight to Texas." Jason hugged her tight again and then released her as Nicole and Jack entered the foyer from the kitchen and Brian entered from the office.

It only took a few minutes to make sure everyone had their belongings packed up and they were all headed out the front door. Brian was anxious to get in the air. While the storm seemed to have finally moved on from Texas, it was wreaking havoc to the east and he wanted to get back to Tennessee.

"Everything okay?" Jack asked Bayleigh as he drove back to his place. With the ice melting, he had decided to take the main road instead of driving across the range so they were already turning off the road and onto the lane leading up to his house.

"I can't say I'm thrilled you're kicking me out but I am looking forward to spending some time with Jason, and getting to know Nicole," she answered, glancing over at him.

He took one hand off the steering wheel and reached over to take hers. "I'm not thrilled either, Bay, but I really..."

"I know. And I think you're right," she broke in, giving

his hand a squeeze. "I think a little space will be good for us. Still doesn't mean I have to be happy about the idea."

Jack brought her hand to his mouth and kissed her fingers. "Then I'll work on making you happy, too."

"I like the sounds of that," Bayleigh teased with a giggle.

Jack smiled at her and parked the truck in front of his house. "Let's get you packed up and moved over to your brother's. If I know him, he'll start calling in about twenty minutes wanting to know why we're not at the hospital yet."

"Is he using this as some sort of payback for anything you did when he and Nicole were dating?" she asked as they headed inside.

"I refuse to answer that on the grounds that it may incriminate me."

"Uh huh. And who was worse, you or Mitch?"

"By far, Mitch, since he's actually related by blood to Nicole and she was living with them at the time," he grinned. "But since Mitch is already married, and has been for quite some time, I think Jason is only out to get me back."

"Do I need to be worried about what he'll do to get you back?" she asked as they walked into the kitchen.

"I don't think so. But if you could put in a good word for me, I'd appreciate it."

Bayleigh rolled her eyes and headed down the hallway. "It won't take me long to get things packed. I'll be ready in just a few minutes," she called over her shoulder.

Within twenty minutes, Bayleigh had everything packed and Jack helped her get it all loaded into her car.

He led the way to Jason's and Nicole's house and helped her carry everything inside and up the stairs to one of the guest rooms.

"How do you know they'll want me in this one?" Bayleigh asked, looking around.

"It's the only one fully furnished, at the moment," Jack explained, setting her guitar down on the bed. "Do you need to change or anything before we head out?"

"Nope, I'm good," Bayleigh shook her head and stepped out into the hallway, waiting for Jack to follow. "I'm ready to head to the hospital, if you are."

Jack nodded and led the way downstairs and out to his truck, pausing only to make sure he'd locked the front door. He glanced over at Bayleigh as he slid behind the wheel and started the engine.

"So, got any plans for this week?"

"Try to write my music, start looking around at possible living and working arrangements. You know, the usual," she grimaced.

"I meant in the evenings, when Jason and Nicole get off work. Do you have any plans for the evenings?"

Bayleigh turned in the seat so she could study him while he drove. "Depends on what offers I get," she raised an eyebrow when he glanced over at her.

"Who do you expect to make offers?"

"Your buddy Paul, maybe? Is he taken?"

"Ha, good luck with him. He's like your friend Brian. He has his hands full with an ex who isn't really an ex," Jack gave a short laugh, shaking his head as he pulled into the hospital parking lot and parked his truck. Turning towards her, he reached out and took her hand in his. "Miss

Morrow, would you do me the absolute honor of joining me for dinner tomorrow night?"

"It would be my pleasure, Mr. Williams," she giggled as she nodded. "Will I need to dress up again?"

"Clothes will be optional," he told her with a wink.

Bayleigh laughed and turned to open her door. "Who said we needed to take this slow? Oh, yeah, that would have been *you!*" she tossed back over her shoulder as she slid out of the cab.

Jack chuckled as he joined her at the front of the trunk. "Can't blame a guy for trying," he whispered in her ear as they turned to walk into the hospital, his hand low on her back. She glanced at him and rolled her eyes.

"Let's go find your family," she told him, shaking her head. But her own arm slipped around his waist as they walked side-by-side into the hospital.

CHAPTER 17

The next few weeks flew by for Bayleigh. The ice storm had been Winter's last hurrah for the Hill Country and Spring had arrived and the Texas Bluebonnets took over the fields. The sight was breathtaking. Jack had taken her out to a meadow on his property where the flowers were so blue and thick, you'd have sworn it was a lake. They'd spent the afternoon cuddled up together on a blanket spread out on the edge of the flowers, talking.

She'd also spent a lot of time reconnecting with her brother and getting to know her sister-in-law. She and Nicole were a lot alike and she enjoyed spending time with her. Most evenings, Jack came over to the house and the four of them had dinner together. And at least once a week, there was a family dinner at 'the main house', as everyone called Helen's and Steve's house.

With Jason's help, Bayleigh had also found a therapist and started therapy for her PTSD. Her panic attacks and nightmares were happening less frequently; she hadn't had a nightmare since shortly after moving in with her brother.

And the panic attacks only happened if a stranger got too close.

But every weekend, she spent a large chunk of time alone with Jack. He usually found things in or around Waketon to show her, but sometimes they'd just spend the day around the ranch. There'd been a few bumps in the road, like the karaoke night they met up with Jason and Nicole and a few of their friends at the bar for night. Unfortunately, one of Jack's former lovers was in also at the bar. The other woman had joined their group and situated herself right next to Jack, her hands constantly touching him.

Bayleigh only tolerated it for a short period of time before she grabbed the woman's wrist as she moved to touch Jack on the chest. Again.

"I am only going to say this once: you touch him again and you may lose this," Bayleigh shook the woman's wrist, making her hand flop.

"Really, Jack. You used to date women with more class. Are you taking on the pity crowd now?" the woman had huffed, flipping her platinum blonde hair back over her shoulder with a practiced move. Her calculating eyes roved over the boots, jeans and western shirt. "Where's your cowboy hat, honey?" she sneered.

"Katherine, I think you need to leave," Nicole told the other woman.

"Good luck with him, honey. He's great in the..."

Jack's hand settled on Bayleigh's thigh as she moved to stand up. "Katherine, you need to think long and hard about what you are about to start here. Don't forget who all is at this table and what is at stake for not just you, but your family," Jack warned, his voice cold.

Katherine stepped back, her gaze moving around the table, seeing everyone's eyes on her. With a huff and another toss of her hair, she stomped off.

Bayleigh watched her go through narrowed eyes, feeling everyone else at the table glancing between her and Jack. She turned her eyes to him and cocked her head to the side.

"You slept with that?"

"Maybe," he answered, his tone cautious.

"How'd you avoid her sinking her claws into you and keeping you?"

"Years of practice with evasive maneuvers," his arm slid around her shoulders and pulled her against his side.

"Funny thing, though...I haven't wanted to use them with you," he whispered against her ear. Bayleigh ducked her head to hide the blush she felt stealing over her cheeks.

Today, he'd saddled up two of his uncles horses and took her on a trail ride around the property. She'd had fun and loved being back on a horse, but was now paying the price. They'd returned to her brother's house so they could clean up before Jack took her 'somewhere special'.

"My butt is not used to being in the saddle," she told him groaning as she moved towards the stairs.

"I can massage it for you," he offered, stopping her with a hand on her arm and giving her a kiss.

"God help me," Jason muttered, walking past them, but giving Bayleigh a wink.

"Paybacks!" Jack called after him, as he bent and swept Bayleigh up in his arms.

"Jack!" she shrieked, laughing as he carried her up the stairs to her room.

"Just trying to help," he smiled as he set her on her feet next to her bed. "Yell down to me and I'll carry you back down the stairs, too," he promised with a wink. "Can't have my girl hurting, now, can I?"

"Bayleigh, I don't know what magic spell you've woven, but please, don't undo it! Jack is so much easier to get along with these days," Nicole laughed from the doorway.

"Too bad love didn't have the same effect on you," Jack muttered, as he turned to frown at his friend. "I'm going downstairs to clean up. How long do you need?" he asked Bayleigh, who was already pulling clean clothes out of the dresser.

"Not long, twenty, no make that thirty minutes," she said, glancing in the mirror and seeing the state of her hair. "I need to wash and dry my hair," she frowned at her reflection. Jack laughed and headed out of the room, Nicole grinned at her and followed him, harassing him the entire way down the stairs, from the sounds of it. Those two really did act like brother and sister most of the time.

Bayleigh glanced at the clock and headed for the bathroom. She would be cutting it close to get her hair washed and dried and be ready to head back out with Jack. He hadn't told her what they were doing next, just to dress casual but warm.

THIRTY MINUTES LATER, Bayleigh eased her way down the stairs. She could hear everyone else in the kitchen, so she made her way down the hallway to the large room in the back of the house.

"Hey, there. Doing ok?" Jack was at her side in an instant, taking her hand.

"Yup. The shower helped ease some of the soreness."

"You ready to take a little ride with me, then?" he asked, sliding an arm around her waist and pulling her a little closer to him.

"Not if it means getting back up on a horse," she raised her eyebrows at him.

"No, just my truck," he assured her.

"You guys better get going if you're going to make it up to the ridge," Nicole interrupted, handing a thermos to Jack. "I made you some coffee, extra-strong. Do you need anything else?"

"Nope, I have what I need," Jack laced his fingers with hers and headed for the back door.

"Be careful and watch your step. There's a bit of a climb," Jason warned, glancing down at Bayleigh's leg.

She shook her head with a soft smile as she answered her brother. "It hasn't bothered me in weeks, Jason. I'll be fine," she reassured her brother.

"I'll help her over any rough spots. I was up there the other day and checked it out. She should be okay," Jack assured him, his hand resting low on her back.

"I'll be fine," Bayleigh smiled at her brother. "Quit worrying about me so much!"

"He can't help it, Bayleigh. It's ingrained in his DNA or something," Nicole told her with a smirk at her husband. "You two get going before you miss the sunset!"

"Thanks, Nicole. We'll see you two later, then," Jack

grabbed the thermos with one hand and Bayleigh's hand with the other. "We have plenty of time to get up there."

Bayleigh glanced over as he drove over the backroads that cut across all three properties. "So, what exactly is this place?"

"Back in high school, there were a few times when things got rough between Ma, Pop and myself. Mostly teenage-angst type crap, but sometimes stuff about my mom would come up. I needed somewhere to go where no one would bother me, where I could just think it through, come to terms with all the shit. I would spend hours up there. The view is amazing, especially at this time of day." He parked the truck at the bottom of a hill and came around to her side to help her down from the cab.

"It's only a short walk from here, but up the hill. Do you think you can make it?" he grimaced. "When I was up here the other day, I made sure the ground was smooth and free of any rocks to stumble over, but I didn't think about you being saddle-sore from our ride."

"I'll be fine, Jack. So, where's this awesome view you promised me?"

"Hold on, I just need to grab a couple of things," he reached back into the truck and grabbed a blanket, folding it over his arm. "I'll leave the thermos down here, for after. Nicole was right, we'll probably need it then." He took her hand and led the way up the hillside.

Jack had been right, it was only a short walk up to the top of the hill where they could look out over the landscape. But man, was her butt letting her know it did not appreciate the abuse she'd been dishing out today. She stopped short when they reached the top of the hill and it flattened out, allowing her to see out over the landscape.

"Oh, wow!" Bayleigh breathed as she got her first look. "This is beautiful!" She moved to edge of the ridge to look out. "I can see why you'd come up here to think. It's so quiet and peaceful," she wrapped her arms around herself as the wind picked up. "Chilly, but beautiful."

"That's why I brought the blanket," Jack moved to stand behind her, his arms wrapping around her and pulling her back against his chest. She relaxed and rested her head against his shoulder. "Are you warm enough?"

"I am now," she nodded, her arms resting on top of his. She could feel the steady rise and fall of his chest against her back. "It's so peaceful," she said again, looking out over the landscape. Jack's arms tightened around her and he pulled her closer.

"Yes, it is. And as beautiful as you," he whispered, kissing her neck and sending shivers of awareness down her spine.

Bayleigh turned in his arms, her hands sliding up his arms to clasp together behind his neck. "Can I ask you something?"

"Anything, anytime. You know that," he answered, his hands going to her waist and pulling her tight against him.

Bayleigh swallowed hard, but kept her gaze locked on his. *Now or never, time to jump.*

"Will you make love to me? Now?" she whispered.

Jack sucked in a breath and his hands gripped her waist tighter. "Are you sure?"

"No, but I know I...want you," *Oh, my God. She did not just about say the "l" word. Not this early in...whatever this was between them.* She bit her lip and looked up at him through her eyelashes, praying she wasn't going to regret this. "I'm more scared of the not knowing and possibly losing out on the best thing I ever had."

Jack groaned and leaned in for a kiss. A toe-curling, sizzling kiss, before grabbing her hand and pulling her down the hillside. "Let's go."

"What about the blanket?" Bayleigh asked, glancing back at the blanket laying in a heap on the ground where Jack had dropped it.

"I'll buy a new one," he told her over his shoulder, not slowing down.

Bayleigh laughed. "What about the spectacular sunset you wanted me to see?"

"They'll be a better one tomorrow. Or, maybe the day after. We'll see when I'm ready to let you out of my bed," he told her, continuing to move towards the truck. He paused beside the front of the truck and turned towards her, his hands settling on her waist again as he stared at her.

Bayleigh waited several seconds for him to say anything, her cheeks growing warm under his scrutiny. "What?" she asked, cocking an eyebrow at him.

"I'm just...I want to make sure there's no signs of a panic attack," he told her, reaching out his hand to caress her face. "I want to make sure that you're doing this for *you.*"

"I'm not doing it for me. I'm doing it for *us*," Bayleigh assured him, turning her head to press a kiss to his palm. "I won't lie and say I'm not scared, or maybe anxious would be a better word. But I trust you, Jack. I'm not panicked in any way."

Jack took in a deep breath and pulled her against him, his head coming down and his lips capturing hers in another one of his bone-melting kisses, his tongue teasing hers. His fingers flexed on her hips, drawing her against him. She felt his erection against her and she ached to settle herself against him.

Bayleigh moaned when he released her, turning to open the truck door for her. "Let's go home," he voice was almost a growl.

"Home?" she looked at him with a frown as she climbed in. After that kiss, and his obvious excitement, he was taking her home?

"My home, Bayleigh, my home. Our first time together is not going to be with you shoved up against the hood of my truck," he whispered with a gentle kiss before turning to help her into the cab of his truck.

"Then let's go home," Bayleigh whispered, sliding across the seat so she could sit next to him on the short drive to his place.

CHAPTER 18

They didn't speak until they were in the kitchen at Jack's house. Jack helped Bayleigh with her coat and then reached to pull her into his arms. His mouth covered hers as his hands moved over her body, eliciting a deep sigh from her.

"Do you want anything to drink? A glass of wine or a shot of whiskey?" he asked, his lips tracing a path along her jaw.

She smiled as she tilted her head, allowing him access to the sensitive spot under her ear. "No, I have everything I need right here," she told him, her hands smoothing over his shoulders before linking together behind his neck.

With one last kiss, Jack took her hand and led her down the hallway to his bedroom.

Bayleigh stopped at the side of the bed, closed her eyes and took a deep breath. Her heart started beating faster as he stepped up behind her, his hands settling on her shoulders.

"You okay? I can still go get that wine," he offered, his lips tickling her ear.

She closed her eyes and took an inventory of her what she was feeling; heart was racing and her stomach was in knots but her breathing wasn't choppy and there weren't any rocks on her chest. Nope, no panic attacks. Just normal 'first time with a guy' anxiety.

"I'm fine," she reassured him, releasing a sigh as his hands began to knead her shoulders. "Maybe a little nervous, but I'm fine."

Jack turned her so they were face-to-face, his hands slipping to her waist, resting on her hips. "Why are you nervous?"

"The only man I've ever been with was Will. I'm not sure what you expect!" she felt her face flame with the admission.

Jack's hands came up and he cupped her face. "Oh, baby. There is nothing to be nervous or worried about. I'm not holding up a scorecard and judging you. I just want to be here with you, showing you how much I want this," he leaned in and kissed her.

Bayleigh opened to him, allowing him to deepen the kiss as her hands settled on his muscled biceps. His after-shave surrounded her, grounding her in the moment. This was Jack, not Will. He wouldn't hurt her in any way. Or leave her hanging. Somehow, she knew that last part to be true.

She realized his fingers had undone the buttons on her shirt and the front clasp of her bra. She gasped as he slid the shirt from her shoulders, the bra straps caught up in it as well. His hands cupped her breasts, his thumbs playing with her nipples.

"Tell me what you like, sweetheart," Jack said as he kissed the sensitive spot under her ear, earning a shudder.

Bayleigh's head dropped back, a silent invitation for Jack to continue. "This. I like this," she whispered as his question finally registered.

Jack chuckled and pinched her nipples, earning another shudder and a gasp. "I can tell." His hands dropped to her waist and he undid the button and zipper on her jeans.

Bayleigh tensed and Jack froze. He eased back, his hands returning to rest on her hips. "Talk to me, Bayleigh," he instructed.

Bayleigh closed her eyes and swallowed. "I'm here. I know it's you. But I've never gotten past this point. I'm waiting for the other shoe to drop, that's all," she opened her eyes and met his concerned gaze. "I'm not saying 'No' and I'm not using my safe word. I don't want to stop," she told him, her voice strong and determined.

"Thank God for small favors," Jack muttered, his hands pushing at her jeans, easing them down her hips. He helped her sit on the edge of the bed and stripped her jeans from her legs, somehow pulling her socks off with them.

"Settle back on the bed, in the middle," he instructed as he pulled his own shirt off over his head. It was his turn to tense as he noticed her eyes going to his scars. And staying there.

Bayleigh scooted back on the bed as she raised her eyes to his. She could feel the tension in him and knew it was because of her fascination with his scars. She couldn't help it. To her, they were badges of honor. Of courage. They had helped make him into the man he was.

"They don't bother me. You have to know that by now," she whispered, holding her hand out. "I just...I know what I went through. All the pain, the rehab. And that was just my leg. I can't imagine what you went through," she told him as he took her hand and slid onto the bed and leaned over her.

He brought her hand up to his lips, kissing the palm before releasing her hand. "I went through Hell, Bayleigh. But I made my way out, just like you will." His fingers trailed a path down the center of her chest, to the lacy edge of her panties. "Do you want to see Heaven tonight?" he whispered as his lips traced the same path his hand had a moment ago.

"Only if you take me there," she invited on a soft moan as he used his tongue to tease one her nipples. She gasped as he closed his lips around it and sucked it, the fingers of his other hand molding and shaping her other breast.

Her hands went between them to stroke his chest, smoothing over the scars, and settling on his pecs, her hands mimicking the actions of his own, her nails digging into the skin. Her legs shifted, spreading apart, as his fingers toyed with the waistband of her underwear.

"Tell me what you want," he whispered, as he moved to lie between her legs, the rough denim of his jeans rubbing against her skin and creating an ache deep inside of her.

Bayleigh bit her lip, her hands smoothed over his chest, found one of the scars and toyed with the puckered skin. "I'm not sure. Will wasn't very inventive during sex," she admitted as she felt her face flame with the embarrassment.

Jack chuckled as he propped himself up to study her.

"I love your blushes," he whispered, his finger stroking a path across her cheekbone down her throat to her chest. "Did you know your breasts blush, too?" He bent his head and pressed a kiss to the tops of her breasts. "So, not inventive, or not attentive?" he asked as one hand stroked across her stomach to her hip, easing down the edge of her panties.

"Uh, both, I guess," Bayleigh shifted her hips, asking without words for him to continue.

"Don't worry, sweet lady. I will be both inventive and attentive when it comes to you," he moved back up to capture her lips as his hands worked to strip her panties down her legs. Once he got them below her knees, she managed to maneuver her legs and kick them off.

"You're overdressed," she told him as her hands went to his belt buckle. He laughed and rolled away from her, quickly stripping off the rest of his clothes. Dropping the jeans over the side of the bed to the floor, he settled himself back against her side, propping himself up on an elbow.

"You're beautiful," his voice was low as he traced circles across her breasts and stomach with the tips of his fingers. "Any areas off limits?" he asked, as his fingers dipped lower, across her pelvic bone.

Bayleigh moaned and raised her hips, begging without words for him to continue. His lips teased hers as his fingers continued to tease and torment her, and then he traced a path to her nipple with his tongue. He rolled her nipple between his lips, using his teeth to bite and then his tongue to soothe.

Her body jerked at the sensations, her legs falling open in invitation. Jack's fingers slid lower, teasing her, as they played with her folds, before slowly inserting his finger in her.

Bayleigh moaned, her back arching and her hips rising off the bed. "More...I need more!" she managed to gasp, her hands pulling on his shoulders.

"More like this?" Jack asked, sliding a second finger in, his thumb resting on her clit and adding to the torment as he pumped his fingers in and out. He loved the sounds she was making as he continued to work her into a fevered pitch. "Or like this?" he added a third finger, earning a long, drawn out moan.

Bayleigh's nails scored his back as she tried to pull him over her. "Please, Jack! I need you inside me, now!" she begged, her hand going to his cock and wrapping around it, stroking him.

"No, baby. This first time is for you," Jack told her, withdrawing his hand and moving his body lower. His hands gripped her hips and held her still as he pursed his lips and blew across her clit.

"J-a-c-k..." her drawn out cry told him all he needed to know.

He slid his tongue along the slit, earning another cry from her. "God, baby. I've been wanting to taste you like this for days," he told her as his tongue lapped at her juices.

"I'm so close," she panted, her fingers gripped his hair as she tried to guide him. Her back arched off the mattress again as she pulled him closer.

"Easy baby, I'll get you there," he slid his fingers back into her, his lips closing around her clit and sucking it into his mouth. Bayleigh screamed his name as Jack continued to pump his fingers into her. His tongue remained on her clit as she rode the wave he'd created inside of her until he felt her body relax back into the mattress, drained.

He rolled away from her to snag a condom out of the bedside table and then returned to her side. Sheathing himself in record time, he moved back between her legs, edging them apart even further, and slid into her with one stroke.

"Easy, baby, you're so tight. I don't want to hurt you," he groaned as she tilted her hips, urging him deeper. He struggled to control the urge to bury himself to the hilt inside of her.

"You're not going to hurt me, Jack," she wrapped her legs around his waist, locking him against her. "Again. Make me come again," she begged, her nails clawing at his back.

"With pleasure," Jack groaned, as he pulled back until he was almost out of her and then pressed back inside, controlling the movement, prolonging the pleasure for both of them. He was desperate to pick up the pace, to start thrusting hard and fast, but he needed her to be ready.

Her nails clawed at his back. "Please, Jack, I need more!" she cried out, her hips moving against him, increasing the pressure on her clit.

"Tell me what you need, baby," Jack whispered against her lips, one hand sliding up so he could cup her breast. His fingers played with the nipple, earning a long, drawn out moan from her. "Like that, do you?" he asked, pinching it between his thumb and forefinger.

"Mm-hmm," her hands drifted down to his butt, squeezing and pulling him deeper. "Now, Jack. I need all of you, now."

"You've got me, sweetheart," he promised, his hand drifting to her hip to make a slight adjustment in their position and then he started moving. He bent his head and pulled her nipple into his mouth, biting her. When her hands came up to his cradle his head to her, he grinned and released her nipple. "Like that, do you?"

"Yesss!" she cried, her body twisting against his, searching for the perfect pressure to make her come again. "Please..." she begged.

"Hang on, babe," he clenched his jaw as his own need for release ratcheted upwards. His hips moved faster, and he could feel her clamping down on him with her vaginal muscles. "Now!" he groaned, as he felt her climax start and allowed his own body to reach his.

BAYLEIGH WASN'T sure how long she laid there, his weight pressing her into the mattress. She may have passed out, she couldn't swear to it though. Her hands stroked over his back, loving the closeness she felt with him.

"You okay?" he pushed himself up on his forearms, his concerned gaze searching her eyes.

"I think I'm perfect," she whispered, smiling up at him.

"I know you're perfect," he bent his head and took her mouth in a deep kiss as he pulled out of her. As he eased off of her to lay beside her on the bed, he caught the slight grimace on her face. "What's wrong?"

"My leg is sore," she admitted and his hand immediately went to her injured leg, his fingers feeling along the injured area to see if they'd reinjured it in any way.

"It's fine, Jack. I just...I used a couple of muscles not used to being worked like that," she blushed.

Jack grinned pressed a kiss to her lips, before he slid off the bed, walking into the bathroom. Bayleigh curled up onto her side, watching him through the doorway as he disposed of the condom and then wet a washcloth.

He walked back into the bedroom and sat beside her on the bed. "Let me clean you up, sweetheart," he whispered, helping her roll onto her back so he could use the warm cloth between her legs. He bent and pressed a kiss to her belly button before standing up.

After tossing the washcloth into the bathroom sink, he returned to the bed, pulling the comforter over them as he reached to draw her into his arms. He sighed as her head found a comfortable spot on his chest and she cuddled into him with a yawn. "Go to sleep, baby," he whispered as he kissed the top of her head. She mumbled something that sounded like an agreement, and within in minutes, they were both sound asleep in each other's arms.

CHAPTER 19

*B*ayleigh woke up and stretched, wincing as more than one muscle protested. She and Jack hadn't left the bedroom last night, except once around two a.m. to raid the refrigerator. That had been the third time he'd woken her up with his touches and kisses. The last time had been around six this morning.

Jack. Her head turned towards the side of the bed. Empty. Sitting up, she looked around the room, spying a robe laid across a chair. With a smile, she threw the covers off and slid the robe on, tying the belt securely around her waist. Stopping in the bathroom long enough to freshen up, she followed the smell of coffee and cinnamon rolls to the kitchen.

Jack had just taken the cinnamon rolls out of the oven and was spreading the icing over them. "Good morning," he greeted her as he set the knife in the sink. "I didn't wake you, did I?"

"Multiple times," she arched an eyebrow.

"Those were intentional and I didn't hear you

complaining," he pointed out, reaching out to pull her into his arms, his head lowering to hers.

Bayleigh laughed and returned his kiss. "No, you didn't wake me. This time," she clarified, smiling.

"How do you feel this morning?" he asked, his lips hovering over hers, as his hand played with the belt on the robe.

"I feel great, but there's a few muscles that are protesting movement right now," she warned him, her fingers latching onto his wrist and holding his hands still.

"I can give you a massage later," he offered, sliding his hands around to cup her buttocks, rubbing them through the cloth of the robe.

"Mmm," her head dropped forward to his chest. "That would be nice," her voice had a huskiness to it that hadn't been there just a moment before.

"We could start it now," his voice was just as husky as he pulled her closer against him, letting her feel his arousal.

"But you made cinnamon rolls. And coffee," she pointed out.

"They'll still be good later."

"True enough but I'm hungry now. And I need caffeine," she laughed as he pouted. "I'll make it up to you later," she promised, standing on tiptoes to press a kiss to his lips.

"I'm holding you to that promise," he deepened the kiss before letting her go. "Let's get you fed. I have a feeling Jason will be by soon to check on you," he turned to grab the rolls off the stove.

"Not if he wants to live," Bayleigh muttered, following him to the table after grabbing the coffee pot.

Jack laughed and set the rolls down on the table, turning to take the coffee pot from her. Grabbing her around the waist, he sat down in one of the chairs and pulled her down onto his lap.

"He's worried about you, Bayleigh," he reminded her, his arms closing around her and holding her close.

"I know, but he's never been like this before."

"You'd never been hurt before. Let him play the role of protector for a while. I can handle him."

"Were you like this when he and Nicole got back together?"

"Honey, I helped push Nicole back at him. He was all set to mess things up again. I was not about to listen to ten more years of her heartache and his grief!"

Bayleigh shook her head and reached for the rolls, picking out the biggest one and taking a huge bite of it, moaning as the sweetness of the icing coated her tongue.

"Only you could make eating a cinnamon roll sexy," Jack muttered, his eyes narrowed as he watched her lick her lips and take another bite.

Bayleigh paused and glanced at him. "Me eating is sexy?"

"It's the way you eat, baby. Licking and moaning... shit," Jack shifted in the chair and Bayleigh's eyes widened as his erection pressed against her.

"You better hope my brother doesn't show up in the next hour," she told him as she tossed the remainder of the roll on the table, stood up and grabbed his hand to pull him to his feet. She dropped his hand and turned to run down the hallway towards his bedroom, laughing, with him close on her heels.

Hours later, Bayleigh stirred in his arms, her eyes fluttering open to see him leaning over her. "Mmm, I could get used to this," she muttered, her hands sliding up his bare chest to slide around his shoulders.

"I could too, babe," he dipped his head and kissed her but kept it brief. Bayleigh frowned at him as he pulled back.

"Something wrong?"

"Not a thing, except your brother keeps texting me wondering when I'm bringing you back to his place," Jack pressed another kiss to her lips. "And I'm getting the feeling he's about to start cleaning his shotgun if we don't head over there soon."

"Jason's a lousy shot, though," Bayleigh reminded him.

"Nicole isn't and she's the one I'm worried about," he gave her a lopsided grin. "Sorry, babe, she has decided it's time for paybacks," his voice held just the slightest amount of regret.

Bayleigh stared at him, confused. "Why would Nicole want to get back at me? I haven't done anything to her. Oh, God, she hates me, doesn't she?"

Jack laughed and covered her mouth with his hand. "Good lord, woman, she's not out to get *you*. She's out to pay me back for all the grief I gave her last year."

Bayleigh's eyes narrowed. "What did you do to her?"

"Just some good natured teasing. Oh, and there may have been a welcoming party on the front porch once or twice when Jason dropped her off 'the morning after'," Jack couldn't hide his smirk as he shrugged his shoulders. "But that was all Mitch's idea. I swear!"

"Sure it was," Bayleigh shook her head, her hands

sliding back to his chest and giving him a shove to push him off of her. "Now that I know what I'm in for when we get home, I guess we'd better get a move on."

Jack rolled over, stood up, and turned to offer her a helping hand. "Shower first? We could save water and shower together."

"Anything to help the environment," Bayleigh agreed with a laugh, following him into the bathroom.

CHAPTER 20

*J*ack dropped bayleigh off at her brother's house on his way into the office. They'd been getting out of the shower when he'd gotten a call from one of his clients who'd insisted on meeting immediately.

"Sure you're going to be okay here?" Jack asked as he walked her up to the door.

"I'm a big girl, Jack. I've stayed alone before. Besides, Jason said he's just doing rounds at the hospital and will be home soon. We're all meeting over at the main house for dinner tonight, right?"

"I'll pick you up after my meeting and you can ride with me. Pack a bag," he responded, kissing her. With a small wave and a smile, he headed back to his truck.

Bayleigh decided to spend the time working on a new song on the front porch. As was often the case, she soon lost herself in the song. Until she heard the sounds of a car driving down the lane. Unable to recognize the car, she set aside her guitar and stood up.

After parking next to her car, the driver opened his door and stepped out. Bayleigh gasped as she recognized him. "You can just stop right there, get back in your car and leave!" she called to her ex-boyfriend.

"Bayleigh! Sweets, I have missed you so much!" Will called to her as he jogged towards the porch steps.

Bayleigh narrowed her eyes and started towards him. "What the hell are you doing here, Will?"

"I need you," he reached towards her, but she brought her hands up between them and shoved him backwards, making him stumble.

"You're full of shit, Will. The only reason you would miss me is if you need something from me." She stood with her feet apart and her hands on her hips. "What the hell do you want?"

"I want you back, Sweets."

"I am not your 'Sweets', Will. I haven't been in over a year. You need to leave."

"Sweets, don't kick me out. I need you back with me. We're perfect for each other. You are everything I need in a woman!"

"Stop calling me that! I am not your 'Sweets', damn it! And if that's really how you feel about me, why did I find you in bed with that slut in London? And all the other times I caught you making out with women after the shows? What are you really doing here?" she asked through gritted teeth, her hands clenched into fists.

Will took a step forward. "Come on, Bayleigh. I'm sorry I wasn't there for you when you hurt your leg, but we were trying to get those gigs lined up to replace the ones we lost when Andrew flaked on us."

"Flaked? The man was going to rape me, Will! And you were more upset over the fact that you lost a gig than that fact!" Bayleigh took a couple of steps backwards. "You need to leave, Will. Now."

Will scowled, looking down at the ground. "I need you to come back, Bayleigh. There's a record label looking at signing us. But you have to be part of the deal."

"Why, I was just a back-up singer, remember? 'Easily replaceable' were the words you used, I believe," she cocked her head to the side, watching him.

Will shifted, his gaze looking everywhere but at her. "They want your songs," he admitted. "The ones that we've always sung on stage."

"The ones you wouldn't use on the demos because they weren't edgy enough for you? Those songs?" her eyebrows went up.

"Damn it, yes, those songs. But I guess even though the band always used them, we don't have exclusive rights to them because I never signed any kind of contract with you for them. I don't understand all of the legalities," he muttered.

"Well, let me explain it to you then. I copyrighted my work. I always do. You cannot reproduce them in any way, shape, or form without my consent." Bayleigh smirked. "Maddie insisted I cover my ass, just in case. Looks like she knew what you were capable of."

"I would have contacted you, worked something out. It's not like I was going to steal them."

"Sounds like that's exactly what you were trying to do," Bayleigh made a show out of glancing at her watch. "Now, your time is up and you are on private property. Leave now or I will call the Sheriff."

Will stepped in front of her, stopping her from walking away. "Bayleigh, I need those songs!" he pleaded, his hand grabbing her wrist, stopping her.

"Have the label contact me. Maybe they're for sale," she narrowed her gaze and twisted her wrist, freeing herself. When he reached for her again, she brought her other arm up and with a move Brian had taught both her and Maddie years ago, knocked him flat. "I think you'd better get in your car and drive away before I find something to use as a baseball bat."

Will stood up and dusted himself off. "This isn't over, *Sweets!*" he yelled over his shoulder.

"Yes, it is, jackass. I promise you, it's over." Bayleigh waited until he was in his car and driving away before she headed into her brother's house. She managed to shut and lock the door before her knees gave out and she sank to the floor.

With a sigh, drew her knees up to rest her head on. She'd done it, she'd stood up to Will. And her past. In a really big way. She'd managed to knock him on his ass. She'd have to remember to thank Brian for showing her that move.

She heard a car pulling up the gravel drive and her heart rate ramped back up. Closing her eyes and saying a short prayer that it wasn't Will coming back, she eased herself into a crouch and looked out the window.

"Oh, thank God," she whispered, forcing herself to stand and open the door. She met her brother on the steps.

"Bayleigh, you're white as a ghost! What's the matter?"

Jason's hands closed around her shoulders. His eyes searched hers. "What happened? Is it Jack?"

"No, I'm fine, Jason," she tried to smile. "Jack had to go into work, he dropped me off a while ago." She took a deep breath and tried to get the pounding of her heart to settle down.

"I had a visitor a little bit ago, while I was waiting for you and Nicole to get home," she turned her head, looking over at her guitar she'd left on the porch swing. "Will stopped by."

"Shit. Are you okay? Did he touch you?"

"No. If anything, he can say I assaulted him. Kind of," she gave a humorless laugh. "He grabbed my wrist and I used a little move Brian taught me. He left after that."

"Which wrist?" Jason took her wrist to examine it. "Why was that asshole even here?"

"Ouch!" Bayleigh winced as he pressed on her wrist. "He wants me back." As Jason's head shot up, she shrugged her shoulders. "Some label wants him and my songs. He doesn't have the rights to my songs."

"Are you going to let him have them?"

"I don't know, depends on the offer I get made, I guess," she glanced over his shoulder and saw the vehicles heading down the lane. "Here come Nicole and Jack."

Jason stepped to stand beside her, his arm around her shoulders as they waited for Jack and Nicole to join them.

"Hey, babe. Get a lot of writing done?" Jack asked as he wrapped his arms around her waist and pulled her up against him.

"Some. I'm having some trouble with a tune, but I'll get

it." She smiled at him. "Did you guys get everything taken care of with your client?"

Jack nodded as they followed Jason and Nicole into the house. "I got your message, you sounded upset."

"Oh, and yeah. Will was here," she turned and faced Jack. "There's a label interested in the band, but they want my songs included."

"Did he touch you?"

"No, I'm fine. He grabbed me by the wrist and I dumped him on his ass. I'm fine!" she insisted as once again her wrist was poked and prodded.

"Did Jason look at this?"

"That's what he was doing when you two showed up," Bayleigh assured him, going up on tiptoes to press a kiss to his lips. "I swear, I'm fine!" she whispered against his lips.

"He left bruises," Jack muttered, raising her wrist to his lips and pressing a kiss to the marks.

"I guarantee you he has one on his butt. He landed pretty hard," she smirked.

"Everything okay out here?" Nicole stood in the doorway to the kitchen. Bayleigh glanced over her shoulder at her sister-in-law and smiled.

"We're fine."

"Coffee's ready when you two are," Nicole smiled and headed back into the kitchen.

"If he comes around again..." Jack started to say.

"He won't. He just wants the rights to record songs he always thought of as his. He'll go back to his agent and tell her he struck out and then the agent will call the label to contact me."

Jack took her hand in his. "I don't know much about

entertainment law, but if you have anything you need me to look over, let me know."

"Thanks. I might take you up on that," she smiled at him as he led the way into the kitchen, pulling a chair out at the table to sink into. Her adrenaline rush had faded and she was still a little shaky.

Her brother handed her a bag of frozen corn and Nicole handed her a towel. Jack took both items, knelt beside her chair and laid the towel over her wrist and then placed the frozen vegetables on it. Jack glanced over at Jason. "Not broken, I take it?"

"Nah. Just bruised where he grabbed her. But if it swells or starts bothering her, take her in for some x-rays, just to be sure."

"Hey, I'm right here, guys. I'm fine! Trust me, after the last year, I know what a broken bone feels like. This is not broken." Bayleigh started to lift her arm off the table Jack placed his hand over it.

"I know you're right here. And I know you're fine. But right now, I want to go rip apart the guy who dared to lay a hand on you. And he just happens to be the same guy who let it all happen the first time around. So, I'm not so 'fine'. And I need to take care of you." Jack held her gaze.

Bayleigh swallowed hard and nodded. "If that's what you need," she whispered, her free hand coming up to cover his. "I'll let you know if it starts to hurt more, then."

"Thank you," he whispered, his forehead resting against hers.

Bayleigh smiled and turned her head to press a kiss to his forehead. "I'm fine, Jack. I stood up to him. I'm getting my life back, one piece at a time."

"That you are, baby."

Jason cleared his throat behind them, causing Bayleigh to jump. "I'd say 'get a room' but knowing Jack, he'd do it. And I'd like to pretend you two just had a pajama party last night, no sex involved."

Bayleigh laughed as Nicole hushed her husband and Jack flipped him off as he stood up. Bayleigh's eyes drifted around the room as they all joked about different things. Nicole caught her eye and winked and Bayleigh smiled back at her.

This was her family and now, it was her home. She had made it back from the edge of the pit and it was time to put the past behind her and move forward. One step at a time.

CHAPTER 21

*B*ayleigh opened her eyes as the last notes faded away and met the eyes of the sound engineer through the glass. The smile on his face told her what she needed to know: that was the one. Her answering smile felt like it was a mile-wide.

"That was perfect, Bayleigh! That gives us eight solid cuts for a demo tape. I can have it ready to give to you by mid-week, if you'd like."

"That would be great, Liam. I'd appreciate it," she slid the headphones off and set her guitar aside.

"It was my pleasure," Liam answered as he opened the door between them. "Sorry I have to rush you through it."

"I'm just glad you found the time to squeeze me in today." Bayleigh slipped of the stool she'd been sitting on and stretched. She glanced over as the door to the hallway opened.

"Oh my, God! Dusty!"

"Bayleigh Morrow! Lord, it's been years since I've seen you. When Liam told me you'd be here today, I had to make sure I got here early. Where have you been, girl?" He stepped into the studio and swept her up into a bear hug.

"England, mostly, with Will." She hugged him back. "But that's over and ancient history and I'm back. Liam is helping me make a demo to send out to the publishing houses."

"Finally got rid of the jackass?" Dusty quirked an eyebrow at her.

"Yes, I did and for good this time," Bayleigh grinned at him. "Enough about my sad life. Just look at you! Mr. Dusty Rhodes, opening act for the hottest act in country music!"

"Luck of the draw, you know that."

She shook her finger at him. "Along with tons of talent and years of hard work. Don't sell yourself short, Dusty," she admonished him.

"Believe me, I don't," he gave her a wink and she laughed.

"Haven't changed, have you?"

"Not a bit," he glanced over his shoulder as a few others walked into the studio. "Come out here and let me introduce you around. You got a few minutes?"

"Sure," Bayleigh finished putting her guitar into its case and slid her music into her bag. She walked out into the sound booth with Dusty and he introduced her to his assistant and his manager.

"Glenn, you need to find out where she signs to publish her songs. I'm going to be looking for some new material for my next album," Dusty turned back to Bayleigh. "I'd like to see what you've got. That is, if you'd be interested in working with me again."

"Are you kidding? I'd love to!" Bayleigh prayed she wasn't dreaming. Write songs and have them recorded by Dusty Rhodes, up and coming superstar? Oh, hell, yeah!

"Sounds like you two already have it all worked out, then," Glenn Marks, Dusty's manager held out his card. "Once you have a deal with the publishing house, let me know. Are you local to Austin, then?"

"I live a few hours west of here, in the heart of the Hill Country, but easy driving distance. I'm staying with my brother for a while until I decide where I want to be permanently."

"Well, keep in touch. Dusty, we need to get into this meeting," Glenn reminded him, with a glance at his watch.

"You go ahead. I'm going to walk Bayleigh out. I won't be long," he promised his manager.

"You don't have to walk me out if you have a meeting," Bayleigh told him as the other men, including Liam, headed for an office down the hall.

"Eh, it's just business. That's what Glenn and Chris are for," he told her as he took her guitar from her and ushered her through the doors and into the hall.

"So, what are you doing here, anyway?"

"I'm going to record my next album in Austin. We're looking at using Liam's studio. And of course, this weekend, I'm playing the Austin Rodeo. You should come check it out. Bring your brother with you, if he wants to come."

"He's married."

"Then how many tickets do you need? I can leave them at the gate for you," he leaned against her car as she unlocked the door with the key fob.

"Four, I guess. But no promises. I'm not sure what we have planned."

"Four it is. And no pressure. I'd love to get a chance to catch up some more." He pulled her in for another hug before he pressed a chaste kiss to her cheek. "I'm glad to hear you left that loser behind you. You've got too much talent to waste your songs on scum like him."

"Thanks, Dusty. You always were good for the ego," Bayleigh opened her driver's door and turned back to him to say goodbye. "I hope I get a chance to talk to you on Saturday, then."

"Here, this is my personal cell. Call or text me. Maybe we can meet up before or after the show," Dusty pressed his business card into her hand, closing her fingers around it.

Bayleigh glanced over his shoulder. "You'd better get back inside. Your assistant just came looking for you."

Dusty laughed and stepped back, allowing her to slide inside her car. She lifted her hand in a wave as she left the parking lot, a smile on her face. Who knew connections made ten years ago in a little hole in the wall dive in Nashville with a bunch of wanna-bes would add up to an invitation to be on what could potentially be a multi-million selling record? She couldn't wait to tell Jack.

"You know Dusty Rhodes and you never told us? Girl, you're holding out on me!" Nicole teased as the two couples checked into one of the hotels in downtown Austin on Friday afternoon. When Bayleigh mentioned she might be able to get tickets to Dusty's show, Nicole had made plans for both couples to spend the weekend.

Bayleigh grinned at her sister-in-law. "Never occurred to me to include that in my references," she teased. "I had no idea he'd be at Liam's the other day."

"Now, who's Liam again?"

"He owns the recording studio I used. He and Maddie were really close for a while back when we were all in Nashville."

Jason walked up and slid an arm around his wife's shoulders. "Okay, we're all checked in and they're taking our bags up to the rooms for us. We've got enough time to rest for a bit before we're meeting Bayleigh's friends for that sound check thing he invited us to."

"Bayleigh's friend who just happens to be Dusty Rhodes," Nicole interjected with a smile.

Bayleigh sighed and looked at Jack. "Is she going to be like this all night?"

Jack shrugged and glanced at his watch. "You ready to head up to the room so we can rest before we go meet these people?" Without waiting for a reply, he marched over to the elevators, stabbing at the call button with his finger.

Surprised at his abrupt tone, Bayleigh glanced at Nicole and Jason, seeing their matching frowns.

"I think we're going to grab a drink in the bar first. You going to be okay with him?"

"Of course," Bayleigh tried to give her brother a reassuring smile as she hurried to catch up with Jack before the elevator doors closed. "You okay?" she asked him, managing to step through the doors just before they closed.

"I'm fine," he leaned his head against the wall of the elevator.

"Then what's wrong?"

"Nothing," he shouldered his way past her as the elevator doors opened on their floor.

Not sure what else to do, Bayleigh followed him down the hallway and waited for him to open the door to their room. She entered behind him and watched as he tossed the keycard on the desk before he stretched out on the bed.

She moved over to stand beside the bed, her hands on her hips. "Are you going to tell me what this is about?"

"I'm just tired, Bayleigh. I just need to take a nap. Can you wake me in a couple of hours so I can take a shower?"

"Jack..."

"I'm tired, Bayleigh. That's all," he grabbed one of the pillows and pulled it over his head, cutting her off.

Bayleigh huffed out a breath and stood with her hands on her hips. "Fine. I'm going back down to the bar with Jason and Nicole."

"'Kay," Jack grumbled from under the pillow.

Throwing her hands up in frustration, Bayleigh stormed back to the door, not bothering to catch it to keep it from slamming. She'd give him his two hours and not a minute more.

Stepping back onto the elevator, she hit the button for the lobby. She found Jason and Nicole sitting at the bar and slid onto a stool next to them.

"Didn't expect to see you back down here," Jason commented after she ordered a glass of wine.

"Neither did I," Bayleigh muttered, taking a healthy swallow of the wine.

Nicole exchanged a look with her husband and jerked her head towards the doors. He nodded and leaned over to kiss his wife before he slid off the barstool. As he passed by his sister, he patted her back.

"Want to talk about it?" Nicole asked, taking a sip of her own drink.

"I don't even know what to talk about, Nicole. You saw what he was like down here, then when we got to the room, he laid down on the bed and said he wanted to take a nap." She took another sip of her wine.

"Did you two have a fight or something?"

"What? No, why?"

Nicole turned to fully face her sister-in-law. "He's been in a mood for the last couple of days. I thought maybe it was something between you two."

"And I was hoping it was something at the office," Bayleigh pushed her wine glass aside. "I don't know what to do, Nicole."

"Well, Jack's the kind of guy who just needs time to work things out on his own, whatever is bothering him." Nicole reached over and put her hand on Bayleigh's arm. "He's a complicated man, Bayleigh. Just give him some space. He'll let you know when he's ready to talk about whatever is bothering him."

Sliding off the barstool, she slid her purse strap over her shoulder. "You want to hang out with me and Jason?"

"No, I'll just go walk around a little," Bayleigh was quick to shake her head. "It's Austin. There's always something to do," she gave her a weak smile.

"You sure?"

"I'll be fine, Nicole. I'll give Jack his space for two hours and then we'll see what happens."

"Come find us if you need anything, Bayleigh. Anything," Nicole gave her a hug.

Bayleigh nodded and watched her sister-in-law walk out of the bar. The bartender pointed to her glass but Bayleigh shook her head. She wasn't one to drown her sorrows in alcohol. But she was one to bury it in the music. And Austin was known worldwide as the Live Music Capitol of the World. She was going to go see what was happening on the streets. Maybe a few hours would give them all a little perspective.

CHAPTER 22

"WHAT THE HELL WAS YOUR problem tonight?" Bayleigh asked, tossing her purse on the small desk in their hotel room.

"Nothing," Jack grabbed a bottle of alcohol out of the mini-bar and poured it into a glass, tossing it back in a single swallow.

"Jack, you didn't talk to any of us all night! I don't even think you talked to Dusty at all!"

"I didn't need to, you talked to him the whole night!" he shot back, reaching for another bottle of the whiskey.

"Don't you think you had enough of that already?" Bayleigh raised an eyebrow.

He opened the second bottle and tossed the cap aside. "I'm not drunk, Bayleigh. Not even close," he downed the second shot.

"Well, you're well on your way, then," she muttered.

"Why don't you go rejoin your friend Dusty? You were pretty close to him the other day," he reached for a third bottle of the alcohol.

"What the hell are you talking about?"

"I saw you, Bayleigh, so don't try to deny it!" he drank the third bottle down.

"Deny what? Are you sure you aren't drunk?"

"I saw you! Outside the studio the other day, here in Austin. You were in his arms, he was all over you!"

Bayleigh stared at him in shock. "You saw what?"

"The day you came to Austin to record your demo, I had to meet a client here. I was going to surprise you, take you out to dinner, something fancier than what we have in Waketon. I got to the studio in time to see you making out with that guy!" he opened the fridge again then slammed it shut. "There's not enough alcohol in this room. I'm going to the bar."

"Wait, Jack! We need to talk about this," Bayleigh reached for his arm but he jerked it out of her reach.

"I'm done talking, Bayleigh. I've been cheated on before by the woman I thought I loved. I should have known better than to trust you!"

"What are you talking about? You *can* trust me! I don't know what you think you saw but it wasn't me cheating on you, or even close! Dusty is a friend, nothing more!"

"Awfully close friend, isn't he?"

"Oh my God, Jack! Nothing happened! You didn't see anything! Dusty, Liam, Will, Maddie and I were all in Nashville together back in the day! We were all friends supporting each other. Dusty showed up at the studio that day and it was the first time we'd seen each other since before I left for England. I have never been interested in Dusty that way. Ever!"

"Actions speak louder, Bayleigh! Last woman who told

me that, I caught sleeping with one of my therapists!" He grabbed the keycard off the desk. "I'll get another room for the night."

"Don't bother! I'm leaving. I won't be with another man I can't trust! Or who won't trust me!" Bayleigh clenched her hands into fists, her nails digging into her palms.

"Fine," he paused at the doorway. "Do you need cash for the room?"

"If I did, I wouldn't take it from you!" her eyes narrowed. "I'll be out of here in thirty minutes or less." Jack nodded and left the room.

Bayleigh closed her eyes and took a deep breath, holding it for a few seconds, praying for calm. The tears were threatening but she forced them back. If she started crying now, she wouldn't stop. He was supposed to be the one, damn it. The one she could count on, the one to be there for her, right through it all.

Opening them back up, she looked around the hotel room. Luckily, she'd only unpacked her make-up and the clothes she'd needed to change into to head to the sound check and the show. Throwing everything back into her suitcase, she sent her brother a text telling him she needed to come to their room for a few minutes.

"Hey, sis. What's up?" Jason opened their door and stepped back to let her enter. "Uh, why do you have your suitcase?"

"I'm leaving," Bayleigh looked over at Nicole. "I found out what Jack's problem is. He thinks I cheated on him."

"What? With who?"

"Why would he think that?" Jason and Nicole both asked at the same time.

Bayleigh held up her hand to stop them from questioning her. "He tried to surprise me at the studio the other day and saw me and Dusty in the parking lot. All Dusty did was kiss my cheek, I swear!" Her voice cracked and she knew she was riding that fine line between holding it together and spending the next three days eating gallons of ice cream and crying. She pressed her lips together and fought to hold it in, to hold it together for just a little bit longer. "I just want to go home and pack. It's time for me to head to Nashville."

"I don't think you should drive that far tonight, honey. It's late and we've already had a long day." Nicole stood up from the couch and walked to them. "Let's go down to the desk, see if there's another room for the night."

Bayleigh shook her head. "We all drove here together. I am not riding back to Waketon in the same car with him."

"You can't take a cab that far, it'll cost too much!" Jason pointed out.

"I can rent a car. It won't cost that much. Or call Mitch or Paul to come get me. Or hell, Brian would fly down to get me if I really needed him to, for that matter, Jason. I have plenty of options," Bayleigh paused to take a deep breath and calm down. "I only stopped by so you wouldn't freak out in the morning. I won't disappear on you, I promise. I'm only going back to your place to pack and then to Nashville."

"That man needs to get his head out of his ass. Let me guess, he's got some issue from his ex-fiancé playing into this, doesn't he?" Nicole grabbed the keycards off the desk, slipping one into her back pocket.

Bayleigh sighed and nodded, wiping the tears off her cheeks. "Yeah, it came up."

Nicole nodded and gave her a hug. "I'm going to go down to the bar and see if I can get to the bottom of this fiasco for you. Hang in there and don't give up on him just yet!"

"Well, he's making it hard not to, Nicole. I think I love him, but I can't go through this again."

Nicole exchanged a look with Jason and then nodded. "I'll be in the bar," she gave Bayleigh's arm a reassuring squeeze and her husband a quick kiss and then headed out the door.

Jason looked at his sister, handing her a couple of tissues from the box on the small table by the door. "So, what do you want to do?"

Bayleigh shook her head. "Get the hell out of here and as far away as possible from Jack, to start with. After that, I don't know," her grip tightened on the handle of her suitcase. "You should go get your wife out of the bar before she and Jack wind up drinking each other under a table," she tried to offer her brother a smile.

"You sure? I can help you get another room," Jason offered, holding the room door open for her as the stepped back into the hallway.

"I'm a big girl, Jason. Time to start acting like one, I guess."

Jason jammed his finger against the call button for the elevator. "Well, you just say the word and I'll take the jackass out back and beat some sense into him. Mitch will probably help me," he grinned at her. "He never needs much of an excuse to go at it with Jack."

Bayleigh shook her head. "Right now, I just want to escape. Fast and far," she told him as the doors opened and she stepped out, right into the solid chest of Dusty Rhodes.

"Hey, girl! Where you headed in such a hurry?" Dusty grabbed her elbows to steady her. "You okay?" his voice dropped when he saw Bayleigh's tear-streaked face and the suitcase next to her. When Bayleigh didn't answer him, he quirked an eyebrow as he looked over at Jason. "Do you really want me and your brother discussing your love life in front of you like you're not here? Because you know I'll do it. You also know I'll call Maddie and put her on speaker phone, and she'll call Jade..."

"Okay, stop already!" Bayleigh grimaced and looked around the near-empty lobby. She allowed Dusty to lead her over to a small alcove, while Jason hovered nearby.

Dusty's hand settled on her shoulder. "Now, what's going on with that man of yours?" he asked and when her startled glance met his knowing look, he shrugged his broad shoulders. "I saw how your guy kept glaring at me all night, and now you're down here with a suitcase, tearstains on your cheeks and your brother looking ready to fight some-one. It doesn't take a genius to figure it out, so go ahead and tell me what this idiot has done."

Bayleigh grimaced and leaned back against the wall, tilting her head back to stare up at the skylight, avoiding Dusty's knowing look. "Jack and I had a big blow up when we got back here tonight. He's got some idea in his head that you and I are, well, um...seeing each other." Bayleigh felt her cheeks growing warm as she said the words. She had never thought of Dusty in those terms, ever. And even if she had, his wife would have scratched her eyes out.

"Well, hell." Dusty glanced over at Jason. "I'm guessing me going up to the room and telling him that he's mistaken wouldn't be a good idea?"

"Not with the amount of whiskey he's probably already ingested by this point," Jason shook his head with a grimace. "Nicole went to check on him in the bar while I came down here with Bayleigh to figure out her next steps."

"What is your next step?" Dusty tilted his head to the side to study Bayleigh.

"Rent a car so I can drive to Waketon tonight so I don't have to ride with Jack tomorrow," she mimicked his look. "Then pack up my stuff and get to Nashville so I can start booking meetings with the publishing houses, sell my music."

"So you're serious about getting the music out there?"

"I told you the other day I was," Bayleigh nodded.

"Then I have a solution for you. Why don't you and Crista drive out to Waketon tonight, get yourself packed up and get back here by one o'clock tomorrow afternoon and you can fly back to Nashville with me tomorrow? I'm signing my deal with Liam tomorrow morning but will have it wrapped up by noon. I'm taking the jet back to Nashville to spend some time with Jade and the kids before the next leg of the tour kicks off."

"Who's Crista?" Jason asked.

"My personal assistant, kid sister, all around nuisance and pain in the ass," Dusty grinned. "She just walked in the door," he waved her over.

"Oh, my God, Bayleigh! How the hell are you? I haven't seen you in forever!" Crista gave Bayleigh a hug as she joined the group. "Sorry I didn't get backstage earlier to see you guys, but keeping this guy's life in order is a job and a half!"

"I can imagine," Bayleigh hugged the younger woman back.

"Speaking of jobs, I've got one for you, Crista. Can you ride back to Bayleigh's home, help her pack up and be back her tomorrow in time to head to Nashville?"

"Uh, sure. Everything okay?"

"No one is coming after me, if that's what you mean. I just need to escape for a while," Bayleigh explained.

"Well, let me head upstairs and change into something more comfortable for driving in and we can head out. You staying here, then, Dusty?"

"Yup. Need my beauty sleep," he gave his sister a wink as she rolled her eyes.

"Bayleigh, you sure this is a good idea?" Jason placed his hand on his sister's arm, pulling her away from the siblings.

"Do you have a better option for me?" Bayleigh arched an eyebrow at her brother. "Crista and I will go get my stuff together, I'll head to Nashville, and Jack can kiss my ass."

"Is that what you want me to tell Jack?"

"I don't care what you tell Jack. He made his decision when he walked out of that room tonight. No, wait, he made his decision the other day when he didn't talk to me about what he thought he saw. I won't stick around and pay for the sins of others, Jason. I've been a doormat in a relationship long enough. It's time for the old Bayleigh to reappear."

"I've missed the old Bayleigh, but I have to say, this new one is a sight to behold," Jason gave her a quick hug. "Drive safe, text me when you get there and again tomorrow before you head to Nashville. And for God's sake, don't be a stranger!"

"I promise, I won't. I'll keep you posted!" she went up on tiptoes to press a kiss to her brother's cheek.

"You coming with us, Bayleigh?" Dusty asked from behind her, as he looped an arm around his sister's neck.

"You'd better believe it!" she stepped over beside Dusty, her arm slipping around his waist. Before she stepped on the elevator, she glanced over at her brother one last time. "I'll be fine, you know. I'm a survivor."

"That you are," he agreed, with a nod. "Take care of her, Dusty." Dusty lifted a hand in acknowledgement, listening to details of some promotional deal Crista was trying to work out.

Bayleigh could see the worry in her brother's eyes, but there was no way she could stay here right now. As she gave her brother one last reassuring smile, the elevator doors closed and she leaned her head back against the wall. She just needed time and space to think. And living with Jason, who was married to Nicole, who was Jack's best friend and business partner, was not going to give her that time and space.

No, she needed to do this. She needed to get to Nashville and get her name and her music out there, get it noticed. And she needed to do it on her own, prove to herself that she had the talent and didn't need to hang onto anyone's coattails to get anywhere. Namedropping might get some doors opened for her, but if she didn't have the talent to back it up, she wouldn't get far.

She'd hoped that after all of that she'd have a life in

Waketon to return to, to keep her grounded. Now it looked like she'd have to find somewhere else to call home and something else to ground her if she needed it.

Dusty glanced over at her as the elevator arrived on their floor and they all stepped off. "You okay, kid?"

"I will be," she nodded. "Just trying to wrap my head around it all."

"Hey, if you want to crash in my room for the night and then we can head out tomorrow morning to get your stuff..." Crista started to offer.

"No, I don't want to chance running into Jack at all tomorrow. He left his truck at Jason's. I think it's best if we head out there tonight. It's not far, only about two hours really. And I just need to throw a few things in the suitcase and grab my music. I only have what I could carry on the plane from England. It's not like it's a lot."

"Call if you need anything," Dusty instructed his sister. "I'm calling Jade, so if I don't answer, call right back."

"Will do. See you in the morning," Crista called over her shoulder as she motioned Bayleigh to follow her down the hallway. "They have most of the band and crew on this floor. Since Dusty was in town all week, the guys have been out partying most nights. And they don't have another show until Wednesday, so they're all out experiencing Austin."

"I appreciate this, Crista." Bayleigh told her as they entered Crista's room.

"No worries. Let me change and we can head out," Crista grabbed some clean clothes out of her own suitcase and headed for the bathroom. "Make yourself comfortable for a few minutes."

Bayleigh eased herself down on the couch in the room and rested her head against the cushions. Her life sure had a way of going from sugar to shit in a heartbeat, and she was getting tired of it. It was time to stand up, dust herself off, and make her own destiny.

CHAPTER 23

"*H*aving trouble concentrating today?" Nicole stood in the doorway to Jack's office.

"And you're not helping any," he growled crumpled up the piece of paper he was writing on and threw it towards the trash can, missing by at least a yard.

Nicole raised an eyebrow at all the other crumpled up balls of paper littering the office. "Are you going to go after her?"

"No," Jack wadded up another piece of paper and tossed it to the floor.

"What if you're wrong?"

"I'm not," he denied, his voice hard as steel. "You saw her that night, getting on the elevator with him and that other woman, arms all over each other."

"And you heard what Jason said about that. Dusty offered to give her a ride to Nashville and his sister was willing to drive out here to get her stuff together so she could go!"

"Yeah, so she could *go with him*! She didn't give me a

second thought, did she?" Jack threw his pen on his desk and shoved his chair back, stalking over to the window.

"You really think that's the kind of person she is? That she can go from being with you to being with someone else in the blink of an eye?"

"She did it, didn't she?" he glanced over his shoulder at her.

Nicole stepped into his office and marched over to him, grabbed his arm and forced him to look at her. "You're being a jackass, and for once, I mean that in the truest sense of the word," her finger stabbed him in the chest for emphasis. "Let me tell you something you don't know, Mr. 'I Always Have To Be Right'. Dusty Rhodes is married, and has been for years. He married his college sweetheart and according to Bayleigh, Dusty and Jade have one of those fairytale romances. He worships the ground Jade walks on and would never do anything to cause her any kind of pain. There has never been any hint of him screwing around on her. Ever." She stepped back from him as he turned to face her fully.

"So why did she leave with him, knowing what I thought?"

"Because you kicked her out, dumb ass! You accused her of cheating on you and wouldn't talk to her about it. You are making her pay for what Diana did to you and Bayleigh knows it! She's not going to stick around and let you dump more of that blame on her, when she didn't do anything wrong!" Nicole threw her hands up and moved over to sit on the couch. "Do you love her, Jack?"

He released a heavy sigh and moved over to sit on the couch beside her. "I thought I was falling in love with her.

Maybe. I don't know anymore, Nicole. I can't get past what I saw!"

"I don't know what you saw, Jack. But you got it wrong. Very wrong."

"He was kissing her!"

"How was he kissing her, Jack? Was it a passionate kiss between two lovers, or a peck on the cheek? Or did you even have a clear line of sight and you're assuming things and flying off the handle based on the actions of a gold-digging ex-fiancé bitch?" Nicole pressed on.

Jack's face went white as her words registered. "I'm a jackass," he groaned.

"I've been telling you that for years," Nicole agreed without hesitation.

Jack's head dropped back against the back of the couch. "How do I fix this, Nicole?"

"You go after her, Jack. You tell her you were wrong. You ask for forgiveness." She stood up and moved towards the doorway, stopping to look back at him. "You grovel, my friend. Just like Jason and I did with each other a year ago. And you pray like hell that she is willing to take another chance on you."

"When did you get so smart?"

"I've always been smart. Just took you a while to realize it," she gave him a smile and went back to her own office.

Jack stayed on the couch and stared at the ceiling, thinking back over what he'd seen. He'd been so shocked to see another man so close to Bayleigh, and then Dusty had leaned in to kiss her. Jack groaned as he admitted to himself that Nicole was right. He hadn't had a clear line of sight and it could have just been a peck on the cheek.

Jack forced himself to his feet and stepped over to his desk and grabbed his keys. "Hey, Nicole. I need to leave for the rest of the day!" he called out as he walked out of his office and into the hallway.

"Okay," she stepped up to her office door, almost as if she'd been waiting just on the other side. "When will you be back?"

"When I convince Bayleigh to come back with me. Can you hold down the fort?"

"That long?" she raised her eyebrows but held up a hand as he started to answer her. "I can manage. Go get your girl. I'll call you if anything urgent comes up," she promised, stepping into the hallway to give him a hug. "Good luck!"

"I think I'm going to need it," he muttered as he hurried through the office.

CHAPTER 24

*B*ayleigh sighed in frustration and set her guitar down on the couch beside her, leaning forward to stare at the lyrics she'd been working on for three days. Tossing her pen down on top of the notebook, she collapsed back against the cushions, leaning her head back to stare at the ceiling.

"Hey, taking a break?" Maddie asked her as she walked into the room, carrying a plate with a sandwich on it. "I bought you a sandwich at the deli while I was there," she set it down on the table next to the notebook.

"You have to be working in order for it to qualify as a break," Bayleigh muttered as she sat up and reached for the sandwich, taking a huge bite. She glanced at the clock over the door and frowned at the time. "I didn't realize it was getting so late."

"Not like you got anywhere to be tonight. Lyrics still giving you trouble?" Maddie picked up the notebook to take a look.

"Hard to find words that rhyme with 'rat bastard', let

alone make that phrase part of a love song," Bayleigh took another bite of the sandwich before setting it aside before she pushed herself to her feet, reaching down for her coffee cup. "Shouldn't you be heading to the bar?"

"That's what assistant managers are for. They get to open and close for me when I decide I don't want to do it." Maddie grinned. "Look, you need a night away from your music. Come with me to the bar. Dusty and Jade might stop by. Maybe you'll get inspired by their love for each other."

"Lack of inspiration isn't my issue, it's the desire to kill the person who inspired it," Bayleigh took a sip of her coffee, grimacing when she realized it was cold. "I mean, how do you write a love song when all you want to do is physically maim someone?"

"So write a song about that, instead. Get it out of your system so we can go get drunk and find you a new man," Maddie advised as she gathered up the crumpled up pieces of paper on the table.

Bayleigh shook her head as she reached down to pick up the sandwich plate. "I'm done with men. Men are trouble. I'm going to find myself my own little house and start adopting stray cats."

"You're allergic to cats," Maddie reminded her as she followed her into the kitchen, tossing the discarded balls of paper into the trashcan.

"So go buy stock in Benadryl and I'll make you rich with my allergies," Bayleigh dumped her cold coffee down the sink, rinsed out the mug and placed it in the dishwasher.

"I've already got enough money to live the life I want,"

Maddie pointed out as she leaned against the counter. "So, you going to come out with me to the bar?"

"Do I have a choice?" Bayleigh quirked an eyebrow at her friend.

"No, not really," Maddie shook her head. "I've let you wallow in your own misery long enough. Time to get back out there, girl!"

"I have not been wallowing!" Bayleigh denied, sticking her tongue out at her friend. "And it's only been a week since I left Texas!"

"Then prove that you're not wallowing! Come to the bar tonight. It's open mic night. You can sing one of your songs and see how it goes over," Maddie implored.

Bayleigh closed her eyes with a heavy sigh. "If I go, will you leave me alone for a few days, then?"

Maddie turned to leave the room but paused at the door to the hallway. "No promises, but I'll try," she wiggled her eyebrows before ducking around the corner.

Bayleigh shook her head and pushed herself away from the counter, resigned to taking a shower and washing her hair and putting on make-up. Sometimes, having a best friend who was an extrovert and just happened to own a bar could be torture sometimes.

BAYLEIGH CLAIMED a seat at the far end of the bar, away from the stage and the crowd around it. She lifted a hand in greeting to the bartender, who'd worked there for as long as she could remember. Names were not his strong point, but if you were there often enough, he knew what your favorite drink was.

"Well, look what the cat dragged in," a booming voice behind her had her jumping in her seat.

"Jesus, Rick. A simple 'Hi' would have been fine!" she turned and gave him a mock glare.

"Maybe, but not nearly as fun," the man winked at her as he leaned over and kissed her cheek before he slid onto the stool beside her. "Why are you hiding back here?"

"Maddie dragged me out here tonight to try and get me out of my funk. I never promised her I would mingle." She picked up the glass of white wine the bartender put in front of her. "Thanks, Tommy."

"Anytime. Usual for you, Rick?"

Rick nodded and glanced around the crowded bar. "She really packs it in on open mic night, doesn't she?"

"Everyone knows she has connections in the business," Bayleigh agreed with a shrug. "It only takes that one song to grab someone's attention and get that deal, right?"

"That's what they say," Rick picked up his beer when Tommy set it in front of him. "So, do I get to hear that song tonight?"

Bayleigh swiveled on her bar stool so she was facing Rick. "What do I get out of it, if I swallow down my fear and actually get up on that stage and sing tonight?"

"You're among friends, what do you have to be afraid of?"

Bayleigh drained her wine glass and held it up to get Tommy's attention, turning herself away from Rick once again. "It's been a year since I got on stage, Rick. And even longer since I was on one by myself," her eyes met Rick's. "The stage was never my life, it was Will's. I just wanted to write the music. But lately, even that's not working out so well," she muttered, turning herself away from Rick once again.

Rick reached over and took her hand in his. Bayleigh clasped it with a death grip as she closed her eyes for a second. "Rick, the last time I tried to get on stage, I had a flashback and a full-blown panic attack backstage. There is no backstage here. If I go into one of my panic attacks, everyone will see it."

Rick nodded, his arm settling across her shoulders, his thumb moving across her knuckles as he looked around the crowded bar. "What if I sat in front, with Brian and maybe we could even coax Dusty to sit up there with us? Would that help?"

"Is Dusty even here? I haven't seen him." Bayleigh's gaze wandered the room, trying to find her friend. "And where's Brian?"

"Brian is sitting with Dusty over in the corner booth in the shadows. We snuck him and Jade in through the kitchen. He's trying to keep a low profile for now. He doesn't want to upstage anyone who's brave enough to get up there tonight." Rick picked up his beer bottle, tipping it towards her in a salute. "We all came out to support you."

Bayleigh stared at him, surprised. "Why?"

"Why, what?" Rick's brow furrowed.

"Why do you care so much, about me and a song I wrote, I mean?"

Rick drained his beer and glanced around the room again. "Because you mean a lot to Maddie and she's really concerned that you're not going to come back from this. And I don't mean the break-up with Will or whatever happened with that dumb asshole in Texas..."

"He's not a dumb asshole," Bayleigh protested, the denial automatic even though it was one of the nicer names she herself had been calling Jack.

"Well, he ain't too smart if he let you get away," Rick pointed out with a raised eyebrow. "So, who are you going to let win? That fucker in England who owned the bar, that dumbass Will, or Maddie and her pushiness?"

Bayleigh laughed and leaned over to kiss his cheek before sliding off her barstool. "Go find a spot up front and you'll find out when I do, I guess."

"Where are you going?" Rick stopped her with a hand on her wrist.

"I'm going to go talk to Dusty and see if he can't give me a better pep talk than that one," Bayleigh gave him a look before she turned and glanced towards the large corner booth that was hidden in shadows. "I evidently have something to prove tonight."

"Now you're talking!" Rick gave her a wink as he motioned to Tommy for a fresh beer. "Brian and I will be standing up there front and center for you. You just keep your eyes on us, and you'll be fine, sweetheart."

"Thanks, Rick," Bayleigh blew him a kiss as she walked away to find Dusty and Jade in their corner booth.

"How IN THE hell did I get talked into this?" Bayleigh glanced around the crowded bar as she waited to take her turn on stage. She was hiding with Dusty in the shadows at his corner booth.

Dusty grinned at her from across the table. "Because

you love me and Maddie and you know how much this means to both of us."

"That may be, but I'm seriously considering running out the back door! What the hell was I thinking?" Bayleigh propped her head up with hands. "I can't do it, guys. I think I'm going to be sick," she muttered, looking around again.

"You're not going to be sick. You're going to pull your big girl panties up and suck it up and get out there and sing that song!"

Jade shook her head at her husband and reached across the table to put her hand on Bayleigh's arm. "You'll be fine, hon. We're going to sit here and watch and cheer you on, and if you freeze, I'll push Dusty out of this booth and he can join you up there."

Dusty caught Maddie's signal from the stage that it was time for Bayleigh to head over and he slid out of the booth, holding his hand towards her to help her slide out. He wrapped his arm around her shoulders and pulled her against his side. "You'll be fine, Bayleigh. Take a deep breath and relax. You're among friends here tonight," he reminded her "You ready to rock this place?"

Bayleigh nodded, a slight grimace crossing her features. "As I'll ever be," she muttered, pasting a wide smile on her face as she watched Maddie walk onto the stage and give the lead singer of the band that had just performed a hug. She made her way along the edge of the crowd and stood at the foot of the steps leading to the stage, waiting for Maddie to introduce her.

"Let's give The Rustler's one last round of applause!" Maddie adjusted the mic stand as she glanced over and made eye contact with Bayleigh. After a slight hesitation, Bayleigh swallowed hard and nodded.

"Now, as you all know, I love to give up and coming singers and songwriters a shot at the limelight on my stage. Well, tonight I'm going to finish off the night a little different. A very good friend of mine left Nashville for a few years and kind of forgot what her music meant to so many of us. Well, tonight she is here, and I talked her into getting up on this stage and showing us what she's got in store for Nashville now that she is back! So, please give a warm welcome to Bayleigh Morrow!" Maddie stepped back from the mic as Bayleigh walked across the stage to the loud applause.

"You're going to be great," Maddie whispered to her as she hugged her tight. "You've got this, girl!"

Bayleigh smiled at her friend. "Just promise you'll hide me somewhere for a few years if I faint or panic, or do something else equally embarrassing up here tonight."

"That's not going to be necessary but if assurances are what you need, you know I've always got your back," Maddie gave her a wink and turned to walk offstage.

Bayleigh looked around the room, her gaze finding and holding Rick's for a moment as she stepped up to the mic, taking a moment to readjust it. With a subtle nod to let him know she was holding it together so far, she took a deep breath and looked up to face the rest of the crowd.

"Thanks, everyone. It's been great to be back in Nashville these last few weeks. I've been busy trying to write some songs, and with the help of an old friend, I've actually completed a couple. This one I'm going to sing for you tonight has already been spoken for by a great guy who wants to include it on his next album. So pay attention and you might just be hearing it on the radio soon!"

Bayleigh adjusted her guitar strap around her neck as she strummed the opening notes to the song she'd finished with Dusty the day before. She let the notes wash over her and lost herself to the music.

It had been a long time since Bayleigh had felt this excitement, this joy, in bringing the music to life. She had poured her heart into writing this song; all the heartache and pain she'd been feeling the last few weeks had come out while she and Dusty had been working on it. If she had any desire to be a performer, this song would be way too personal to give away to anyone else.

Less than five minutes later, the applause was thunderous as the last notes faded away. Bayleigh opened her eyes and looked towards where her friends were standing. Dusty had left the safety of his shadowed booth and was standing just in front of it. He caught her eye and gave her a thumbs up, the grin on his face telling her all she needed to know.

As she turned back towards the crowd, a figure standing near towards the back of the room caught her attention. Maybe it was the cowboy hat he had on, but something about him made her think of Jack. Bayleigh squinted, trying to see through the haze the bright stage lights cast over the room but whoever it had been faded into the crowd and Bayleigh lost sight of him.

She raised her hand in acknowledgement of the crowd as she stepped back from the mic and released the guitar strap from around her neck. Maddie stepped back onto the stage, stopping Bayleigh's exit with a hand on her arm.

"I told you, you didn't need anyone to hide you. You nailed it!" Maddie gave her a quick hug before she released her friend and stepped up to the mic once again.

Bayleigh heaved a sigh of relief as she set the guitar down that she'd borrowed and moved offstage as Maddie introduced her house band to finish up the night of live music. She grinned when she saw Rick standing at the bottom of the steps, waiting for her.

"You did good, kiddo." Rick told her as he held out his hand to help her down the steps. "Feeling okay?"

"I feel like I need a shot of something stronger than wine," Bayleigh told him, accepting his hand as he led her back to the corner booth Dusty had been hiding out in all evening. She was a little amazed no one had figured out who was hiding there tonight, but didn't hesitate to take advantage of the anonymity of it.

"That little performance calls for a celebration! We need tequila!" Jade raised her hand and waved one of the servers over, asking for the best tequila Maddie stocked and all the extras needed to do shots.

Dusty turned towards Bayleigh as she slid into the booth. "You rocked that song. Still sure you want to give it up?"

"I'm positive. I have no desire to be up on that stage any more than necessary!" Bayleigh told him as the waiter returned with the tequila and shot glasses. She laughed as Jade quickly set up the shots for everyone to do.

"How drunk is she?" she asked Dusty.

"Not very. No one has recognized me yet and for once, we're getting to have a true date night." Dusty picked up the shot glass his wife set in front of him and raised an eyebrow at her. "I'm not going down alone, you know."

"I'll do one shot, that's it," Bayleigh agreed with a laugh, reaching for her own shot glass. "You know I'm not into tequila shots."

"No, but I remember those Jell-O shots Maddie used to make and how you'd put them away."

"Yeah, back when I was in college and didn't care how I felt the next day," Bayleigh grinned at Rick as he slid into the booth on her other side. "Bottoms up, boys!" she slid another glass in front of Rick, as Maddie slid in on his other side. Maddie shook her head as she took in the shot glasses, but reached for one of her own.

Jade glanced around the table to make sure everyone had a shot glass. "Okay, everyone ready? Remember how to do this? On three...lick, salt and...go!" Jade called out as they all licked the salt off the back of their hands and tossed back the shots of tequila and reached for the lemons.

"God, I hate tequila," she shuddered as she and Rick both set their glasses on the table, stuffing the used lemons into them. Jade laughed at them as she set up the next round for her and Dusty.

"Yeah, can't say I'm a fan, either," Rick agreed, his eyes roaming over the crowd. "So, not trying to put a damper on things here, or scare you, but I noticed a guy watching you while you were getting ready to go on stage, and I don't think his eyes ever left you while you were up there singing." He tilted his head in a brief nod to his right. "He's over against the wall again, staring at all of us, but I'd bet his eyes are watching you more than us. Any idea of who he is or do Brian and I need to pay him a visit?"

Bayleigh shifted in her seat so she could see who Rick was talking about. "Well, shit," she muttered, drawing back into the shadows once again. "What the hell is he doing here?"

"Who's here?" Brian asked as he stepped up to the table.

"That guy holding up the wall," Rick's eyes flicked back to the stranger as Brian also shifted to see around everyone.

"Isn't that the dipshit you left in Texas?" Brian asked, turning back around to face Bayleigh.

"That's Jack? Holy hell, he's hot," Maddie told her as she caught sight of who they were talking about.

Bayleigh groaned and buried her face in her hands. "I was hoping it wasn't," she muttered.

"You knew he was here?" Dusty glanced at her, surprise evident in his voice. "Jack's here? Should I go talk to him, try and set things straight?"

"I saw a guy when I finished singing that I thought reminded me of Jack, but I didn't get a good look at him. I was hoping it was just a coincidence. And no, I don't want you to go talk to him." Bayleigh picked her head up and looked across the table at her friend. "You're trying to maintain a low profile tonight, remember?"

"Do you want one of us to get rid of him?" Rick asked, indicating himself and Brian by jerking his thumb between them.

Bayleigh shook her head. "No, I don't want a scene. Just get me out of here so I can go back to the apartment."

"I'll go talk to him. Take her out through the kitchen," Brian told his friend, stepping back from the booth.

"Brian, I mean it. No scenes!" Bayleigh hissed at him

before he walked away. He raised his hand in acknowledgement as he walked towards Jack.

"Bayleigh, you sure? I mean, he came all this way to see you," Jade reached across the table and put her hand on Bayleigh's arm.

"Then he can wait another day or two. Because right now, I don't trust myself not to hurt him," Bayleigh told her friend as Dusty chuckled beside his wife.

"Leave it alone, Jade. Bayleigh knows what she's doing. No Regrets, right, kiddo?"

"Way to throw my own song back at me, Dusty," Bayleigh gave her friend a smile. "I'm not saying I won't talk to him, Jade. I'm just saying I can't right now," Bayleigh told her friend before turning to look at Rick and Maddie. "I'm ready to go while Brian has him distracted."

"I'll meet you in the kitchen. Just let me tell Tommy I'm out of here," Maddie slid out of the booth and headed towards the bar and her assistant manager.

"Okay, let's see if we can get you out of here without him seeing you," Rick slid out of the booth, using his size to block any view Jack might have had of the table. Using the crowd to his advantage, he led the way to the kitchen where they met Maddie.

"You sure you want to leave?" Maddie asked her as she led the way out to her car.

"I'm sure," Bayleigh nodded her head. "If and when I talk to him, it will be in private, not in a bar where a thousand strangers are around to hear it, and not when Dusty is around to grab everyone's attention and have some trade rag run a story on it just because he happened to be here.

Last thing he and Jade need is someone to start a rumor that he's cheating on her with me."

"I'll make sure Dusty stays away from him, and Brian will keep Jack occupied for a few minutes so you two can get out of here. Text me when you get back to the apartment," Rick told Maddie as he opened her driver's door for her.

Maddie rolled her eyes as she slid behind the wheel. "I'm a big girl, Rick. I can take care of myself."

"I know. Doesn't mean I can't care, though." Rick told her, looking across the seat to Bayleigh as she slammed her door. "Make her text me."

"One of us will text you, Rick. Thanks for getting me out of there," Bayleigh shook her head at the interaction between the two.

"Drive safe," Rick instructed, stepping back from the vehicle as Maddie started the engine.

"When are you two going to stop dancing around each other and just get together?" Bayleigh asked as Maddie pulled out of the parking lot and headed towards her apartment complex.

"When Satan orders a ski lift," Maddie told her, cutting across two lanes of traffic and taking a sharp right turn.

"You ever going to tell me what happened between you two?"

"Nothing ever happened, nothing ever will. He's still mad that I didn't listen to him about Nicholas," Maddie shrugged as she pulled up to the security gate for the apartment complex.

"The way he is around you, though...Maddie, I don't

think it's anger," Bayleigh shook her head as her friend parked the SUV.

"He's just still overly protective of me, like he is with you."

Bayleigh pursed her lips. "No, he's different with you. Maybe you need to take some of your own advice. Quit running from him all the time."

"Yeah, well, easy enough for you to say. You're not the one who made such a complete mess of your life."

"Really, Maddie? You want to start arguing over who screwed up more?" Bayleigh raised an eyebrow.

"I'm the one who got pregnant by a two-timing jackass!"

"I'm the one who left the country with a two-timing jackass, almost got raped and didn't tell her own brother, not even when I was alone in a hospital bed with a broken leg needing surgery to put pins in it!" Bayleigh reminded her.

Maddie sighed and leaned her head against the head-rest. "So now what?"

"Beats me. I just ran out of a bar trying to avoid my problem," Bayleigh reminded her, grabbing her purse and opening the SUV's door. "If either one of us were drinkers, I'd say let's go get ripped."

Maddie laughed as she exited the vehicle. "If we were going to do that, we should have stayed at the bar. Selection of alcohol is much better!"

Bayleigh laughed as they headed for Maddie's apart-ment. "We could always call Rick, have him bring a couple of bottles over."

"The idea has merit," Maddie let them into the apartment and tossed her keys on the small table by the door. "It's been a long day. I'll stay up and chat if you need to, but I'm exhausted and I'm not sure how much I'll be able to process, or for how much longer."

"You go on to bed. I'm ready to crash, too," Bayleigh admitted, smiling over at her friend. "Who's going to text Rick?"

"I'll do it," Maddie double checked the lock and her security system and said good night.

Bayleigh went towards her own room, pulling her phone out of her pocket as it buzzed with an incoming text message.

I was wrong. I just want to talk. Please call me ~ Jack

Bayleigh stared at the message, her fingers hovering over the delete button. With a sigh, she typed out a message and hit send before she could talk herself out of it. She quickly changed into her pajamas and then slid into bed. This was not a night sleep would come easy for her, she knew.

CHAPTER 25

*B*ayleigh slept in the next morning, waiting until almost nine before she left the safety of her room. She was sitting at the kitchen table with her coffee mug, staring out the window but not seeing anything. When Maddie entered the room and said her name, she was so startled, she jumped, almost dumping her hot coffee in her lap.

"'Leigh, your phone has been ringing for the last thirty minutes! Please, either answer it or turn it off!" Maddie set the phone on the table beside her. She stood beside her friend's chair, studying her. "Did you get any sleep?"

"Not much. I kept thinking about what I should do about Jack," Bayleigh picked up her coffee but set it down again without taking a sip.

"And what did you decide? Because I'm guessing that's who is calling every five minutes this morning," Maddie poured herself a cup of coffee and joined her friend at the table.

Bayleigh glanced at the call log and nodded. "Yes, it's

him. And one from Jason." She buried her face in her hands. "I haven't decided anything, yet."

"But you love him, right?"

Bayleigh nodded without looking up. "Yeah, more than I've ever loved anyone else before."

"So, what are you going to do about that?"

"I don't know, Maddie," Bayleigh finally looked up. "He's the one who was wrong, not me."

"Well, if he's trying to ask for you to forgive him, he's not going to get very far if you don't answer your phone," Maddie pointed out as the phone began to ring again. She raised an eyebrow as Bayleigh declined the call.

Bayleigh shook her head as she caught her friend's look. "Jack texted me last night after we got back here. He says he's sorry and he wants to talk." She sighed heavily as her phone beeped with a voice message. "I'm not ready to talk to him, Maddie."

"Do you believe him? That he's sorry, I mean."

"Me trusting and believing him wasn't the issue, remember?" There was a note of bitterness in Bayleigh's voice.

Maddie nodded and leaned back in her chair, watching her friend from across the table. "Okay, here's the deal. I'm not going to give you any other details, and you're not allowed to ask questions. But let me put it to you this way," Maddie waited until she was sure she had Bayleigh's attention.

"Do you want to be like me and Rick? Always knowing the chance was there and you blew it? And then being too much of a coward to ask for another chance?" Maddie pushed her chair back from the table and stood up.

"So it's not just that you wouldn't listen to him about Nicholas?" Bayleigh asked, narrowing her gaze.

Maddie sighed heavily, remembering what she'd told her friend the night before. "Not entirely, no. And that's all you're getting!"

"But what do I do, Maddie? It's not like I'm the one who needs to be forgiven. I can't throw myself at his feet and beg him to take me back and forgive me, now can I?"

"No, but you're not giving him the chance to do it, either." Maddie pointed out as she walked towards the doorway.

"So you think I should talk to him?"

Maddie paused and looked back at her friend. "That, my friend, is a decision only you can make for yourself. I'm just pointing out that you are at a crossroads and you have to decide which way to go." She glanced at her own phone in her hand as it buzzed. "And now Brian is texting me that I need to call him. You up for going to the bar with me again tonight?"

"I'll check my calendar, make sure I don't have anything more pressing," Bayleigh told her and laughed as Maddie gave her the finger. "What time do I need to be ready to leave?"

"Around four, I guess. It's a Saturday night, so I like to go in a bit earlier than I normally do. Or I can see if Brian and Rick are going to be there. I'm sure one of them will give you a ride, if you want."

"I can ride in with you. If I decide to cut out, you can get them to give you a ride home," Bayleigh raised her eyebrows when her friend's gaze narrowed. "What?"

"No matchmaking," Maddie warned, her eyes still narrowed.

"Of course not," Bayleigh tried to look innocent and knew from her friend's expression she was failing. "Fine, I'll stick around the bar until all hours of the night."

"You could always take the stage," Maddie suggested as she headed down the hall to her room.

"Not bloody likely," Bayleigh muttered to her friend's back as she finished off her coffee. Glancing at the clock, she decided to try and take a nap before she had to get ready to leave with Maddie. At least tonight she could just claim her seat and the bar and stay there.

CHAPTER 26

ayleigh had managed to snag a table across from the bar and in a corner. Rick and Brian had joined her as soon as they'd arrived. Brian had brought Kaitlyn, his on-again, off-again girlfriend, and Rick was busy trying to talk Maddie into joining them. Maddie and Kaitlyn were busy trying to scope the room for a man for Bayleigh.

Bayleigh shook her head as she watched a young man approach Maddie. Her gaze narrowed as Maddie started nodding enthusiastically and pointed towards their table.

"Rick, I swear to God, if she's sending him over here to talk to me, you'd better be prepared for me to crawl into your lap and start making out with you," Bayleigh muttered as the man started making his way to their table.

Rick set his drink down and shook his head. "I can think of a few worse things," he winked at her as a shadow fell over the table. Brian's eyes went wide as he took in the man standing next to their table.

"Miss Morrow? I'm David Wilson, one of the signing

agents for Nashville Music House. Have you heard of us?"
He held his hand out to shake hers and then handed her a
business card he withdrew from his pocket.

Bayleigh tilted her head to the side as she reached out
to take the card. "I've heard of your company. What can I
help you with?"

"I happened to be here last night and I heard your song.
You have a lot of talent."

"Thank you." Bayleigh dipped her head in acknowledgement.

"Now, I understand Dusty Rhodes has already
optioned that song from you, but with talent like yours,
there's bound to be a whole portfolio sitting around waiting
for someone to snatch it up. Am I right?"

Bayleigh glanced towards Maddie who was still
standing near the bar. "I'm not sure I'd say I have a whole
portfolio, but yes, I have written other songs," she answered
the man in front of her.

"I'm interested in hearing them, if you're interested in
selling them. If you've heard of us, then you are aware of
the caliber of the artists we pitch to," he nodded at the card
in her hand. "You have my card. My assistant will be glad
to set up an appointment for you, if you call her."

"Thank you, Mr. Wilson. I will think about it."
Bayleigh nodded, as she glanced at the card in her hand.

"You do that. It was a pleasure to meet you."

"Same here, Mr. Wilson."

Bayleigh looked around the table at her friends as the
other man walked away. "You guys can pick your chins up
off the floor now," she told them with a laugh.

"Bayleigh, that man is one of the top recruiters for his

music publishing house! He pitches music to all the big names in Nashville, on like a daily basis!" Kaitlyn told her, leaning forward to make sure Bayleigh could hear her.

"I know who he is. I saw him sitting here last night," Bayleigh admitted.

"Then how can you sit here and simply say you'll call him? I would have been pulling out songs left and right on the spot to sell to him!" Kaitlyn shook her head in disbelief.

"Yeah, for someone who's been dipping their toes in the water for a decade, you're awfully calm," Brian agreed, looking across at her.

Bayleigh forced herself to unclasp her hands and hold them up to show everyone how much she was shaking. Rick laughed and nudged her shoulder with his. "You and your poker face," he shook his head.

"Now, someone please tell me I didn't stutter or say something stupid, please? Please tell me I didn't just blow it?"

"You were calm, cool and collected. I would say you nailed it," Brian told her with a wink as his sister joined them.

"Holy shit, 'Leigh! I about died when David Wilson approached me! Did he make the offer right here?"

"No, he told me to call his office and set up an appointment." Bayleigh looked over at her friend. "You didn't set this up, did you?"

"No, I swear! I knew he was here last night but I thought he had left before you took the stage," Maddie insisted as she took the seat between Bayleigh and Kaitlyn. "How can you be sitting here and not freaking out? One of the biggest recruiters in Nashville just told you he is interested in your songs!"

Bayleigh laughed and out her hand for her friend to see. "I'm freaking out on the inside, see?"

Maddie took Bayleigh's hand and squeezed it. "Well, this calls for a celebration, don't you think?"

"Anything but tequila," Bayleigh agreed.

"How about a shot of Jack?" a voice asked from above them. Bayleigh froze and glanced up at the man who'd stepped up to the table.

"Jack," her whisper was lost in the noise of the bar. She wasn't positive, but she was pretty sure her heart had just skipped a beat. Bayleigh squared her shoulders and stared at the man standing beside the table.

"I think I'd rather take a shot *at* Jack. Got your pistol on you?" she asked Rick. She caught the grin that Brian was quick to cover.

"Do you want us to make him leave?" Rick asked her as he eyed Jack, distrust evident on his face.

Bayleigh swallowed hard and looked at her friends, her eyes locking onto Maddie, who gave her an encouraging smile. "Time to pick which road, I guess. But I can have him tossed if you want me to," Maddie leaned in closer to whisper for Bayleigh's ears alone.

Bayleigh shook her head and looked towards Jack. "No, I'll talk to him. Could you guys give us a few minutes, please?"

"You sure?" Rick looked between the two.

Brian clapped his friend on the back and pulled him to his feet. "C'mon buddy. You can be a watchdog from a stool at the bar. Let's go figure out what Maddie has hidden behind the bar that we can pilfer from as a celebration."

Bayleigh smiled her thanks at her friends and watched as Jack settled himself in the chair across from her. "What are you doing here?" she asked him, the smile fading from her features.

Jack cleared his throat and looked down at her hands clasped together on the table before he raised his eyes back to her. ""Baby, I've missed you so much. I can't tell you how sorry I am that I pushed you away. I drove all day to get here yesterday."

Bayleigh swallowed hard. "And that's supposed to make it all better now?"

"No, but it's supposed to at least let me get a foot back in the door," Jack admitted. "Jason and Nicole pounded it into me before I left Texas that apologizing was only the first step of many I would need to take if I wanted to win you back. Nicole assured me there would be a lot of begging and pleading involved as well, at least on my part. But I guess you're the one who has to decide if I'm worth another chance. I was so wrong to say what I did to you," Jack's voice was rough with emotion.

"Wrong about what, exactly?" Bayleigh steeled herself against the emotion. *Be tough*, she told herself.

Jack leaned forward, a hand near hers but not quite touching her. He stared down at their hands but didn't speak. Bayleigh could feel her heart rate increasing just from his nearness. She loved this man, more than anything, but if he didn't trust her, there was no hope.

Jack's eyes raised and met hers. "I was wrong about pushing you away, forcing you to leave, not talking to you for days, and assuming that Dusty was more than just a friend. All of it, Bayleigh. Everything and anything that made you leave me. I'm sorry for all of it."

Bayleigh pressed her lips together. It would be so easy to just accept it and ignore the hurt that was still so raw and fresh. But she'd always done that with Will, and look at the mess her life had turned into.

"And the next time an old friend greets me with a hug or a kiss?" she asked him, her eyes straying to see her friends at the bar.

"I'll hang around, get an introduction." Jack moved his hand a fraction of inch, still not touching her, but she could feel the heat of his hand now. "Bayleigh, I have so many issues when it comes to women. My therapist had a field day with me this week when I went in to talk to her." Jack moved his hand closer so that he could reach out and touch her with one finger.

Bayleigh looked down at their hands before looking back at him. "How does that make it right?"

"It doesn't and I'm not trying to make excuses. I just know I can't lose you," he covered her hand with his. "Please tell me I haven't completely fucked this up," he begged.

Bayleigh took a deep breath and looked away. She saw Rick and Maddie together at the bar, so completely perfect for each other but for whatever reason, unable to get past their complicated history and be together. And then there was Brian and Kaitlyn, another match made in heaven, but the two of them were still working their way through hell to get to each other. She thought of her brother and Nicole and all they'd gone through before reconnecting.

Bayleigh could see Maddie watching her from the bar and remembered the conversation she'd had with her earlier. She was standing at that crossroads now and she needed to pick which direction she would be heading. One path would be with Jack at her side, maybe not forever, but at least for now. The other was without him and alone. "*Some choice,*" she thought as her focus returned to Jack.

"I don't know what I want to do, Jack. I need time to think."

Jack took a deep breath and nodded, his eyes never leaving hers. "I won't give up, Bayleigh. I know I screwed up. I know I hurt you." He glanced over at her friends and then around the bar. "I also know we're not going to solve everything between us tonight in a crowded bar with your friends watching every move. Can I take you somewhere more private?"

Bayleigh's eyes traveled the same path Jack's had just a moment before. She took a deep breath and looked across the table at him. "I think I need time alone to process, Jack," she saw the hurt in his eyes. "I just got out of a relationship with a guy who didn't care about what I wanted, who tried to control me and who my friends were. I can't go back to that. I won't go back to something like that," Bayleigh swallowed past the lump in her throat. "I need to make sure I'm doing what's right for me now."

Jack took a deep breath and nodded. "I've got a hotel downtown for a few days. Can I at least call you?" he reached across the table and cupped her cheek with his palm. "I just miss you, Bay."

Bayleigh closed her eyes and gave a short nod. "I'm not making any promises," she warned as she opened her eyes and looked into his. "You can call me as long as you're not trying to pressure me."

"I promise, no pressure," he agreed in an instant. He glanced over at the bar again. "So, what's Rick story? Why the watchdog attitude?"

"He's overly protective of me and Maddie. And if you think he's a watchdog with me, you should see him with Maddie," Bayleigh looked at her friends and shook her head. "One of these days, those two are either going to spontaneously combust around each other or kill each other," she looked back at Jack. "You're welcome to hang around with us tonight, if you'd like, but I'm not sure what kind of reception you're going to get from them."

Jack sighed with regret and leaned back. "I know, and I can't say I blame them. But if it means time with you, I will put up with any attitude they want to dish out." He knew he'd at least gotten that answer right when she smiled.

Bayleigh turned and waved her friends back over. Maddie slid back into the chair next to her and bumped shoulders with her friend. "Everything okay?"

"I'm trying to pick a path," Bayleigh muttered back, accepting the glass of wine Rick held out to her. She noticed Brian had grabbed a beer for Jack. "I'm not going anywhere anytime soon, though."

"Ah, playing hard to get. Good plan," Maddie teased, clinking her own wine glass against Bayleigh's. "Make him work for that forgiveness."

"I'm not playing games, Maddie," Bayleigh denied, her voice pitched low to prevent it from carrying across the table. "I just need more time."

Maddie nodded and gave her friend's arm a sympathetic squeeze. "I know, sweetie." Maddie's gaze flicked to Rick before coming back to Bayleigh. "Just be careful. Time doesn't always work in your favor."

"One of these days, you're going to tell me that whole story," Bayleigh told her, shaking her head.

"Maybe when I'm ninety," Maddie agreed, shaking her head. "So, 'Leigh, any chance I can get you back up stage tonight?" she asked, raising her voice.

"Hell, no. One near panic attack a week is enough," Bayleigh shot the idea down with a laugh. "Your band can provide the entertainment tonight,"

Bayleigh was able to relax and enjoy the evening with her friends, not quite ignoring Jack, but not being overly attentive either. Rick and Brian talked business with him, discussing different aspects of the legal system while she, Maddie, and Kaitlyn dissected different people in the bar.

Bayleigh glanced at her watch, surprised to see how late it was getting. She and Dusty were supposed to meet the next morning at his studio so she could work on some songs with him. She tapped Maddie's arm and pointed at her watch.

"I have that session with Dusty in the morning. I need to get going," she pushed her chair back and looked around the table. "Sorry to break it up, guys, but I need to head back to the apartment."

"Do you need to take my car? Brian or Rick will give me a ride, right guys?" Maddie asked them.

"Of course. Unless you want one of us to drive you home, 'Leigh," Rick agreed.

"No, I'll be fine taking Maddie's car," Bayleigh stood up

and grabbed her purse, checking to make sure she'd tucked her phone inside.

"I'll walk you out," Jack stood up as well. "I think I'm ready to call it a night as well."

"I'll try to keep the noise level to a minimum when I get home," Maddie told her with a grin. Being a night owl, Maddie sometimes forgot others didn't share her nocturnal habits.

Bayleigh grinned back at her and said her goodnights to everyone else at the table. She turned to walk out, Jack at her side. She led the way over to her car and hit the button on the key fob to unlock it. After she opened the door, she turned to face him.

"Thank you," she told him, resting one hand on the car door.

"For what?" he quirked an eyebrow.

"Staying and getting to know my friends, even though they were a little on the rude side at first," she gave him a small smile.

"It's okay, I understood. I'm glad you have friends who look out for you," Jack stepped in closer to her. "I'm glad you let me stay," he whispered, as his hand came up to cup her face, his thumb caressing her cheek. "I'm going to kiss you."

Bayleigh's eyes widened as he announced his intentions but didn't step away or try to stop him. Her eyes closed as his mouth closed over hers. His scent enveloped her and she moaned, sinking into his kiss. Her hands fisted against his chest as she lost herself in the moment. *This is what I missed,* she thought to herself, kissing him back.

"Come back to my hotel with me," he invited between kisses.

Bayleigh tore her mouth from his, dragging in a ragged breath. "I can't, Jack," she pushed against his chest and he took a step back. Bayleigh felt the chill in the air as she lost his body heat. She inhaled and forced herself to look him in the eye. "I've let my emotions rule me for far too long. The first twenty-two years of my life, I did whatever my parents asked of me, including going to college and getting a degree. Then, it was all about Will and his band, and keeping the peace. I need this time alone, Jack, to make sure that I'm doing what *I* need for a change."

Jack took another step away from her and nodded. "I'm not giving up, Bayleigh."

Bayleigh took a step back towards him, her hand reaching up to cup his face. "I'm not asking you to, Jack. But I need some time to figure it all out." She sniffed and shook her head. "You and I were a whirlwind back in Waketon, that instant attraction and everything that happened that threw us together. I need to get my balance again. There's so much at stake and I don't even know how to work it all out. I just need..."

"Time. I get it, baby. Really, I do." Jack reached up and covered her hand on his cheek before he turned his head and pressed a kiss to the palm. "Just don't forget that some-where during that whirlwind, we fell in love. So while I will respect you and give you the time and space you're requesting, I am not giving up on us." He dropped her hand and stepped away from her. "I'm going to catch a flight back to Texas tomorrow but I'll call you sometime tomorrow afternoon."

Bayleigh nodded as she blinked back the tears. She wanted to believe she was doing the right thing, but good God her heart was killing her right now! "I do love you, Jack," she whispered as she looked down at her car keys.

With a low growl, Jack stepped up to her and pulled her against him. "I don't care what else you think about me, or our time in Waketon. But believe that I love you, too, Bayleigh Morrow. And I am *not* giving up on us. Ever. You want time, you've got it," he dipped his head and kissed her again.

"Now, get in your car and drive away before I kidnap you," he whispered against her lips a moment later as he released her.

Unable to stop the tears this time, Bayleigh did as instructed. Jack rapped his knuckles on her roof and stepped away as she turned the key in the ignition. She dried the tears and waved her hand in a wave as she shifted into gear and drove out of the parking lot.

JACK STARED after the taillights until the car turned a corner and disappeared. Time and space to think, that's what she was asking for and even if it killed him, that's what he was going to give her. He looked around the parking lot and back towards Maddie's bar, an idea taking shape in his head. Knowing he was risking his health and safety, he turned to go back inside to talk to Brian and Rick, hoping they wouldn't try to kill him on sight.

CHAPTER 27

Two weeks later, bayleigh let herself into the apartment and called out a greeting to Maddie as she kicked off her shoes. She'd spent the morning at the recording studio with Dusty, making changes to one of the songs they'd been working on together.

"Oh, good. You made it home before I had to leave," Maddie stepped out of the kitchen. "You have a package on the table and the curiosity has been killing me all afternoon."

"Package? What kind of package?" Bayleigh asked stepping into the kitchen.

"Well, envelope, really." Maddie laughed as Bayleigh picked up the large envelope.

"Oh, my God, Maddie! It's from David Wilson!" Bayleigh stared at the envelope.

"I know. And from the size of that thing, I'm betting it's a contract," Maddie told her with a laugh. "Now, open it!"

"I'm too afraid to," Bayleigh admitted with a shaky laugh. But she took the letter opener from her friend and sliced through the layer of tape on the flap. With a deep breath, she slid the papers out, reading through the letter quickly. With a gasp, she handed it over to Maddie. "Holy shit," she breathed. "Tell me I'm not dreaming!"

Maddie scanned the letter and then looked at the other documents in Bayleigh's hands. "I think we're both having the same dream," she looked at her friend. "You did it, 'Leigh. You just landed your first contract!" she squealed, throwing her arms around her friend.

Bayleigh laughed and hugged her friend back and then grabbed the documents back. "I need to find an entertainment lawyer to review this for me, just to make sure it's all good," she shook her head. "Wow. I mean, I knew he liked the music, but I figured I'd get the standard contract and be forced to sign an exclusive agreement. But this," she tapped the stack of papers. "This is amazing!"

"I told you, you've got talent, girl! And with Dusty already snatching up those three songs, the word is out on the street that you are the one to watch!"

Bayleigh shook her head. "It's too much to take in," she muttered, sliding the papers back into the envelope.

"Hey, I thought this is what you wanted?" Maddie's voice was filled with concern as she put her hand on her friend's arm.

"It was, I mean, it is! It's just..." her voice trailed off and Maddie shook her head.

"Too many changes in such a short period of time?" Maddie guessed, her voice soft and knowing.

Bayleigh sighed and nodded. "Something like that," she agreed, tapping the envelope against her palm.

Maddie smiled and slid her arm around Bayleigh's

shoulders, giving her a quick squeeze. "Look, you have a few days to think it over. David's one of the best, but he's certainly not the only game in town. You won't do much better than the contract you have in your hand, but no one said you have to sign the first deal presented to you."

Bayleigh took a deep breath and nodded. "You're right. I'm going to go make a few phone calls. Maybe Nicole knows someone I can talk to about the contract. I'll meet up with you at the bar later, okay?"

"You bet," Maddie gave her another hug. "I need to get going. Call if you're going to be more than a couple of hours!"

Bayleigh waved her friend off and wandered over to the living room to look out the window. With her forehead pressed to the smooth windowpane, she watched as the cars whipped by on the street below. It still hadn't sunk in yet that she actually held a songwriting contract in her hand. One that allowed her to retain the copyrights and didn't limit her to being exclusive for the publisher.

She knew it wasn't a contract offered lightly; most new songwriters had to either be exclusive to the publisher for a few years or give up the rights to the songs they penned, at least until they had proven themselves. She wasn't going to have to do either of those. She was coming to the table with songs already being cut by the likes of Dusty Rhoades, not to mention writing songs with him.

Her phone buzzed in her back pocket with an incoming text message and she tugged it out to check it, smiling as she saw her brother's name.

"Just checking in. Are you doing okay?"

Bayleigh hit the tab to place a call to her brother instead of responding and waited for him to answer.

"Hey, kiddo! I just texted you," Jason's answered on the first ring.

"I know, I thought I'd call instead of texting back. Do you have ESP or something?"

"No, why, is something wrong? Is that leg bothering you again? I can call..."

"Jason, stop! I'm fine," Bayleigh laughed as she cut him off, both a little amused and guilty that her brother's first thought was along the lines of her being in trouble. "I just had some news from that publishing house I talked to, that's all."

"Well, what did they say?"

Bayleigh loved that her brother was as eager to find out the news as she was to share it with him. "I'm in, they offered me a contract!" She had to take the phone away from her ear as he shouted his congratulations.

"So now what?" he asked, once he had calmed down.

"I don't really know. They just sent the contract to me today to review. I guess I need to find an entertainment lawyer to review it and then decide if it's what I want."

"Well, I know two really great lawyers here in Waketon who know a thing or two about contract law. I bet they'd even give you the family discount. I know Jack would."

Bayleigh shook her head at her brother's tactics. "I don't know, Jason. That would be a little awkward. I mean, we haven't really talked since he left here two weeks ago."

"Because you told him to give you some space and time, Bayleigh," Jason pointed out. "Look, Jack's a pretty private guy and he sure as hell isn't going to come talking to me about how he may or may not have broken your heart. But you have that man tied up in knots, little sister."

"I'm not trying to," Bayleigh whispered into the phone.

"I know that and so does Jack. And I know you want some space to figure things out. But sometimes, all that space does is create more problems. Trust me on that one. I refused to back down when Nicole left me all those years ago and it took us ten years to find our way back to each other."

"I'm not asking for years, Jason! I just don't want to jump from one fire into another!"

"I know, kiddo. And I do understand. I'm just saying that sometimes, it's better to just lay it all on the line and go for broke. Jack's just trying to give you what you want but he can't read your mind."

Bayleigh sighed and laid her forehead against the window pane. "Why does life have to be so complicated?"

"Keeps things interesting," Jason responded. "I'm sorry, Bayleigh, but my nurse just told me my next patient is ready. I can call you later if you still need someone to talk to," he offered.

"I'm fine, Jason. But could you have Nicole call me so I can see what she thinks about reviewing the contract for me?"

"Be happy to, sis. I'm really proud of you, you know."

"Thanks, big brother. I know you are but it's still nice to hear," Bayleigh told him before disconnecting the call. She dropped down onto the sofa, staring at her phone in her hand before she dropped it onto the cushion beside her.

She rested her head against the back of the sofa and stared at the ceiling. Times like this, she needed her mother back. Her mom always had the answers when it came to guys. The only time Bayleigh hadn't listened to her had been when she started dating Will. Her mother had tried to warn her that Will wasn't the one for her, he only cared about himself. But Bayleigh hadn't wanted to listen at the time. Will was *fun* and *edgy* and had that 'bad boy' image down pat.

But then her mother had gotten sick and Bayleigh hadn't wanted to be left alone, so she'd continued to date Will. And for a while, she'd thought he'd cared about her as much as she thought she'd loved him. It had become clear pretty soon after her mother's death that he'd been more concerned about the money he'd thought she'd come into. But even with that revelation, Bayleigh had stayed with him.

Because she didn't want to be alone.

She stared at the room around her. Now here she was with the biggest news of her life, and she was still all alone. Only this time, the guy in her life was interested in more than just her inheritance. Jack was only interested in her.

Snatching up her phone, she placed a call to Maddie as she quickly grabbed the essentials and threw things into a suitcase. "I'm going home, Maddie," she told her friend when she answered her phone.

"About damn time. I love you, 'Leigh, you're the sister I never had, but I gotta tell you, I was beginning to wonder about your sanity after I met Jack. That man loves you."

"I know. I'm questioning my own sanity at the moment. I just hope I didn't blow it," Bayleigh snapped the suitcase closed. "Any idea when the last flight to Austin leaves?"

"No need to worry about that. Rick was here and I

wrote it out on a napkin for him. He should be at the apartment in about twenty minutes and he'll fly you all the way to Waketon," Maddie told her.

"For once, I'm not even going to argue about it. Tell Brian bye for me, would you, please?"

"Of course. Take care of yourself, Bayleigh. You deserve every bit of this success and happiness, you hear me?"

"Right back at you, Maddie. One of these days, I'm going to get the full story out of you."

"Oh, look, my bartender needs me. Gotta go be a bar owner now. Take care, 'Leigh. Love you!"

Bayleigh laughed as she disconnected the call. Now that she didn't have to rush to get to the airport to catch a flight, she paused in her frantic packing and took a deep breath as she took stock of what was in her suitcase and what she was missing. She repacked it neatly and added a few more items and then grabbed her computer bag and made sure her sheet music and laptop were in there, setting both bags and her guitar case near the front door.

CHAPTER 28

*R*ick had her at the airfield where he kept his plane, had the preflight check done and the flight plan filed in record time. Within forty minutes of getting to the airport, they'd been in the air. From there, flight time was a little over two hours.

"Did you talk to him?" Rick asked, checking the instruments as he flew.

"I'm too afraid to, to be honest. What if my brother is wrong and Jack's not tied up in knots over me? What if he hates me?"

"Love and hate are two sides of the same coin, Bayleigh. You have to care about something in order to hate it. Be more worried about him being indifferent," Rick suggested.

"Is that why you haven't given up on Maddie? She's not indifferent?"

"Maddie and I, we're a whole different ballgame," Rick frowned. "One of these days, she's going to break and tell me why she won't let me in."

"I always assumed you two had some fight or something," Bayleigh admitted.

Rick shook his head as he answered, "No, no fight. No argument, no disagreement, nothing. It just seemed to change overnight. For a long time, I thought it was because Brian and I went after that douchebag she'd gotten pregnant by, but she's not mad at Brian. Hell, I don't even know if she's mad at me. I don't know what the hell you'd call it."

"If she ever opens up and tells me, I promise I'll figure out a way to clue you in," Bayleigh reached over and squeezed his hand. "I've never met a couple more suited to each other. Well, except maybe Jason and Nicole," she amended.

Rick grinned over at her as the tower in Austin checked in with him. He keyed the mic and answered them and then motioned to her safety harness. "Buckle up, little lady. Austin just informed me that we're going to hit some turbulence as we approach Waketon. They have storms in the area but nothing that will keep us from landing. I'll have you on the ground in less than thirty minutes and we can figure out the rest of the plan from there."

"Are you going to stay the night?"

"I am now," he check a few of his gauges. "There's a storm front I checked on before we took flight. I knew we'd get to Waketon ahead of it, but it's moved in a little faster than I thought it would. I could do it if I had to, but there's no reason for me to hurry back," he flipped another switch. "I'll call Brian and give him an update and then I'll check into a hotel. I always keep a change of clothes on board, so it's no big deal."

He hadn't been kidding when he'd warned her they

were going to hit some turbulence. If she hadn't tightened her harness, she was pretty sure her head would have hit the ceiling a couple of times, and a few other times, she probably would have been dumped on the floor.

They landed in Waketon without any problems and Bayleigh helped Rick secure the plane for the night. She could see the flashes of lightening as it danced across the sky in the distance. Rick went inside the hanger to talk to the guys inside and then they walked around to the front of the building and the parking lot. She glanced over as a truck pulled into the parking lot and she smiled as she recognized her brother.

"Hey, Jason! Thanks for coming to pick us up," she greeted him as she gave him a hug. "This is Rick, Brian's business partner and a great friend to have in your corner. Rick, my brother Jason."

The two men shook hands and Jason grabbed a couple of the bags Rick set on the ground. "Come on, we need to get home before this storm hits. It's triggered a couple of tornados north of here already and I want to be off the road and safe before it gets here," Jason told her as he led them over to his truck.

"Yeah, the tower out of Austin advised me of that. I adjusted our path a little to stay out of its way. If they'd given me any indication it would be here before us, I would have stopped in Austin for the night," Rick answered as they loaded the bags in the extended cab. Rick slid into the back seat and Bayleigh took the passenger seat.

Bayleigh glanced at her brother. "You didn't tell Jack I was coming back, did you?"

"You asked us not to, so no, we didn't," Jason shook his

head as he headed for his home. "How long you going to make him wait to find out?"

"Not long. I don't want to give myself a chance to chicken out," Bayleigh admitted.

"Trust me, Bayleigh. You chicken out and I'm hauling your ass over there myself. No way in hell I'm letting you do to this poor guy what Maddie's been doing to me for the last couple of years," Rick muttered.

Bayleigh shook her head as Jason threw her a questioning look. "I guess that settles it then. Do you think you can drop me off at his place?"

"Don't need to, he's still in the office," Jason jerked his chin towards the building coming up and sure enough, Jack's truck was still parked in front and a light was still on in the front area. "Do you want me to stop?"

Bayleigh took a deep breath and nodded. "Might as well get this over with now." Her brother whipped the wheel and they turned into the lot.

She looked at her brother and he gave her a knowing smile. "He won't turn you away, sis. But if you need me to come get you, just call."

"Thanks, Jason. And Rick, thanks for flying me out here tonight."

"Anytime, 'Leigh," Rick pushed open his door, giving her a hug before sliding into the front seat.

"Go put your man out of his misery, Bayleigh," Jason told her with a wink as Rick moved to shut the door. "Talk to you tomorrow."

Bayleigh raised her hand and stepped back from the truck, already turning to head up the steps that led to the front door. She heard her brother pull out of the lot and back onto the highway as she stepped up to the door.

Her hand was trembling as she turned the doorknob, remembering the very first time she'd ever entered this office. She smiled as the bell sounded above her head and she heard the muttered curse coming from Jack's office and she took a couple of steps into the room.

Stopping just shy of the receptionist's desk as she heard Jack coming down the hallway, she waited for him to see her.

"Can I help..." his voice trailed off as he realized who was standing there. "Bayleigh!"

"I'm sorry to barge in on you like this but I seem to have lost my way and I was wondering if you could help me?" her eyes drank in the sight of him, from his mussed up hair and short sleeved golf shirt to the well-worn, tight jeans.

Jack glanced from her to the large window behind her and back. "What are you doing here, Bayleigh?"

Bayleigh's heart dropped to the floor. Jason was wrong, Jack wasn't tied up in knots over her. He was pissed at her. He didn't want her anymore. He didn't *love* her any more. Her eyes filled with tears as she stared at him.

"I-I," she stammered out, stopped took a deep breath, started again. "I had some news today, some wonderful, awesome news and when I looked around to share it with, I had no one," she looked at him but his face was impassive. The man could be carved from stone.

"Maddie not around?" he quirked an eyebrow.

"She was there, and I even called Jason. And they're happy for me but it's not the same as sharing it with the man I love," she held her hand out to him in a silent plea.

Jack ignored her outstretched hand and stepped past her towards the door. Bayleigh's head fell forward and she bit the inside of her cheek to keep from sobbing. And then she heard the *snick* of the lock and the *thud* of the deadbolt being turned. She spun around to stare at Jack as he advanced on her.

Startled, she backed away from him but soon came up against the desk. Jack didn't stop until he was standing in front of her, hands braced on the desk on either side of her hips.

"I'll ask you again, why are you here?" his voice was low, demanding.

Bayleigh took a deep breath and laid her heart completely out there. "Because I love you and I miss you and I needed to be with you," her eyes never strayed from his, begging him to believe her.

Jack reached out and trailed his fingers down her cheek. "What changed?" he asked.

"I opened my eyes and saw what I was missing," she answered, the honesty of her answer reflected in her eyes.

"And what was that? What are you missing?"

"You. I'm missing you," her voice was a whisper as she forced the words out. "And I need you, Jack. I need to know that I have you in my corner and by my side to pick up the pieces when I fall apart." Bayleigh kept her eyes on his as she nuzzled her cheek against his palm.

"Did you have any nightmares in Nashville?" his voice was still low, but it had become softer.

"Not like the ones I used to have but I had a few dreams," she admitted, her voice just as low.

"I'm sorry I wasn't there when you needed me," his

thumb stroked across her cheek. And Bayleigh knew he wasn't kicking her out.

"I'm so sorry I pushed you away," her eyes filled with tears again.

"You had every right to," he shook his head as his other hand came up to rest on her hip, drawing her closer. "Are you here to stay? I mean, are you coming home? Oh, hell, I don't know what I'm trying to say," he cursed.

Bayleigh giggled and stepped closer, pressing herself against him. "I'm here to stay, if you'll let me. I landed my contract, which I need you and Nicole to look over for me before I sign it, but I can make my home base Austin and only fly to Nashville when I have to."

"You got the contract?" his arms slid around her waist, holding her to him.

"I did," she nodded. "I was going to call you but I decided I didn't want to be alone anymore. I wanted to share the news in person and celebrate with someone who loves me."

Jack's mouth covered hers and he kissed her as he pulled her against the hard contours of his body. Bayleigh sighed and leaned into the kiss, her hands sliding up his chest and linking behind his neck.

They broke apart when his cell phone rang. With a muttered curse, Jack pulled it out of his pocket. "Yeah, Nicole, what do you want?"

Bayleigh could hear her sister-in-law's laugh over the phone. "You either need to close the shutters on the windows or take Bayleigh into your office, my friend. I've had four calls already from people in town, wanting to know what's going on with you and Bayleigh," Nicole told him. "And you'd better do it quick before one of the callers tells Jason and not me!"

Bayleigh groaned and buried her face against Jack's chest. Jack's arm tightened around her as he told his friend what she could tell the callers and hung up. "You okay?" he asked her as he felt her shoulders shaking.

She tilted her head back and looked at him and he realized she was laughing. He smiled at her as he stepped back from her and took her hand. "Let's go home, baby."

"I like the sound of that," Bayleigh agreed, linking her fingers with his.

CHAPTER 29

*J*ack helped her into the cab of his truck and glanced up at the sky. The storm clouds were rolling in and the wind had picked up. He hurried around to the driver's side and climbed in, reaching over to grab her hand. "So, I've got a surprise for you when we get back to my place."

"Oh, I just bet you do," she waggled her eyebrows and he chuckled.

"Get your mind out of the gutter," he muttered as he started the engine and put the truck in gear. "I'm doing some remodeling on the barn."

"Remodeling the barn? Why?"

"Well, a couple of new friends of mine had some suggestions as to what a home office would need to look like and I thought my barn would be perfect for what they're suggesting. But we can still change things if you don't like it."

"If I don't like it? Why would I have any say in the matter?"

Jack shook his head and gave her fingers a squeeze. "Maybe I just care what you think," he told her and she squeezed his hand back and smiled at him.

"So, this contract of yours. What's it entail?" he asked as they drove.

"Well, I think it's a pretty sweet deal. Most new songwriters have to sign an exclusive contract with a publishing house, and most of the time, the house retains the copyrights to any songs that are written during the term of the contract. In return, the artist basically get a steady paycheck for the duration of the contract."

"So is that what you got?"

"No, I'm not giving up any copyrights and I don't have to be exclusive. The downside is, I don't have a steady paycheck every two weeks but it means I can sign multiple contracts or just showcase songs to certain houses when I want. Or pitch them to artists directly, or write with other artists when the opportunity comes up. The sky is the limit for me now."

"You mean, like what you and Dusty just did for his album?"

"Sort of. Dusty and I have known each other for years and we used to write together back then, too. But him wanting the one song I had written plus writing three more with me, well, that should open a lot of doors in town. At least, I hope it does," Bayleigh admitted as she glanced at him out of the corner of her eye. "Is that going to cause problems?"

"No, it won't," Jack promised, steel in his voice as he brought her hand up to his lips and kissed her knuckles. "I'm not saying I won't screw up again because we both know I will at some point, but I can promise you it won't be some petty jealousy issue."

Bayleigh nodded and glanced out the window. "But I do get the jealousy part, Jack. It was the lack of trust that bothered me."

"And I get *that*. I trust you, baby. I swear I do," his fingers tightened around her hand again as he made the turn off of the highway and onto the road leading back to his house. They were silent for the last few moments of the drive, until Jack stopped the truck in front of his barn.

He turned to face her in the small confines of the cab of the pick-up, taking both of her hands and holding on. "I know I can't erase the hurt I caused. But I want to make it up to you and show you that I trust you," he paused, looking down at their linked hands. "I know you're going to have to travel sometimes to make this dream of yours work. And I know that you keep saying you can work anywhere, but we don't have any kind of sound studio here in Waketon that would work for your needs. And I don't like the idea of you 'commuting' to Austin all the time for that." He dropped her hands and turned to open his door, reached back for her hand and pulled her out behind him.

"So, when I was in Nashville, chasing you down, I talked to a few people there and found out what you would need to have a home studio. Brian talked to Dusty and I was able to go see his set-up and then he gave me Liam's name and number. Liam helped me figure out how to do this. But like I said," he told her as he led her to a door on the side of the barn and opened it. He reached in and flipped a switch and waited for her to look inside. "We can change anything you don't like."

Bayleigh's eyes were huge as she took a step inside the new 'office space'. "You built a studio?" she turned back to him.

"I wanted you to have your own space, somewhere you could escape to anytime you wanted to write, without distractions. And I didn't want you to have to drive all the way into Austin every time. I get that you're still going to have to go into Austin or off to Nashville, or hell, I don't know, maybe even back to London at some point, but at least this way, you can have the basics laid out. At least, that's what Liam said you could do. He assured me you'd know how to use all of this," he gestured towards the sound board and computer set-up along one wall.

Bayleigh laughed and nodded before launching herself at him. "Oh, yeah. I know exactly how to use all of this!" she told him, kissing him. "You did this, for me, not even knowing if I would come back?"

Jack nodded and then looked a little sheepish. "Well, I was going to use it to lure you back here, if you hadn't come back on your own," he admitted. "I figured you could live with Jason and Nicole but this would be at your disposal. And then I'd use my charm to win you back."

A gust of wind slammed the door shut and Jack glanced around. "Let's get up to the house before it starts raining," he suggested, turning off the lights and re-opening the door. He made sure everything was secure and then took her hand and steered her up to the house. They made it to the porch just as the first raindrops fell and Jack hurried her inside before the downpour started.

"I want to check the weather report, see what we're in for," Jack muttered as they headed into the kitchen. The lights flickered and then went out. "Or maybe not," he grimaced.

"Now, this has a familiar feel to it," Bayleigh laughed, stepping closer to him. "Do we need to bring in firewood and make up a bed on the floor of the living room?"

Jack laughed and picked her up, striding down the hall-way. He had her naked and situated in the middle of her bed in seconds. "This time, we're riding out the storm in my bed," he told her as he tore off his own clothes. "God, I missed you. You're so beautiful," he told her in-between kisses. His hand came up to caress and shape her breast and Bayleigh arched her back.

"I missed you, too, Jack," Bayleigh told him on a sigh as his thigh insinuated itself between hers. She parted her thighs to accommodate him and sucked in a breath when she felt his fingers touching her, finding her slick and ready for him.

"God, baby, you're so wet," he groaned, his forehead dropping to hers. "I didn't want to rush you this time. I wanted to wine and dine you, prove to you how much I love you," he whispered against her lips, all the while his fingers were doing magical things to her, making her even wetter.

"Wine and dine later. I already know how much you love me," Bayleigh managed to answer as his lips closed around her nipple. "Please don't tease me!" she begged as her hips started to move under him, as his fingers continued to caress and torment her.

"This first time is going to be hard and fast," he warned as he positioned himself, ready to slide into her.

Bayleigh smiled at him. "You can make it up to me on

the second, then," she moaned as she raised her hips for his thrust.

"Count on it," Jack grunted out the promise as he slid into her. Bayleigh's breath left her in a rush of air and her fingernails dug into his shoulders. Jack stilled his movements and he lifted his head, a frown on his features as he looked at her. "You okay?"

Bayleigh smiled and nodded, her hand coming up to caress his cheek. "It's just...tight," she shrugged, unable to come up with a better word. "But I swear to God, Jack, if you don't start moving, I'm going to show you a few self-defense moves Brian taught me and I'll take over this show!"

Jack threw back his head and laughed before he repositioned her hips and pulled back until he had almost withdrawn from her before he slid back in, exquisitely slow, which earned another low moan from Bayleigh. Jack's fingers flexed against her hips at the sound and he thrust again, deeper this time.

Bayleigh gasped and her eyes widened which caused Jack to smile at her. "I take it you like that?" he whispered against her lips as he moved his hips again.

"Oh, God, yes, Jack! Don't stop!" she begged as her body raced for that peak, desperate to reach it. Her fingernails scored his back as she raised her hips to meet his thrusts. "Please, Jack," she panted as she wrapped her legs around his hips.

"Hang on, babe. I'll take care of you," Jack reached between them and flicked her clit with his thumb. The motion had her arching up against him. With gritted teeth, he held off on his own release. He felt the tremors start and he moved his thumb harder, faster, in time to the movement of her hips. She tightened around him and he knew she'd reached her peak. The tingle started in his spine and spread, and with a shout, he followed her over that peak.

BAYLEIGH WOKE UP, her head pillowed on Jack's chest. She felt his hand rubbing up and down her back. She could still hear the storm raging outside and burrowed closer to Jack.

"You okay?" he asked, his hand stilling in its soothing motion.

"I'm fine, just a little cold," she admitted and he immediately pulled the blanket higher, tucking it in around her shoulders.

"Better?"

"Just being here with you is better," she snuggled in closer. "Where do we go now, Jack?" she asked, her voice soft.

Jack sighed and his arms tightened around her. "Where do you want to go?"

Bayleigh knew what he was asking and for the first time in a long time, she wasn't afraid to give the answer in her heart. "I don't want to go anywhere anytime soon," she assured him. "I'm obviously going to have to make some trips back and forth to Nashville, once I sign that contact. But I want to make my home here, with my family close to me." She tapped his chest with one finger, letting him know she was including him in that last part.

"I'd like that," he admitted, his voice low. He shifted

and grabbed her left hand with his right, sliding something over the knuckle of her ring finger. "I had this in my pocket that day I tried to surprise you in Austin. It's probably why I was so ready to think the worst of you—all that baggage I carry around from before, I guess. My therapist said my sub-conscious has been waiting for you to 'betray me' I think was how she put it. Even though I knew you would never do that, that part of me I keep buried is always waiting for the ones I love to leave me hanging."

Bayleigh gasped as she looked down at the biggest emerald she'd ever seen and blinked back the tears swimming in her eyes and making it difficult to see. She bit her lip and looked back up at Jack. "Jack..."

"Don't say no, Bayleigh. Tell me you need to think about it, tell me you need to talk to Jason. Tell me you need me on my hands and knees begging you, but please don't say no!"

"I CAN'T SAY anything right now," she told him. She felt him tense and a shuttered look came over his face as he steeled himself for rejection. "Because you haven't asked me anything yet, Jack!" she whispered, her hand coming up to stroke his cheek. "You have to ask to get an answer," she prompted as his eyes lit up and he smiled at her.

"I saw you that night in the bar before you took the stage, and I knew what it took for you to get up there to sing that song. I swear, all I could think was that it should have been me sitting there, building you up and waiting for you to get offstage so we could celebrate. Instead it was a group of your friends, who were intent on keeping me away from you. And I let them, and not just because your two self-proclaimed bodyguards have concealed weapons." Jack sighed and his hand stroked over her cheek. "I know I fucked up, Bayleigh, but I swear to you, I won't make the same mistake twice."

Jack picked her left hand up and kissed her knuckles, his thumb rubbing over the ring finger. "Bayleigh Morrow, I will thank God every day of our lives that you came back and are willing to give me a second chance. One I'm sure most women will tell you I never deserved. And I sure as hell don't deserve a woman like you. But I love you. You make me complete. Will you do me the honor of becoming my wife?"

Trying hard to stop the flow of tears, Bayleigh managed to whisper "yes" between sobs. "I love you, too, Jack. I was miserable in Nashville," she whispered as he wiped the tears from her cheeks.

"God, Bayleigh, I was miserable here. I was so afraid I'd lost you," he whispered, rolling her to her back and leaning in for a kiss.

"You can't lose me, Jack. I'm here to stay. Besides, if you try to run now, I'll hire Brian and Rick to haul your ass back to me," she threatened with a smile.

"Same goes, baby. Same goes," Jack assured her.

"We need to tell Jason and Nicole. And the rest of the family," Bayleigh reminded him between kisses.

"Power's out. I can't find my car keys in the dark. Cell phone died, can't charge it," Jack muttered as he kissed her shoulder.

"Think they'll buy it?"

"I don't really care, do you?" he whispered, covering her body with his and sinking into her.

And Bayleigh found she didn't really care, either.

THREE DAYS LATER, Jack and Bayleigh returned from Vegas, wearing matching smiles and wedding bands, much to their family's delight.

ABOUT THE AUTHOR

Kelli grew up all over the East Coast but her family finally settled in Cincinnati long enough for her to finish high school and college. She has always loved to read books and write her own stories. In high school, she used to pass around the latest chapter of the story she was writing for her friends to read. There is more than one high school teacher out there that can probably remember telling her to put the book down and pay attention to the lectures.

Graduating from the University of Cincinnati with her BS in Nursing, she left Ohio for Texas and the U.S. Army. She received a medical discharge for a knee injury, but was able to meet the man she'd one day call her husband first-- thanks to some mutual friends who insisted they would be perfect together. And what do you know--they are!

She continued to read books by the dozens and write her own stories. And then one day, a friend dared her to enter a contest. She didn't win, but the feedback she received from the judges convinced her that maybe people were interested in the stories she wanted to tell. She still lives in Central Texas, with her husband, two children and 2 dogs.